SO FADES MY LIGHT

Kay Winchester

Robert Boyd, the kindly much-loved Vicar and part-time novelist, lives with his acid-tongued sister in the village of Brookfield-under-Woke, in less-than-harmonious circumstances. They quarrel endlessly about his star-struck daughter, Hazel, who lives for good times and wants more of everything. Lady Lassett, the Vicar's friend and the lady of the manor, invariably causes sparks to fly in the village with her bluntness. Into this country idyll comes Andrew Farrar, escaping from London society, and hoping to find the tranquillity he needs to come to terms with his failing eyesight . . .

SO FADES MY LIGHT

Kay Winchester

APR 2 1991

Curley Publishing, Inc.
South Yarmouth, Ma.

Library of Congress Cataloging-in-Publication Data

Winchester, Kay.
   So fades my light / Kay Winchester.—Large print ed.
      p.   cm.
   1. Large type books.   I. Title.
   [PR6073.I476S58   1991]
   823′.914—dc20
   ISBN 0–7927–0517–3 (lg. print)   90–48139
                                                                          CIP

© 1948

Published in Large Print by arrangement with the author.

Printed in Great Britain

ONE

Two things happened one sunbathed April morning in Brookfield-under-Woke. The Vicar and his sister quarrelled, and a car—the most luxurious, long-nosed model imaginable—piled up against the carved stone wall of the ancient churchyard. Of the two events, the quarrel at the Vicarage was the more significant.

Robert Boyd, the big, handsome Vicar of the two parishes of Brookfield and St. Mary's-on-the-Heath, faced his elder sister with something approaching an angry glint in his eyes. Little Winnie Ogg (who had brought the bread from her father's shop, and been summarily dispatched back there with one of the loaves because it was burnt) stood for a second outside the parlour window and watched him.

She heard him say, distinctly, before she turned to scuttle off with the news: 'Once again, Frances, will you kindly mind your own business!'

1

Frances Boyd, thin and faded, and some ten years older than her brother, also showed more spirit than usual.

'It *is* my business, Robert, as long as I keep on the none-too-pleasant task of running your house for you. Here am I, trying to make both ends meet, while you spend a fortune which you haven't got, on that pampered daughter of yours! It isn't fair!' She gasped a little, at her own temerity. She wasn't afraid of him, and often spoke her mind, but on any other subject than Hazel. Her brother was touchy, where his only child was concerned.

She licked her lips, and took up the cudgels on behalf of someone else. 'Besides, there's Elaine.'

Her brother looked at her, and some of the anger died out of his eyes. They could hear, in the sudden cessation of their own angry voices, the regular tapping of Elaine's typewriter in the Vicar's study, where she was working on the notes of his latest novel.

'I know your work is good, Robert,' his sister went on, in an altered tone, 'but will it be good enough to make the kind of money you want? You ought to pay Elaine more money, you know you ought! She could make a very good wage if she went to work in a town.'

'I know that,' he said gruffly. 'I've told her I can't afford to pay her any more, but she always says the same thing. She's our flesh and blood, and she wants to make her home with us, even if the wage is poor. There's no sense in flogging the matter.'

'Then if you can't do more for Elaine, at least abandon this idiotic idea of sending Hazel to a finishing school. It isn't necessary! It's—it's mad, that's what it is!'

Elaine heard their voices, and guessed the cause. This disagreement (it could hardly be called a quarrel, she reasoned, in two such normally good-tempered people) had been boiling up for days. Weeks, even. It drew nearer with every letter from Hazel, eternally wanting more money, more clothes, more of everything so that she could compete with the other girls at her expensive boarding-school. Why the Vicar hadn't sent his daughter to a cheaper school was beyond his young cousin. The schoolfellows of Hazel came from wealthy families, with whom he was constantly trying to keep pace, with an alarmingly depleted purse.

She watched the baker's child run by, and thought regretfully that it would soon be all over the village. It was some time since she had taken the loaves in, which meant that since then Winnie had been listening at the parlour window. You had to be so careful in a place like Brookfield, if you didn't want to start gossip. So little happened here. News of 'words' in the Vicarage was news indeed.

Little Winnie Ogg worked fast. From her father's shop she doubled back to the Stores, where old Harris' youngest, a mite of two, played in the centre of the road in preference to the pavement or the grass patch in front of the shop.

'Back on the pavement!' Winnie shouted, lifting the dirty-faced child up the steep kerb. 'Yer'll get run over!'

'Shan't!' the mite returned smartly, dropping down into the road again.

'They're 'avin' a fight, up at Vicarage,' Winnie gasped, darting into the shop and out again.

' 'Ere, 'ere, 'ere, not so fast,' Harris said, lumbering out from behind a keg of soft soap. 'Oo's 'avin' a fight?'

'Vicar 'n Miss Frances!' Winnie, with more calls and little time, yelled.

'What about?' Harris called patiently, from the door of his shop.

4

'Miss 'Azel,' was the reply, before his informant darted up the road to Eb Wilkins' forge.

'Oh, aye, so it's come to that, 'as it?' Harris observed, moving back slowly into the shop to make way for a customer.

'What's that, Mr. 'Arris?'

' 'Avin' a row up at Vicarage over that baggage, Miss 'Azel,' he said, as he weighed sugar.

'Oh, are they?' Miss Christmas, the local dressmaker, blinked excitedly. 'Well, I'm not surprised. Bleed 'er pore father's pocket dry, afore she's finished, the 'ussy! My pore work isn't good enough for 'er, if you please! Oh, no, she must go to the big shops in London, and for why, that's what I say. For why?'

He wagged his head sagely. 'Come to no good, that girl! But Vicar was wrong, aye, 'e was way off the mark, the way 'e brought 'er up! Good fella, the Vicar, but I always say— 'e was wrong!'

Miss Christmas hastily agreed, and hurried from the shop, to carry the news to little Miss Trigg who was in the act of shingling the head of the sewing-woman at Walpole House. Shingling might be decades out of date in the big cities, but it was still the vogue in Brookfield. It was easy to keep tidy and in waves, but more to the point was the fact that it was about the only style which Miss Trigg could manage really well.

Lady Lassett was enjoying what she termed one of her blank days, and Walpole House was quiet. Her ladyship yawned over the current novel sent by a book society in London, and yearned for local news. The Vicarage row, over by the time she heard of it, was delivered to her via her maid (from the sewing-woman) and via the butler, who said he had been informed (he hoped incorrectly) by the chauffeur, when getting the car filled up at Eb Wilkins' place.

'The telephone and cable services have got nothing on this village,' her ladyship remarked, as her maid fussed around the big dressing-table, trying to get her mistress to look less horsey and more like the niece of a duke.

'Oh, stop fussing me, girl. Damme, let me be comfortable. Where's my old tweed—no, not that monstrosity. My old one, the one that smells of pigs and stables. I want a walk. I think I'll pop over to Brookfield and see what it's all about. Though I suppose Elaine will have cooled them both down by now.' She grinned reminiscently. 'Damned long time since Robert Boyd got wild. Gad, I remember the last time——'

She broke off abruptly as she noticed the expectant look on her maid's face. 'If you think I'm going to tell you about it,' she told the girl, 'so you can broadcast it around before lunch, you're mistaken!'

She didn't get as far as Brookfield, however, for trouble in the Walpole stables claimed her, and finally she was tempted to go to a neighbour's house to inspect a new litter of spaniel pups.

Robert Boyd didn't know how near he came to having the atmosphere of his house charged with electricity again, for where his old friend was, sparks invariably flew. With the best intentions in the world, Judy Lassett rubbed the fur the wrong way.

Robert's temperament was peacefully inclined, and he and his sister were good friends again before mid-morning, though (as Judy Lassett suspected) this was largely due to Elaine.

'Robert,' she said, poking her head round the parlour door, 'sorry to butt in on your fireworks, but I'm stuck. Your writing doesn't improve, does it?'

7

She quirked her eyebrows at them both and grinned comically, and the tension eased. Robert nodded briefly at her. 'All right, I'll come to your rescue.'

She vanished discreetly, and he turned to his sister. 'I can't quarrel with you, Frances. I'll do as you say. We'll think no more about sending Hazel to a finishing school. But in return, do please stop harrying me about the girl. You know my reasons for spending so much on her. I beg of you, let's leave it at that.'

'Yes, Robert,' she sighed, but was glad enough to relinquish the fighting stand she had, for the moment, adopted. Any attempt to ease Robert of his finances was a perilous business, and the fact that he was writing books—successful and popular books—to supplement his income, did little to relieve her mind. His expenses far exceeded the sum total of his literary earnings, and as she turned back to the kitchen, Frances Boyd had the uneasy premonition that this morning's heated discussion was a fair sample of others to come.

TWO

ELAINE HARCOURT paused in her work and looked out of the window. The Vicarage garden was filled with tulips this year, and blazed scarlet, yellow and gold. She rested her chin on her hands and drank in the colours with a little sigh of pure pleasure.

The early April sunshine touched the keys of her typewriter and made them glint. Her hair, short and curly, such a light brown that it was almost rusty gold, caught the sunshine, too, and made a glowing halo—her one beauty.

The Rev. Robert Boyd looked up from the littered roll-top desk where he sat working at the far window. 'What is it, my dear? Are you stuck again?'

She grinned guiltily.

'No, Robert. Not really. Your new novel's going to be a winner.' She paused, and reflectively studied the page of shorthand notes. 'Robert, I think I'd work better if I could take a walk. D'you mind?

9

It's no use—this wonderful weather's got into my system. I want to be out in it!'

He burst out laughing. 'Oh, is that all? Good gracious, child, you had me worried for a moment. As a rule your attention wanders only when I turn out poor work.'

She regarded him affectionately. 'Don't you worry, darling. This stuff's good, and I mean it!'

'It's got to be good,' he said, with a sigh, and returned to his work. 'Cut along and get your walk, child.'

She tidied the papers on her desk, slipped the cover on her machine and went out. On the way through the house, she called out to Frances.

'I'm going out to blow the cobwebs off,' she said.

Frances Boyd, in the same pale shade of blue which she had favoured as a girl and had never quite been able to discard for a more mature colour, came to the kitchen door.

'Will you be long, Elaine, dear?' she asked, surprise in her voice.

'Don't tell me—I know! It's only mid-morning and I should be working,' the girl grinned. 'Robert intimated I'd better clear out and whip up a desire for work—or else!'

Frances bit back a smile, and nodded. 'Don't be late for lunch. It's rabbit to-day.'

She watched the girl pull on the shabby brown beret and shrug herself into the same old tweed overcoat she'd had since she came to the Vicarage three years ago. It did seem a pity that one young girl couldn't have more of the good things of life, while another had everything.

Her brother must have had the same thoughts in his mind, she concluded, as she took in his mid-morning cup of malted milk.

He was standing in front of a studio portrait of his daughter propped on top of one of the low glass-fronted book-cases. By all accepted standards, Hazel was very good-looking and well-groomed: too well-groomed for a girl still away at boarding-school.

Frances tightened her lips. All her displeasure of an hour ago came back. 'Here's your milk, Robert,' she said severely.

He started guiltily, and frowned. He never cared to be caught looking at his daughter's portrait.

'I was just thinking. This is, after all her

last year at school. She'll find it very dull when she comes home, won't she?'

'Why should she?' Frances countered, with the sharp note back in her voice. 'The Vicarage is a big enough house for half a dozen girls her age. (I know that, only too well—I have to run it!) And goodness knows, Brookfield's a very nice village. Oakbridge's near, too. It isn't every village that has such an up-and-coming town on its doorstep!' She paused, still indignant. 'You fuss her too much, Robert. I know I said an hour ago that I wouldn't mention the subject again, but I can't help it. You're making a rod for your own back, mark my words!'

She retreated before he could reply, and he sighed in sheer relief. He didn't want a re-opening of that painful scene.

He took his malted drink over to Elaine's desk, and sat down in her chair to read through the typescript of his new book as far as she had gone with it. It was true what he had said: it had to be good. He was depending on it. Up till now, he had done well enough with popular adventure stories. But now he must be more ambitious. His expenses were such that he had to produce something far above his previous work.

But was it good enough? Was Elaine

right?

Elaine herself was certain she was right. As she strode along, up lanes and down by-ways, nodding to this or that member of the parish, greeting farm hands and labourers at their work, she was thinking all the time of her cousin's new book, and the 'feel' of it. It's good, she decided happily.

Robert Boyd was such a dear. Her second-cousin, and her only living male relative, he had taken her into his own home three years ago, at her own request. She had been home from school a matter of weeks before her parents were killed in an accident and, apart from Robert and his sister, there was no one else to whom she could turn.

Robert, at that time, was struggling along with his books and his parish work, getting help where he could, and sending his MSS. out to be typed. The result was inferior and expensive, and she had offered to take over all his secretarial work in exchange for a home.

The Boyds had made her very welcome. In his heart, Robert Boyd hoped that she would prove to be a companion to his daughter Hazel, during her holidays, and when she finally came home from school. Hazel had made it very plain that she was dreading her return to Brookfield village, to 'stagnate', as she put it. Hazel wanted wonderful clothes and a gay life, and as far as her father's limited means would allow, she had been getting it. Her companions came from wealthy homes, and unwittingly encouraged Hazel's love of luxury and good times.

'How came Robert to send her to such an exclusive school?' Elaine had once asked Frances. 'Surely there are good schools at lower fees?'

Frances Boyd had sniffed in righteous indignation. 'It wasn't my brother's wish, as you may imagine. D'you remember Elizabeth?'

'Hazel's mother? No, not very well. I met her twice before she died. Why?'

'Her family were very well-off, and she had the same extravagant tastes as Hazel. That's where the girl gets them from, I suppose. When Elizabeth lay dying, she begged that Hazel should go to that school when she was old enough. She said her parents would settle the fees, as it was their wish, too.'

'So they should, if they were well-off!' Elaine put in, with indignation.

'Yes, well, I don't know where Elizabeth

14

thought the money was coming from, for she must have known how things were at her home. When Robert went to see them about it, he had a shock. It appeared that the good style of living they kept up was all a sham, and they hadn't got enough money to settle their own bills, let alone send Hazel to school! They said as much to Robert.' Frances had sucked in her lips angrily at that point. 'It should have been enough for Robert, but oh, no! He had promised his dear wife, so what must he do but saddle himself with school fees and goodness knows what else! You know what he's like. He says if he cuts down Hazel's requirements, it will only be carrying out his promise to the letter, and that won't do. He insists on bringing Hazel up as her mother would have wished, and now you know why he works himself to a shadow, keeping up his output of saleable books!'

At first Elaine had been worried, but finally she had dismissed it with a smile. It was true in a way that Robert was worried over bills, but Frances always made it sound worse. She got so anxious about the Vicar and her niece. But now it seemed it went deeper than she had at first thought. Robert and Frances had quarrelled, and she couldn't bear that. It was understandable in a way, Elaine felt, that Hazel wanted pretty things and nice people to be with. Hazel was that sort of person. She'd find Brookfield dreadfully dull.

Elaine herself loved the village. Before her parents died, she had lived in a smoky Midland town, and had gone to school in the bleak moorlands some twenty miles away. Brookfield represented beauty and peace to her.

She loved every stick and stone of it, in good weather and bad. She liked the people, from Lady Lassett, who organized the church bazaar and sat on most of the committees, to old Grannie Geddes who scrounged from everyone and was said to make the most intoxicating red currant wine in the county. She liked living at the Vicarage, she liked the Boyds and her work, but most of all, she liked the Vicarage library. Her passion for books had got her into awkward situations in the past, and the latest and most awkward of all situations was her friendship with Charles Ramsey.

THREE

ELAINE was on the point of turning back from her walk as she reached the gates of the Walpole estate, when Lady Lassett overtook her and invited her up to the house for coffee and a chat. She liked the girl, but she also wanted news of the Vicarage row, and knowing Elaine, it would take time and patience to get it out of her.

'You haven't been to see me lately, my dear? Why?' Judy Lassett asked in her abrupt manner. 'Don't tell me young Ramsey takes up so much of your time?'

Elaine flushed. 'Of course he doesn't. We're just friends. The fact is, Robert and I have been so busy lately, and there doesn't seem a lot of time. How's Peter?' she asked, adroitly changing the subject.

Lady Lassett snorted. 'My young brother is much the same as usual, thanks! Spends far too much time on books and not nearly enough time on games. Sport is what he wants! Make a man of him. He'll be a cissy

17

if we're not careful! Young idiot—don't wonder Robert's gal is losing interest in him.'

Elaine said, 'I don't think Hazel's losing interest in Peter. It's just that they grew up together and, well, take each other rather for granted.'

'Peter doesn't take Hazel for granted,' his sister said, severely. 'Still, they're little more than children. Expected home soon, isn't she?'

Elaine was saved the trouble of answering, by their arrival at Walpole House, the white-pillared Georgian Mansion at the end of a fine old avenue of red beeches. Once in the drawing-room, however, her hostess returned to the attack.

Elaine watched her nervously, as she poured coffee and looked down her long nose at the girl. Judy Lassett was a sturdy little woman who rode like a man and did almost everything in a determined masculine manner. Her bright little black eyes reminded Elaine of a robin; they snapped and twinkled, and missed very little.

'Now, about this Charles Ramsey. Keeps a bookshop, heh?'

'Yes, Lady Lassett. A good-class bookshop, in Oakbridge High Street.'

'H'm. Is that what upset Robert this morning?'

'No,' Elaine said, with truth, and momentarily caught off guard.

'Ah, keeping mum, eh? What's Robert feel about your marrying into trade?'

'But I'm not,' the girl protested. 'I mean, we're not engaged or anything. Just friends?'

'Nonsense! Gals like you don't see fellows like Charles Ramsey three and four times a week without there being something in the wind. No smoke without fire, y'know! Heh? Besides, it's around all over the place!'

'Then I shall have to stop the story,' Elaine said heatedly. 'Honestly, Lady Lassett, there's nothing in it. I just see Charles so much because—well, he's got a bookshop and I love books and can't read enough. We're good friends, and it's been fun helping him work that shop up from a poky little secondhand place. We've been nearly three years at it—in fact, since not long after I came here. I've loved every minute of it, but that's all there is to it. No romance or anything!'

'Does he want you to marry him?' Robert's old friend asked shrewdly.

19

The girl flushed a little. 'Well, yes, I think so,' she admitted reluctantly, 'but he knows I don't want that. I can't think who put the story about. I wish people wouldn't gossip so.'

'So do I!' Lady Lassett commented. 'Though what we should do without gossip in a place like this, I can't think!'

The butler knocked discreetly at the door and announced that there was a telephone call for her ladyship, and while Judy Lassett was out of the room, Elaine studied a new picture of Peter Walpole, propped up on his sister's desk. He was a nice youth, with the long oval face, dreamy eyes and sensitive mouth of the poet.

'He looks kind,' Elaine murmured, and for the moment she envied Hazel. 'Brainy' too. I bet he'll get on, sport or no sport!'

'Ah!' Lady Lassett bustled in, talking rapidly as she came. 'See you've found that young scamp's latest picture. Pretty, isn't he? Ought to have been a girl!' Without waiting for Elaine to answer, she went on, 'Here's a tit-bit of news to put your possible engagement in the shade, my girl. Don't say nothing ever happens in our part of the world. It does! There's just been an accident, outside your own door—and you,

you little ninny, are miles away and missed it!'

'Accident? Not Robert?' Elaine gasped, her hand at her throat.

'Robert! Good lord, no! Think he can't take care of himself better than that?' Judy Lassett exploded. 'No, my gal, it's a good-looking fella from London, run into the churchyard wall, in his car. Damned good car, too, so they say.'

'Ran into the wall! Was he drunk?'

'Drunk, my eye! No, he was trying to avoid that dirty little shrimp from the Stores—what's the child's name?—Meggie Harris! Ought to be horse-whipped, the way they let the brat run about the street. Saw it coming to her, ages ago. Nearly ran her down meself, once, on my bicycle. Well, they won't learn, these people!'

She finished her coffee, and said to the subdued Elaine, 'Now you cut along and find out some more about it, then come over to-morrow and tell me. Remember—get all the details or I'll have to come down myself and worry Robert, and he won't care for that, now he's so crazy about this book nonsense of his! Adventure-writing Vicar, if you please!'

But it was a tolerant smile which played

21

round her mouth as she said it, and Elaine wondered if there was any truth in the story that Judy Lassett nearly married Robert herself years ago, before Robert became infatuated with the pampered Elizabeth and forgot his horse-riding friend.

FOUR

ANDREW FARRAR subsided into an easy chair by the bright wood fire in the bar parlour, and relaxed. 'Leave me alone,' he had said repeatedly, in a dull sort of voice, and he was conscious of someone in the background murmuring something about shock, and that the fellow was best left alone for the time being. That was Dr. Everton, who had administered to him when he was first brought in; Andrew, while not being actually unconscious, had certainly no clear recollection of what the man looked like, but recalled his gruff, yet not unfriendly voice.

A large, pot-bellied man with a creased brown face and laughing eyes, and an air of leisurely authority, had made up the fire, furnished him with another drink, shooed the rest of the stragglers out, and followed them.

Somewhere beyond the bar parlour their voices rose, going again over the details of

23

the accident. It was, apparently, an event in their lives. Nothing, he heard them say, had happened like it since Tom Jelks had fallen into the threshing machine nine years ago come Easter Monday.

One voice held forth on the way the car—Andrew's car—had come hurtling round the corner at sixty miles an hour. (That's a lie, thought Andrew, savagely. I was nosing gently round that corner.) Another voice drew attention to Meggie playing in the road, and yet another angrily asserting that she had not been in the road at all, but on the pavement, where the car had shot up the kerb, owing to the tremendous speed it had been travelling.

'Out of control, 'e wor!' said someone else, and two others shouted, 'No!'

A woman's voice broke in, with the information that little Meggie had been in the road for the purpose of rescuing a ginger cat from an untimely death, and for a few minutes the truth of this unlikely statement was fiercely contested.

Not a word was said in sympathy with Andrew himself. No one seemed to think it likely that he felt ill through the effects of a near-accident, or that he was possibly angry at the unnecessary damage to his car. On the other hand, there was much hopeful talk of compensation; compensation for any resulting damage to Meggie and compensation for the Vicar for a new wall round the churchyard. No one seemed to have any idea where the compensation was likely to come from, nor did they care. It was something new to talk about, and there was plenty of speculation and lively discussion.

Andrew, listening for a time, at last wearied of the repetition, and let his thoughts slip elsewhere. For a time, they slipped back to Town, a smart flat in Mayfair, where Sandra had strode up and down a pale mauve carpet, like an angry tigress, before she paused in front of him and returned his ring.

He took it out of his pocket, where he had been carrying it ever since, and looked at it, wonderingly. Two superbly-cut emeralds. Well, they did say that green stones were unlucky, didn't they? Who had first told him that? Idly he searched back down the passages of time, and recalled at last hearing a maid talking to his old nurse, and both women had wisely agreed that green stones undoubtedly brought ill fortune. Andrew, at seven, had been tremendously impressed. Andrew, at twenty-seven, was still impressed. Luck was against him, all round. Green stones.

He slipped the ring back in his pocket, and leaned back again, watching the fire, still conscious of the eager, wrangling, repeating, speculating voices beyond the door, but not paying too much attention to them. The fire was of much more importance. It behaved in a queer manner. It changed from a spitting mass of clear-cut flames to a blurred splotch of coral-pink light, which still moved but no longer kept to clear-cut particles.

He leaned forward, and rubbed his eyes. His heart started an anxious, uneven tattoo, as he started the routine of looking, shutting his eyes, then looking again.

'Must keep steady,' he muttered thickly, and leaned back in his chair, eyes closed, forehead damp, hands clutching the arms. Presently he cautiously opened his eyes again, and looked. The mass receded, leaving darting flames. He identified the different colours, and finally picked out a faint curling trail of smoke from a slender stick that was too damp to burn well. The sickly thundering of his heart-beats eased up, and he sank back again, exhausted.

'Mustn't get upset like this,' he whispered. 'Must expect it.'

They left him alone for an hour, then sent a buxom little body in a tight, shiny brown frock and check apron, to tell him dinner was ready, and that it was a cut off the joint and two veg. and would that do?

He looked up into her fat round face, and wondered where he had seen those laughing eyes before. They were alight with curiosity, as she took in the lean length of him, the straight black hair and dark brown eyes, the fine lines of nose and jaw.

'You could do wi' a bit of fattenin', sir,' she said critically.

'Who the devil are you?' he asked, frowning, still trying to remember of whom the eyes reminded him.

'Prue Chibbetts,' she told him, hands on hips, and without a trace of embarrassment. 'What's yore name, sir?'

'D'you work here, or something?' he asked impatiently, ignoring her question.

She tossed her head. 'I live here! Father's landlord of The Crown, same as my grandad wor!'

'Oh, yes,' he breathed, placing her at last as the daughter of the man who had settled him in this room in peace and solitude. 'Seth Chibbetts, licensed to sell wines, spirits, and tobacco. Well, you'd better bring me the food, then, and set about fattening me.'

'You staying 'ere, sir?' she asked incredulously.

'I can hardly go with my car in that condition,' he reminded her gravely. 'Do you know it isn't possible to drive a car with a smashed bonnet?'

'Aye, sir, I drive one meself,' she told him, with a slight lift of the chin. 'Don't I walk out with Eb Wilkins at the garage?'

'Really!'

'Eb reckons it's a town job, and they'm towing it to Oakbridge soon as lorry comes over from the farm. Eb reckons you'll be staying at the Royal Hotel in Oakbridge, seein' as this is only a beer-house, with only one room over stables free.'

'I see,' he murmured. 'Well, you tell your Eb to keep his reckonings to himself, and then go and intimate to your father that I'd like that room over the stables—indefinitely!'

As his decision undoubtedly gave more food for audible thought, he decided after lunch to go out for a stroll. There was silence as he walked through the knot of people at the door of The Crown, but when he was well away from them, he heard their voices raised again in eager speculation. A walk through the village enlightened him; his appearance was indeed an event.

The inn was thatched and gabled, and stood just above the village green. There was a pond, and two upright struts which he later discovered to be part of the original structure of the old ducking-stool. A fine old oak reflected its boughs in the water, and one or two ducks splashed among the reeds at the edge.

Brookfield had two streets, the one which wound through the cluster of old thatched cottages and shops, the other going straight out of the centre of it, where the church and Vicarage lay well back from the road, in line with two or three larger houses, the dimensions and acreage of which grew as they got nearer to the outskirts of the Walpole estate. The smallest of them housed the doctor; the largest was closed for most of the year, and belonged to a retired actress, who spent her old age between her pseudo-Tudor 'cottage' in Brookfield and her ornate villa in the South of France.

Andrew Farrar walked slowly through the village and back again, and liked what he saw. He was enchanted with the butcher's shop in the side of the slaughter-house; the Stores, which sold groceries, kitchenware and garden utensils, drapery and clothing, sweets, tobacco and also acted as Post Office; the church, with its separate Norman tower with the crimson creeper doing its best to cover the grey stonework, and the carved flowers and gargoyles in the churchyard wall which had suffered rather badly from his collision. It was all so unspoiled. Even the sign in one of the cottage windows, intimating that Miss Muriel Trigg undertook to permanent wave between the hours of eleven and five, and that Jonas Trigg's hair-dressing saloon was now approached from the back door, did nothing to mar the rural scene.

The garage he finally ran to earth next to the blacksmith's forge. The proprietor of the petrol pumps was also the blacksmith; horses had to wait for petrol tanks to be filled, lorries for horses to be shod, whichever arrived first. The petrol pumps were sheltered beneath an ancient red-tiled roof which was held up in turn by the main structure of the forge on the one side, and Eb Wilkins, Senr.'s house on the other side; wheels and hammers cheerfully leaned against the scarlet painted sides of the

30

pumps, while a new jack rested with easy familiarity against the side of the anvil.

Andrew smiled, and walked back to The Crown. Here he stopped to look at the gilded sign outside, and noticed for the first time the row of geraniums in the green painted boxes above the porch.

'Yes,' he murmured, 'I'll stay here, I think. As nice a place as any, to——' He broke off, and stared down at two fat white pebbles, which were doing their best to run into each other and dissolve into a blurred lump. He shuddered, recovered himself, and strode back to the inn.

That evening he joined the others at the bar. A few of the men, farmers by their appearance and conversation, were drinking out of metal tankards with lids. A few played darts, and invited him to join them. He refused brusquely, and gave no reason, and they returned silently to their game.

A man in shabby tweeds, a black vest and dog collar, stood at the bar, listening with an amused air to Seth Chibbetts' account of the last rat hunt. Occasionally he took a pull at a glass of ale. As Andrew Farrar moved up to the bar, he turned round and introduced himself as the Vicar of the parish.

'I trust you're no worse for the accident,' he said courteously.

Andrew crisply assured him he was feeling no ill effects, and ordered whisky. He wondered what Sandra was doing now, and had a swift mental vision of her behind her own little cocktail bar, mixing drinks with exotic names, while she smiled languidly on them all. Her hair, Andrew remembered, was the colour of new rope. Ash-blonde, the Society columnists called it, and her eyes were the sultry blue of cornflowers seen through a heat haze. While he mentally jeered at himself for being a poetic fool, he was conscious of a new pain somewhere inside him. Not the dull, aching pain which came with thoughts of his future, but a new pain which was embodied in the bitter-sweet memory of Sandra Standish and this unknown man who was coming back from abroad, for whom she professed greater interest.

With the cheerful clink of glasses over the counter of The Crown, came a memory of a similar clink of glass at one of Sandra's parties, the last one he had been to. Two months ago. Sandra had been by the piano, singing in that sweet, husky voice of hers. She wore, with an amount of elegance and casualness which made enemies of most of the women in the room, a new dress designed in Paris. Andrew didn't know the technical name for it, but connected it with old pictures of Spanish princesses in billowing white. There was very little bodice and no visible means of support, but there was a lot of skirt, and somewhere near the hem it was bunched up beneath a great tawny yellow rose. Sandra wore a daring dress with terrific effect.

Zillah Carey, Sandra's best friend, in a classic black gown, told him in her brittle small voice, 'Sandra's after something, darling. Watch out when she starts wearing a rose within reach of your big feet,' and her tinkling laughter had made him want to choke her.

His co-director had placed a fat, hairy hand on Zillah's bare shoulder, and the pair had moved off. Andrew had stayed and watched Sandra. He didn't remember what she had said to him afterwards, or if he ever found out what it was she had wanted. He remembered only the picture of her as she stood there, and the sound of her voice, and as he stood by the Rev. Robert Boyd at the bar of The Crown, he tried to imprint it on his memory in case he never saw it again.

Sandra was very lovely.

The Vicar said, 'I understand you're going to stay here for a time. We're rather rural, I'm afraid. D'you care for that?'

He nodded. 'I want quiet,' he said curtly.

'Make him comfortable, Chibbetts,' the Vicar told Seth.

'Aye, sir. Missus says he's to have the best front. Prue here has been up to her tricks again, touting for the Royal in Oakbridge. Don't you believe my darter, sir. We won't put you over no stables!'

The Vicar chuckled. 'Still trying to angle for the proprietor of the Royal, is she?'

Seth grinned broadly. 'Likes two strings to 'er bow, does our Prue, though I think she'll wed Eb Wilkins in the end.'

The Vicar said suddenly, 'Come over to the Vicarage for supper. My sister will like having you.'

'D'you usually invite strangers into your home within five minutes of meeting them?' Andrew returned harshly.

'No,' the Vicar replied, in a level tone. 'But I watched you to-day, when you went past our gate. You interested me. I'd like a better opportunity than this of having a quiet chat with you. It's also in the nature of a welcome to Brookfield, as you say you're

34

staying for some time.'

'I'm sorry. That was damned churlish of me. Yes, I'll come,' Andrew said.

Elaine was at the church hall, helping with the laying out of stalls for the jumble sale.

'Vicar's just gone by with chap from accident,' a grubby small boy said succinctly, as he stumbled by with an armful of clothes he had collected at the last moment.

Elaine smiled across at the baker's wife, over a pile of children's underwear. 'My cousin loves new faces,' she said.

'They do say this fella's good-looking miss,' was the reserved response. 'And plenty o' money, to judge by the motor what 'e wantonly smashed into churchyard wall.'

'We don't know whether he did it wantonly or purely by accident,' Elaine said severely. 'And I'd better go home, I suppose, in case the Vicar's asked him to supper.'

Robert Boyd was in the study with his guest when Elaine burst in. They were talking about books in a desultory way, and the Vicar was putting a sheaf of new notes on Elaine's desk. Her first glimpse of

Andrew Farrar was that of the back of his head and part of his lean profile, as he stood by the bookcase studying the portrait of Hazel.

FIVE

'HAZEL's coming home at Easter,' Frances said, a week later, as she carefully folded the letter and put it back into the envelope.

'Is that from her?' Elaine wanted to know, without looking up from spreading marmalade on toast.

Frances frowned at the Vicar's untouched egg, and leaned over to adjust the little cosy. 'Robert's breakfast will be spoiled,' she fumed. 'Odd, the way old Job Tampin always gets a relapse just before the Vicar's breakfast is ready. No,' she said, finally answering the question, 'Hazel hasn't written to me since I last ventured to remind her that her father wasn't made of money. It's from the headmistress. It seems they're to have a fancy dress ball before close of term, and it is imperative that Hazel's costume costs more than her dress allowance will stretch. I wonder why that should be?'

'But, Frances, Robert can't send her any

more money—he's got an overdraft already!'

Frances looked up, startled. 'Has he? I didn't know!' She worried her napkin into a series of creases, then impatiently flung back her chair and went over to her own little bureau. 'I've got my savings—though it does seem hard to squander so much on such a frivolous thing as fancy dress.'

Elaine got up and slipped an arm round the older woman's shoulders. 'It's wrong, too. I won't let you do it. Look, I'll tell you what. We'll get Amelia Christmas to get her ideas going—she's really quite good, you know, for a village dressmaker—and we'll make it a super effort by buying extra-good material for it in Oakbridge. How's that?'

The girl's voice was eager and at the same time appealing. Frances smiled uncertainly.

'We may think it's a good plan, my dear, but will Hazel! It's got something to do with having the name tag of a big dress house just inside the back of the neck, it seems.'

'The snobbish brat!' Elaine exploded. 'Just how much is this going to cost, and what's it supposed to look like, anyway? I bet old Christmas could make one just as good!'

'I'm afraid Miss Christmas won't need to be bothered, dear. You don't understand—they've got the costume already! This is the bill,' she faltered, undoing the letter again, and passing the bill over to Elaine.

'De Bruy Becke of Paris, London and New York,' Elaine read aloud, with a gasp. 'Help, has she lost her mind? Oh, Frances, what's Hazel thinking about?'

She read through the items. 'I don't get it—it's just a Persian Princess. We did that at my old school—one of the girls asked her mother to make it. It was quite pretty, and very effective. But this is just daft! Listen—silver tissue, ice-blue crepe, hand-embroidered with silver thread and seed pearls. Frances, it's about time that spoiled brat came home!' She returned to the bill. 'Good grief, look what it's costing!'

Frances nodded. 'Hazel's account, the letter says, is about fifteen guineas short. I just don't know what to do, short of dipping into my savings,' she said helplessly.

'No! No, you mustn't do that. Wait a minute, while I think,' Elaine said. 'Look, don't let's tell Robert. I'll get the money for you, somehow. Don't you worry. Then later, if Robert's new book is a success, we shall be able to tell him, and perhaps it won't be so bad. Besides, we might explain to Hazel, and get her to sell the costume. She won't need it again, will she?'

'No, I don't think so, unless she insists on having an expensive portrait taken, wearing the thing,' Frances Boyd said, with a wry smile. 'Elaine,' she began again, hesitating.

'Yes, Frances?'

'I don't usually pry into your affairs, my dear, do I? But just this once . . . where are you going to get the money?'

Elaine stared at her.

'I mean, Elaine dear, you're not going to ask Mr. Farrar to lend it to you, or anything like that?'

Elaine laughed sharply in sheer relief, and at the ludicrous idea of approaching Farrar for anything. 'Good heavens, no! It's all I can manage to wish him good morning without getting snubbed for it!'

'He snubs you, dear? Why should he do that?'

Elaine shrugged. 'Oh, I don't know. Perhaps I'm a bit pushful. Perhaps he just doesn't like girls with freckles. I don't even know why I bother about him, but the fact is, he strikes me as being a little lost, lonely. Oh, it may be my imagination.'

'I must say he's been quite courteous to me,' Frances said, wrinkling her brow. 'And I know he likes Robert. I believe he's made friends with Israel Lincoln, too.'

'Oh, that's just because Israel's the organist, and Robert discovered that the distant Mr. Farrar loves music. I don't know why I bother with the man, but I expect the next time I see him I shall stick my neck out, and wonder why I get a bucket of cold water flung over me!'

Frances looked wonderingly after her, as she picked up her things and slammed out of the room. It wasn't like Elaine to bother so much about any one person, nor to be snubbed—if it were true. Everyone liked Elaine. She was easily the most popular girl in the district. Perhaps this young man was interested in a particular girl, and just didn't notice others. But it was a bad sign for Elaine to take his lack of interest like this. She forgot the bill from Hazel's headmistress, and set to work worrying about Elaine, and determining to speak to the Vicar about it.

He, too, looked worried, as he settled down to eat his cold breakfast. 'Old Job died this time,' he told his sister.

Frances snorted. 'So it wasn't a false alarm to-day!' she said tartly. 'They've sent for you so many times and spoilt your breakfast, that I began to be quite cross.'

'Where's Elaine?' he wanted to know.

She told him what had been said about Andrew Farrar. 'Is it true, Robert? He looks too nice to snub anyone.'

'He's an unhappy man, Frances. I found out last night that his fiancée has jilted him. He didn't say why, but he carries her ring about with him. Perpetual reminder, I suppose.' He thoughtfully lit his pipe, and murmured, as he got up, 'Elaine is a very attractive young person, and a very persistent one,' and his sister got the impression that despite his apparent interest in books to the exclusion of everything else, there was little he missed after all, and that he, too, was worried about Elaine.

He went to his study, and found that Elaine's typewriter was still covered. She arrived, flushed and breathless, an hour later, and looking rather cross.

'Sorry I'm late, Robert. I'll work it out the other end of the day, to make up.'

'You don't need to do that, my dear. Your working time has always been elastic, though you chose to keep rigid office hours.

But I do like to know if you aren't going to be at hand.'

She didn't answer, and he studied her curiously. She ripped three sheets of paper out of the machine, spoiled. She seemed to have difficulty with her shorthand notes, and finally knocked over the pen-tray, spilling a shower of paper clips and pins over the carpet.

'Let's knock off for a bit and have a chat,' he suggested. 'Did you hear that old Job Tampin has died this morning?'

She looked up, startled. 'No, I didn't. How funny—I always thought he was strong as a horse, and just made a show of being ill. I'm sorry,' she added, hurriedly.

He turned away to hide a smile, and offered: 'Mrs. Ogg says we've seventeen and sixpence more than at the last jumble sale. Things are looking up.'

'How nice, Robert.'

'And Judy Lassett's offering a boy's bicycle as a special prize, to act as incentive to the Cubs to fetch and carry at the Garden Party in June. (I think it's one of Peter's bikes he grew too big for, but it should be in good condition and quite acceptable.) Oh, and old Mrs. Geddes is offering three bottles of red currant wine against one last time, for the Sale of Work.'

'Things *are* looking up!' Elaine said, trying to be enthusiastic.

'But not with you, eh, my dear?' he observed shrewdly. 'Come on, now, get it off your chest. Why this wild dashing about before anyone else is up?'

She thoughtfully put the pen-tray back, and said hesitantly, 'Robert, when you've got money coming to you, by a legacy, isn't it all right to get a loan on it? Sort of on your expectations?'

'Well, it depends,' he said carefully.

'What does it depend on?' she wanted to know, and there was still that heated tone in her voice.

'Suppose you tell me what it's all about, instead of asking me difficult questions?'

'Well, I get fifty pounds and the proceeds of the old house when I'm twenty-one, don't I—from Father and Mother?' she said, with difficulty. 'I wanted to borrow on it, but the bank wouldn't let me. Robert, there's no doubt about my money—I know I'm going to get it. There's only four months to wait, and I wanted to sign an undertaking that I'd pay it back? Good grief, Mr. Cheddle knows me almost as well as you do, but——'

44

The Vicar chuckled. 'Elaine, you're supposed to be my private secretary, and you don't know any better than that! You can't go to a bank and borrow without security and, besides, you're a minor!'

She shrugged impatiently. 'Oh, I know that, Robert—but that only means big banks, where they don't know you personally. I wanted to put down a copy of the letter from the solicitors saying I was to have it—that'd be security, wouldn't it? Well, enough for a potty little bank like the Oakbridge one.'

He wasn't smiling at her now. He looked old and tired. 'I suppose you must want money pretty badly, to go to such desperate lengths. It's no good my asking what you want it for, or how much you want?' he hazarded.

'I want fifteen guineas,' she said, in a stifled voice, 'and I can't tell you what it's for, Robert. I didn't really want to mention it, only I thought—well, you know old Cheddle so well, and I wondered if you could speak to him for me. He's only being uppish, you know.'

'No, my dear. He isn't. He's the manager of a small town branch of a very big and important London bank. The size of his branch doesn't lessen his responsibility. You should know that. You shouldn't be misled, either, by the fact that we all know each other so well here, and mostly use each other's Christian names. We've still got to render businesslike accounts to our superiors, who, unfortunately perhaps, aren't on such an easy footing with us.'

He paused, and considered her mutinous little round face, and thought with a pang how young she was after all, and how little she had had out of life. Like his sister, he felt suddenly that it didn't seem right that Hazel should take so much, and take it for granted, while her cousin should have nothing at all.

'You know, Elaine, I said at the beginning that you would one day want money of your own, but you insisted on coming here to work for me.'

She was out of her chair in a flash and by his side. 'Oh, no, Robert—don't say that! It isn't that at all. To tell you the truth, I don't want this money for—for myself—' She broke off, flushing. 'That's not true, exactly. It is for myself, but I'm so ashamed of wanting it because I might have known how you'd feel. Believe me, it's for an important purpose, not for anything frivolous. Oh, I can't explain—'

He stroked her hair. 'It isn't enough to work in return for a home and the pitiful pocket-money I give you. I can't do more, my dear—you know that. I would, if I could! But that needn't stop you from going to work elsewhere. Why don't you try and get a well-paid job in a town? You could, you know! You could always come here for week-ends, and feel free to come back at any time you wanted to. But you must have money, my dear. You can't go on like this.'

'No, no, Robert, you don't understand,' she cried, clutching his arm as though to force him to see her thoughts. 'It's not that I want a job with money—I don't. I'm so happy here. I wouldn't want to work in a town and live on my own, and I love the village and the people and everything. I'd never get work I loved like yours, either. It's just that it's so aggravating that I've got this money due to me and can't touch it just when I need it.'

'I could lend it to you,' he began doubtfully, and she could almost feel him anxiously going over his overdraft.

'No, Robert. I know you can't do it. I'm so sorry I had to tell you all this. But you did ask me—oh, I've made a mess of everything.'

He suggested that they both forget it for the time being, and perhaps he'd think of something, and she agreed. But the work didn't go so well, and they were both glad when Frances beat the gong for lunch.

Twice Elaine had caught him looking extremely worried, and she could have kicked herself for being so clumsy in letting him know she wanted money. She might have known how he'd take it, for he had often tried to raise the subject of his dissatisfaction with their mutual arrangements in the time she had been with him. She had always known it had worried him, and now he had some tangible incident to pin down, to prove that he was right and that she was not managing too well without a set wage.

When their work was over for the day, she put on her outdoor clothes and quietly took the old bike and went back to Oakbridge. Charles' shop was still open, though most of the other shops were preparing to close. She propped the bike outside his window and ran into the doorway, where she collided sharply with a customer who was coming out.

'Oh!' she gasped, recoiling.

He was a tall man, and almost knocked the breath out of her, and as his back was to the light, it was a moment or two before she recognized him.

'Oh, it's you, Mr. Farrar! I wanted to catch the shop before it closed.'

'Not at all!' he said, bowing distantly, and stood aside for her to pass.

She flushed a little, but said determinedly, 'Good night, Mr. Farrar!'

His good night was as stiff as his expression, as he walked quickly off into the April dusk.

Charles Ramsey had come forward, and was watching the incident curiously.

'Do you know that man?' he asked her sharply.

He was a thick-set young man, with sharp, inquisitive features, sandy hair, and bright eyes which were more green than grey. He wore glasses in a thick horn frame, which added to his already bookish appearance, and he had an irritating trick of leaning forward a little, chin out and eyes anxious, as if for ever anticipating the wishes of his customers.

Elaine frowned a little. 'Oh, he's new to the village. Staying at The Crown,' she said carelessly. 'Charles, I want to talk to you.

Can we go into the office?'

'Well, can't you wait till I shut the shop? I may lose some business, you know.'

'Oh, all right, but I have to be back for tea,' she warned, and stood by his side till the town clock struck six. Then, and not a second before, would Charles put up the shutters and close the shop door, and all the time he had stood waiting for possible customers, he had been thinking (she could see) about Andrew Farrar.

Once he had said, 'It's odd that you should know the man by name, when I hadn't even an inkling that there was anyone new in Brookfield,' and she had answered impatiently, 'Why is it odd when I live so near The Crown, and you've only been in the village twice since he's been there? Besides, he's a friend of Robert's.'

'But the Vicar is so much older than my late customer,' he fretted, and just before the clock struck six, he had said again, 'Strange that the Vicar should have a friend so much younger than himself.'

'Charles, if you don't stop harping on that stiff-necked individual who just went out of your shop, I shall scream!' she warned, and at that he looked a little relieved. Obviously Elaine wasn't attracted,

50

or she wouldn't speak like that of the man, he reasoned.

'Now, Elaine,' he began, as she followed him into the tiny room at the back of the shop, where his chair was pulled up neatly to his tidily-kept desk, and another small chair stood ready for possible invasion. 'To what do I owe the honour of this visit?'

He smiled brightly at her, and took off his glasses to polish them on an immaculate white handkerchief which he kept tucked up his sleeve.

'Charles, can you lend me fifteen guineas?' she began, without preamble.

Her shock tactics had worked with him before, over the matter of loans of books, but she had never had occasion to mention money, and from the first she could see that her usual methods weren't going to work this time.

The smile fled from his face, his eyes popped and his jaw dropped. 'Fifteen guineas?' he whispered.

'Yes,' she said firmly. 'As you know, I'm expecting a small legacy in four months' time. I'll repay you then. I'll sign a note to that effect, if you like,' she finished.

He sat staring at her for a bit, then deliberately finished polishing his glasses, and took time to settle them on the bridge of his nose. He then picked up a pencil, and pulled forward a neat pad, and sat at the ready.

'I don't think I recall much of this legacy, Elaine. Where is it to come from?'

'You know—I told you,' she said impatiently. 'From my parents—the sale of our old house and all that. It was held in trust for me till I was twenty-one.'

'Then you've been having interest on it all this time?' was his next question.

'What's that got to do with it?' she exploded. 'Help, I'm only asking for the loan of a paltry fifteen pounds odd!'

He patted her hand. 'Don't be upset, Elaine. I'm a business man, and I must know how I stand to lose or gain by whatever transaction I handle.'

'It's not a transaction!' she said heatedly. 'It's a request for a small loan, between friends, that's all. If you don't want to lend it to me, say so, and I'll ask someone else!'

He put down his pencil, and folded his lips in tightly. 'I haven't said I won't lend it, Elaine,' he said cautiously. 'The fact is, I've always thought very highly of you, and to tell you the truth, I'm rather disappointed in you. Nice girls don't ask men for loans of money, you know!'

'Who's asking *men*?' she fumed, glaring at him. 'I'm asking *you*. You're supposed to be my friend, and you've always said I'm to come to you whenever I wanted help—anything at all! Well, I do need help and I've come, like you said. What are you going to do about it?'

'You're so violent,' he protested, mopping his forehead. 'It's a most regrettable trait in you. Now, this request for fifteen guineas, that isn't a small sum, Elaine. What would you want it for? Something very important, I feel sure!'

'Of course it's important, or I wouldn't degrade myself in asking for it. *Begging* for it!'

'Well, I shall have to know what it's for,' he murmured.

She considered the point. It just wasn't possible to tell anyone, least of all Charles. She couldn't have said why she felt like that about him, for he had always seemed most trustworthy. It was just that he had that irritating quality of holding an inquest on the most simple request. If she told him about Hazel, he would probably feel it his duty to go and tell the Vicar, and presume to lecture Robert on his daughter's extravagance. Then the fat would be in the fire!

She swallowed and determinedly told a lie. 'If you must know, I want a new suit—badly—and I simply can't afford it. I shall be able to buy a complete outfit when I get my legacy, but even *you* can't feel too happy about being seen out with me in these shabby old things!'

His face cleared. 'Elaine, why didn't you say so at first? That simplifies everything. Now, the tailor along the way is a good friend of mine, and we'll have you measured, and I shall be happy to present it to you to celebrate our engagement!'

He made elaborate and complicated notes on his little pad. 'We'll have a new hat with it—it should all come out of the fifteen guineas, with perhaps a little over for shoes and handbag. I can do it cheaply.'

'Charles, doesn't it strike you that you're presuming? I like to do my own shopping—and I don't care for your tailor friend. All I am asking you is to make me a small loan which I'll repay. And besides, we're not engaged!'

He stared again, and there was a suggestion of unfriendliness in his face.

'I took it for granted that you'd altered your mind about that,' he said slowly. 'I mean you can't ask me for money, and still refuse to marry me, can you?'

'Can't I!' she said furiously. 'Watch me! You're so mean, I'd think twice before I got engaged to you anway! I'm never going to see you again, Charles Ramsey!'

She stalked to the door and wrenched it open. He was there almost as soon as she was, holding it against her. 'Don't—don't say things to me like that, Elaine. You upset me. Excuse me—I must have a tablet. My heart, you know!'

She paused, scared a little. He did look queer. She followed him to the back of the shop, and watched him fuss with a tablet and a glass of water, before she spoke again.

'I'm sorry, Charles, I didn't mean to upset you. But you make me so angry.'

'Then you'll take back what you said?' he asked eagerly. 'Look, I'll lend you the money, and we'll say nothing about being engaged. Not for the present, anyway,' he compromised, and went over to his safe. She stood by, fascinated at his slow and precise movements, unlocking the safe, moving out neat packages, counting out the notes one by one, securing with a rubber band and marking the paper round the rest of the notes, putting everything back again, and carefully locking the safe. He ought to have been a bank clerk, not a bookseller, she mused.

She took the money gratefully enough, though she was surprised at Charles' insistence on her signing an undertaking to return it as she had half frivolously promised, and putting it carefully away in a clean envelope in the safe before he locked up. Finally, he entered the whole transaction in his diary before her eyes.

She felt a little sick, and somehow trapped. She went out to her bicycle, and rode away without a backward glance.

Charles Ramsey stood watching her, and there came an unbidden thought in his mind that she had never bothered about new clothes for him. It was a coincidence that she should do so now, he decided, at the same time that a prepossessing stranger appeared in the village. He recalled, too, the look on her face when Farrar had rebuffed her in the doorway of the shop.

SIX

ZILLAH CAREY stepped carefully out of the low, tiny body of the garishly painted racer, made an effusive farewell to her escort, and ran up the two steps into the hall of the expensive block of flats in which Sandra Standish was at present housed.

Sandra, in a cream and jade patterned house-coat, moved away from the window. 'You needed a corkscrew to get out of that, my pet, didn't you?' she observed with a faint smile.

Zillah grinned and threw down her new fox. 'It's handmade,' she explained, referring to the racer. Then, with an ecstatic look (and now referring to her escort) she said: 'He's a pet.'

'A little young for you, don't you think?' her friend murmured.

'I like 'em young. I train 'em myself,' Zillah said, airily, and added, 'His father's got pots of money.'

'How do you find them?' Sandra asked

57

wonderingly. She sat down on the table edge, and said, 'Well, what's this wonderful letter you'd had which won't wait till I see you this afternoon?'

Zillah whipped it out of her muff-bag, with a triumphant gesture. 'From the Merryweathers,' she whooped.

'From the *who*?'

Zillah wasn't deceived by Sandra's mystified voice, and knew very well that the other girl remembered the rather noisy and vulgarly wealthy family they had met at a party the year before.

'Pip and Squeak Merryweather, darling. Willie's divorce party, fun in the Blue Room, the new house at Brookfield with those awful green tiles—you *must* remember!'

'Oh, yes, I recall . . . what about them?' Sandra yawned.

'They've got *Andrew* down there—or at least, they've *seen* him there!' Zillah crowed.

Sandra looked wary. She swished over to a settee and sprawled on it, studying her nails, before answering.

'What about it?' she drawled, finally.

'*Dar*-ling—I thought you were *crazy* to know what had *happened* to him!' Zillah protested.

'Naturally, poor lamb,' Sandra said carelessly. 'He's not safe to be about alone.'

'Not safe? Why?' Zillah breathed.

'Oh, you know the story of that old accident. The one he had at that last school, when he hurt his head. It's going to affect his eyes, it seems, after all these years.'

Zillah opened her pillar-box red mouth. 'You mean he's going to be *blind*?' she squeaked.

'Oh, don't be dramatic! It'll affect his sight, but how much, they can't say.'

'How'd you know all this?' Zillah probed.

Sandra shrugged. 'Oh, the usual source. Andrew consulted Bubbles Burke's new husband—he's a big bug in the optical way, apparently. You know Bubbles, always snooping. When Andrew went there, she had the added incentive of knowing him well, and listened in so eagerly that she got all her facts wrong. At least, she said there was to be another consultation, but that couldn't be so, because Andrew never went again.' She sucked in her lips, angrily. 'But there was something said, and it was serious. They told him at the time of the

59

accident that it would probably muck his sight up, and I only found that out when he came back from seeing Burke. To think Andrew had the nerve to get engaged to me without letting me know a word about it! He might have warned me!'

Zillah chirped. 'Well, perhaps he was in love with you, darling. It's no fun to have to lead your bloke about on a bit of string, but I must say it takes nerve to chuck his ring back at him. If it were anyone else but you, angel, I'd say it was the act of a stinker, you know!'

'Oh, shut up! It wouldn't have been so bad if he hadn't lost his money. He could have had a man to wait on him, and we could still have had fun in our separate ways. But having to pinch and scrape—not me! I've had to do that all my life—I would be a mut to run into that again!'

'Money?' Zillah repeated, catching the essential word. 'What about his money?'

'He's been losing on horses in a big way, and his investments went flop. And now his eyes are all wrong, and he won't wear glasses, and he'll have to give up his work. Didn't you know?' Sandra said, wearily and with more than a trace of bitterness.

'Are you kidding?' Zillah squeaked

delightedly. 'It's all in the game—they're all doing it! I must say I didn't think old stick-in-the-mud Andrew would try it out, though.' She started to laugh, little tinkly peals of laughter which had always irritated Sandra, and affected her so strongly now that she shouted at the other girl to stop it.

'You little fool—what are you blathering about? What game? Who's playing it?'

'Everyone in our crowd,' Zillah spluttered. 'It's Willie's book, you know. The one about How to Make Friends or something silly. It says if you want to prove your friends are really friends, just tell 'em you're going to lose all your money. If they leave you, they're stinkers. If they stick by you, they're True Blue. Everyone's tried it, only most of us knew what it was about, and we all got voted True Blue. Didn't you *know*, darling?'

Sandra stared at her.

'Andrew's stinking rich,' Zillah crowed. 'He's got pots more money than he ever had, now his uncle's snuffed out. (The one that lived in Rhodesia or the Gold Coast or somewhere.) Gosh, you're cuckoo! I'd have stuck to him if he'd lost both arms and legs as well, if I'd been you,' Zillah said fervently.

Sandra clutched her shoulder. 'You're not making this up?' she insisted.

Zillah shook her head. 'What happened to his ring? Did you really chuck it back at him?'

'Why?'

'Oh, I just wondered whether he took it, or whether he walked off in scorn and left it, because that ring'll be worth something.'

Sandra worried her hair. 'I don't know. I threw it down somewhere, I think. It should be here—that damned girl never dusts anywhere.' She scrabbled among the things on the small table near where Andrew had stood that day. It wasn't among them. 'He must have picked it up.'

'He would,' Zillah said, disappointed. 'He's always the little gentleman. He'll probably carry it about with him, and keep reminding himself of his misery by looking at it.'

'I wonder,' Sandra said, thinking quickly. 'I wonder if I could get him back?'

Zillah knew better than to hazard an answer, but sat quietly and waited. Suddenly Sandra whirled round on her, with the old show of temper which her friends knew well, and expected sooner or later in every disappointment which Sandra had.

'You little idiot, why didn't you warn me about Willie's miserable book, and what the others were doing? How was I to know? Making a fool of me like this? Look what I've lost through it! It's all your fault! What are you supposed to be my friend for, I should like to know? What are you going to do about trying to get Andrew back? It was all your fault that I lost him!'

Zillah listened patiently until the tirade was over, then said brightly: 'If I could only be sure where that ring was, I could make a plan of campaign. He's probably pawned it, or thrown it in the river. If he's still keeping it, I think I know what to do.'

At that moment the ring was rolling gently down a bank, coming to rest at last against a large lump of rock. The twin green stones winked with a rich, glowing colour against the greyish-white behind them, and the young grass around was almost faded in comparison.

Andrew watched it with a curious fascination and made no attempt to pick it up. Instead he said, without his usual harsh tones, 'You really are a clumsy young woman!'

'Oh, I *am* sorry, truly I am,' Elaine stammered, flushing, and it was she who ran down the bank and retrieved it for him. 'I only grabbed your arm because—well, you were standing rather near the edge—'

'You thought I was going to jump in the river?' he asked, with a twisted grin. 'No, I'm not that kind of a person. I simply haven't the courage to take my life.'

He held his hand out for it, and as she dropped it into his palm, she said softly, 'Isn't it a beauty? I hope it isn't damaged.'

'Do you?' he looked curiously at her, and she returned his look fearlessly. For her, there was something hauntingly sad and lost in his dark eyes, but for him there was something new and very appealing in a woman who could look him straight in the eyes with such frank friendliness.

'Sit down,' he said. 'Oh, go on—sit, sit! I know I've been damned rude to you ever since I first saw you, and I apologize, if that's what you want. That's right, show you've forgiven me by sharing the grass with me.'

She watched him sit down beside her, with a mixture of interest and uneasiness. She had heard him converse pleasantly with the Vicar, but had never had the experience of hearing him talk easily with her. The harshness had vanished, but he was still very much on the defensive.

He made an effort to explain. 'It wasn't really rudeness as such. Just a fervent desire to keep away from women.' He searched her face to see how she was taking it. 'You're a very persistent specimen. How many times have I snubbed you?'

'Twelve,' she admitted. 'I counted them.'

'Yes. I thought you'd do that. Well, you've won. Satisfied?'

'In a way,' she allowed, adding, 'I was going to give you up, though. No one's ever snubbed me before, and it's not a nice feeling. I tried to win your friendship, because you gave it to others—Robert, Frances, Israel Lincoln. You looked such an interesting person. Then, when you snubbed me in the doorway of Charles Ramsey's shop, I determined to have no more to do with you.'

'H'm. Ramsey, eh? Friend of yours?'

She hesitated. 'No. No, he isn't,' she said, the second negative being firmer than the first.

He looked down at her and wondered. 'Oh, it wasn't Ramsey who made you change your mind about me, then?'

'No, it was Robert,' she admitted

frankly. 'He told me a bit about—that,' she said, nodding at the ring he still toyed with between thumb and forefinger. 'I hope you don't mind my mentioning it. Only, you see—well, it sort of justified your being so horrid to me. If I'd been treated like that, well, I wouldn't want anything more to do with men, if you see what I mean.'

'I do see,' he told her.

She pulled her knees up, and cuddled her arms round them, resting her chin on top. The fresh breeze ruffled her rich brown crop of curls, and her eyes had a far-away look. She seemed a long way away from him, and he was conscious of a need to bring her back.

'So you hope the ring isn't damaged, do you?' he murmured.

'Oh, yes,' she told him earnestly. 'Can you tell, or will it have to go back to a jeweller's?'

'Oh, I think it'll stand up to it,' he assured her. 'Any idea of its value?'

'Oh, no,' she laughed. 'I've never had any jewellery in my life. I know what I like, without knowing why. I don't know what you call the setting or those stones, but I feel inside me that it's a lovely thing,' she explained, with a hint of embarrassment at her own ignorance.

'No idea of jewellery values, eh? How refreshing,' he mused. Suddenly he thrust it at her. 'Here, you have it! You would like it, wouldn't you?'

The smile vanished from her face, and a look of faint distrust appeared, a little hurt look with it. 'You're laughing at me,' she told him. 'Perhaps I oughtn't to have taken any notice of Robert after all.'

He pulled her down as she started to scramble to her feet. 'Oh, lord, I didn't mean to do that! Don't be offended. Look, all I meant was this. This ring belonged to a spoiled, lovely creature who had so much jewellery that this was just another ring to her. She knew values, too, and probably felt that it wasn't worth her while to take care of. Now I meet someone who likes it because it is a lovely thing in itself—don't you see? I thought it would be in better keeping with you. Precious stones like to be liked. (That's not my own—I heard an old jeweller say that once, and it struck me as being a bit of rare wisdom.) I just offered it to you on the spur of the moment. I'll take it back, if you don't like the idea. But don't look like that.'

She relaxed a little. 'Well, if that's

true—'

He assured her it was, and she sat down again.

'In any case, even if I knew you well enough to take it, Mr. Farrar, I couldn't, you know. It's unlucky to wear someone else's engagement ring.'

'Even if the owner rejected it?' he asked, with his old harshness coming back.

She nodded. 'It's an old superstition. You have to have the stones put into another setting, to make a fresh ring of it.'

'I see.' He put the ring back in his pocket. She wondered where the case was, and decided that he must be very hurt not to bother about losing the value of such a thing either by giving it away to the first stranger who came along, or by running the risk of losing it out of his pocket.

'They brought your car back to-day,' she told him, making conversation. 'It's at Eb Wilkins' place. Have you seen it yet?'

'No,' he told her, without much interest.

'They made a fine job of it in Oakbridge. They can do most things in Oakbridge, as well as they can in London,' she boasted.

He looked quizzically down at her.

'Well, *almost* as well,' she temporized, with a grin.

68

'You're a happy soul,' he said, taking in every detail of her face as if seeing it for the first time. 'What's the secret?'

'I don't know,' she said slowly. 'Life's good, you know. I suppose it's because everything and everyone are so nice to me, that I'm happy. I can't help being happy.'

He looked covertly at her shabby coat and worn shoes, and wondered how her shapely legs would look in sheer silk stockings, instead of that curious cotton mixture stocking which most of the women seemed to wear down here.

'Don't you ever yearn for a job in Town, and a good time at night and at the week-ends?' he wondered.

'Robert's urging me to consider the same thing,' she told him. 'He's my second-cousin, you know, and he seems to think there's more to be had in Town than here. That's strange, I think, because Robert is such a wise person, as a rule.'

'What makes you so sure that he isn't being wise about this?'

'I know a girl who got a job in Birmingham. She was at school with me, and her parents died, too. She's better trained than I am, and she gets a good wage, too. She lives by herself in a bed-sitter, and packs the bed up in the day-time and pretends it's a couch. She has her food all by herself in crowded teashops, and has to make her own breakfast and supper and do her washing all in that one room. She goes to the pictures once a week, and dancing on Saturday. She says Sundays ought not to have been invented, they take such a long time to get through.' She raised clear grey eyes to his. 'What's she got that I'd care to swap all this for?'

He followed her fond glance round the sweep of countryside; on tiny farms and thatched roofs, a red church top here and a grey spire there; banks of blue-green woods, and the sudden silver gleam of water.

'Shut your eyes,' she commanded, 'and listen to it. Then stuff your ears and just smell it all. Then pinch your nose as well, and lie down with your face on the grass so you can do nothing but *feel* it. Ever tried feeling grass and soil and water, when all the other senses are shut up for a time?'

He did as she told him, then looked at her again, as if he saw her for the first time, and found her good.

'It seems to me, Mr. Farrar, that when you want a glamorous dance frock, you have to take the grey streets, the loneliness and the bed-sitter with it,' she said, dismissing the subject, and scrambling to her feet. 'I'll be late for lunch. Coming?'

SEVEN

ELAINE'S remark about Sundays intrigued Andrew Farrar, and as Easter drew near, and succeeding Sabbaths drew him closer to the Vicarage family, he began to understand.

Brookfield had a special atmosphere on its seventh day. The inhabitants wore the clothes of their labours during the week, and put them aside for decent black on Sunday. Eb Wilkins' father looked strangely unfamiliar in stiff collar and funereal coat and trousers instead of the open shirt and old leather apron. Harris, without glasses and pencil behind ear, and Ogg, without a liberal smearing of flour over face and bare arms, were strangers.

From his seat in the Vicarage pew, Andrew watched them covertly, though with less comfort than his former place at the back of the church. His feelings were of warmth and interest rather than amusement. They were the first real people he had ever known.

Some of the pews were longer than others, and all had a small gate at the end. On the top was a tiny metal frame, in which a card was slipped with the family's name, though Robert had told him humorously that very few of the pews were paid for any longer.

Ogg the baker had one of the biggest pews. He came in first with tremendous ceremony, followed by wife and tallest child, the rest going down in size until the tiniest tottered along, clutching the end of her brother's jacket. With unfailing regularity this tiny mite's knickers slipped down, and it was the weekly routine for Mrs. Ogg to turn round and pass the word down the line to the last-child-but-one to pull up the offending garment before they took their places.

Lady Lassett occupied the small pew across the aisle from Andrew, but Dr. Everton occupied a large one, to accommodate his wife, her mother and unmarried sister, his old father and his five children.

Andrew had lately slipped into the habit of calling for Frances and Elaine, who went early just behind the Vicar. On his first two Sundays in Brookfield, Andrew had attended church with the Chibbett family, whose pew was at the back, but now it was understood that this rule should be broken. Yet he missed the old vantage point, and to make up for the uninterrupted view of the congregation streaming in, he found himself forming a new habit; that of sitting with eyes closed, trying to recognize footsteps and voices. (Just to save the indignity of looking round, he told himself—not with any thought of future need.)

Grannie Geddes was easy to recognize. She almost always dropped her bag of brandy balls brought to while away Robert's sermon, and their familiar tinkle and plop as they met the stones and rolled in all directions, never varied.

Miss Christmas rustled into church, a walking advertisement for her little dress-making establishment. Miss Trigg and brother Jonas also advertised, via the seductive display of formal iron waves and gleaming hair oil. Both smelt aggressively of lilies of the valley, from brilliantine and setting lotion. One of the Triggs (Andrew could never find out which, but he suspected Miss Muriel) wore squeaky shoes.

Dr. Everton had a trick of clearing his

throat as he sat down in his pew, and growled a warning to his family who, at the given moment, all knelt together with a tremendous clattering of Sunday boots, and all miraculously finished the entering-church prayer at the same moment and clattered up on to the seat again. The old grandfather blew his nose like a fog-horn at this point, and Andrew caught himself wondering with a smile whether that was the pre-arranged signal. The young Evertons were nice children, all disconcertingly alike. If you looked along their pew, they all looked straight at you with the same movement of the head, and stared back like a row of young owls.

'You like church, don't you?' Elaine asked him one day, as they sat side by side with only a preoccupied Frances as their nearest neighbour.

'Well—' Andrew hesitated, 'I like this one.' He felt the warmth of it all surging round him, and without being able to pin it down to any one thing, he saw it in many of the intimate little details around him.

The small boy (ginger-headed brother of the tiny girl Andrew had almost killed not so long ago) moving slowly across the altar steps, lighting the candles, a boy unfamiliar in his little black vestments and surplice, with fresh-scrubbed face, and hair starting straight from his head after contact with the pump. The tulips from the Vicarage garden mingled with hothouse flowers from Walpole House, on the high altar. The burnished glow of the altar brasses, provided (he knew) by the hands of the Vicar's sister the day before. The crochet edge of the altar cloth, the fine work of the baker's wife and the sewing-woman at Walpole House. The fine old stained-glass window over the high altar, provided by the rich of the parish; the old carved screen and the collection of pictures depicting the Twelve Stations of the Cross, provided by the labours and ingenuity of the poor. And perhaps symbolizing the whole of this heart-warming atmosphere was the swelling crescendo of Israel Lincoln's own fugue from the organ loft.

St. Chad's belonged to the people of Brookfield, and it was kept going by their love and devotion. Courting still started with the young sparks waiting outside to look over the young women as they came out in their colourful best. Robert prayed for his people in sickness and in health, baptized their children, confirmed and married them, and presided at their decent burial. Under Robert's guidance were their problems and their pleasures, and St. Chad's was the centre of their lives.

Andrew reflected that in his world, church was merely the backcloth for smart weddings. Christenings, too, perhaps, and for important funerals. Otherwise church was a shocking bore. He wondered how Sandra would fit into all this, and how Willie and Zillah and the rest would be, if they were transported here at this moment. For a second he heard Sandra's bored drawl, Zillah's metallic tinkle and Willie's stutter. He shut his eyes, and tried to push out the unwelcome memory. It was spoiling everything.

As Robert came slowly in, and the congregation rose, Elaine whispered: 'You've got the wrong place. Sunday before Easter, you know!'

He looked down at the open page, and the letters started to dance and go into that confused blur which was beginning to haunt his waking hours. He shut the prayer book with a snap. 'I don't need it,' he whispered shortly.

'You can look over mine,' she said, but there was an odd expression on her face.

Frances leaned forward to see what the whispering was about and noticed the way Elaine was looking, but said nothing. Later in the day, however, when she had a moment to speak to the girl, she said, 'Why were you looking so queerly at Mr. Farrar? It's not like you to stare so, my dear! Not only in church but over lunch too!'

'I'm glad he's gone out with Robert for a walk,' Elaine answered worriedly. 'I wanted to ask you about him. I think there's something wrong with his eyes.'

'With his eyes? Oh, no, I don't think so,' Frances said, struggling to recollect any odd thing about them. 'Whatever made you think so?'

'He couldn't find the right place in the prayer-book, and sometimes I've noticed he stops and stares hard at things, as if he's trying to get his eyes to focus right.'

'Well, dear, what if that is so? He may need glasses. He may even have consulted an optician already, and he's probably trying to make do until his glasses come,' Frances said, comfortably.

'Oh, perhaps you're right,' Elaine breathed, with relief. 'I was rather worried, for a moment.'

Frances glanced sharply at her, and

hoped that Elaine wouldn't make her anxiety public in other directions. Things could get rather tiresome if that odd Mr. Ramsey was to hear of it.

EIGHT

THE following week Elaine and Robert worked all day and all through the evening, too, in an effort to clear everything up before Hazel came home. Hazel hated to see people working, and kept up a constant stream of interruptions and small crises, to divert attention to herself. Otherwise, she was apt to feel 'out of it'.

The night before Good Friday, utterly exhausted but completely happy, Elaine and Robert tidied the study, and prepared to go and meet Robert's daughter at Brookfield Halt. Elaine looked at her cousin fondly, but with a trace of uneasiness. He was sheet-white and rather slower in his movements. Robert had always been such a hale and hearty man, yet when she spoke to Frances about him, his sister always brushed it aside with the assurance that he was bound to feel tired, under the strain of so much work.

She sighed. 'Robert, you've worked too

hard these last few weeks. I wish you'd leave more to me.'

He smiled a little and shook his head.

'At least why don't you try and get a curate, Robert? The parish work is too much for you, you know it is!'

'What, with two rural churches to see to? My dear, whoever heard of such nonsense!' he gently reproved, but even his voice had an exhausted quality in it. 'Where did you put my sermons?'

'In the top drawer on the left. In separate envelopes. The ones for St. Chad's are on the top.'

'Bless my soul, what a girl you are for efficiency! ''Sermons for St. Mary's-on-the-Heath, Good Friday and Easter Sunday, Evensong.'' ''Sermons for St. Chad's, Brookfield-under-Woke, Good Friday and Easter Sunday, Matins only,' '' he chuckled, in mock dismay, reading the under-lined information on each envelope. Then the smile faded from his face, as he murmured, 'I wonder if Hazel will go to church this Easter.'

They walked across the meadows to the Halt, half-way to St. Mary's. It was a soft, mild Spring evening, full of pearly greys and cloudy pinks, which echoed themselves in pond and brook, and made the green of the young grass and leaves a washed-out drab by contrast, and the distant banks of the woodlands a smoky blue. The air was full of the sounds of running water, distant bells, and the soft lowing of cattle being settled for the night.

Elaine thought of Hazel, who had all this by right; who had been born here, and who would probably stay here for the rest of her life if she married young Peter Walpole and settled up at the big house. Judy Lassett always said she'd clear out the minute her young brother brought a wife home, and Elaine suspected that she would be more than ready to join her late husband's family up North. The Lassett family lived for hunting, and their part of the country offered more opportunities than the Brookfield district, for anyone of Judy's keenness.

Elaine sighed. She'd miss Judy Lassett, and somehow she just couldn't see Hazel as the mistress of Walpole House. She looked at Robert, and decided that he must be worrying about Hazel, too.

They walked down the crazy flight of steps which were little more than slabs of flat stone let into the earth at intervals, and finished off by a tottery rail of rustic wood. The platform was deserted, although the signals indicated the proximity of the local train. Old Tim Jimpson was probably having his supper, or putting in a bit of work in his garden at the back of the cottage.

'Robert, you are happy about the book, aren't you?' she said, suddenly, in an effort to switch his mind from its present anxious groove.

He looked surprised. 'Yes, my dear, I think so. I'm glad it's finished, too, and packed off to those film people. Though I'm not at all sure that it *is* film material—I've only your assurance that it is.'

'And you're not too sure we did right in choosing those particular people, eh? We've never heard of Pennington Pictures Inc. so they just naturally can't be up to much!' she gently teased him.

He smiled faintly. 'As a matter of fact, I have heard of them before. From our mutual friend, Mr. Farrar,' he began hesitantly. 'It was of him I was thinking,' and he looked down into her bright young face with an expression she couldn't fathom.

She began an eager stream of questions, just as old Tim came hobbling out of his

83

front door.

' 'Ere she be, sor,' he cackled, hovering unsteadily on his bandy old legs. 'Dang me if she ain't late agin,' he added, irritably, as the local from Belminster reluctantly steamed in.

Elaine waited anxiously (more anxiously than she realized) for the first sight of Hazel, and as the girl stepped off the train towards the far end, Elaine's heart sank. Hazel had changed a great deal since the last time she came home. She had changed almost unbelievably, Elaine miserably decided, and stood there waiting. Robert waited, too, instead of striding eagerly forward as in the past. To both of them, it was rather like meeting a stranger, a stranger one felt one wouldn't particularly care for.

Hazel Boyd had grown tall and lithe, and walked with the supple grace of a panther. She'll make a film actress all right, Elaine admitted miserably to herself, and didn't dare look at Robert.

He watched his daughter with misgiving as she strolled towards them, and he noticed that she had the poise and assurance of a woman of twenty-five, and dressed with the sophistication of that age. Her black hair was elaborately piled on the top of her head, and above it sat a bit of fur and velvet which he supposed could be called a hat. He didn't know what Miss Trigg and Miss Christmas would say, but he felt sure that neither they nor the rest of the parish would feel it was the sort of head a country Vicar's daughter should present to the world.

With a sinking heart he noticed how her frosty blue eyes raked them both expertly, and saw how shabby they were, and it was with no great joy that he kissed the skilfully made-up cheek she presented to him. She merely held out a casual, suede-gloved hand to Elaine, while she talked to her father, hardly looking at the other girl as she tossed her a casual 'Hallo.'

'Up to the last minute I was going to stay in London for Easter, Daddy, but it fell through, so here I am, in the dreariest place on earth, for a long, long week-end!'

Robert looked frankly hurt at that statement, but his daughter didn't seem to notice. She was already calling out to old Tim, who hovered nearby, registering disapproval.

'Hey, Jimpson—my hand luggage. Quickly! Two cases and a hatbox!' Turning to her father, she said, 'I hope the trunks have arrived!' and didn't seem to expect a reply.

The old man retrieved her belongings without hurry. The local usually hung about at Brookfield Halt long enough to make it staggeringly late at the end of the line. There was no need for rush here. He came in his own good time, only too well aware that Hazel Boyd was standing impatiently tapping her toe on the flagstones. He juggled with the expensive lizard-skin articles as though they were so much paste-board, and he could see that Elaine was feverishly making conversation so that her cousin shouldn't notice how roughly he was treating the baggage. Ultimately he did as he was requested with them—took them to the top of the steps and half-dropped them—and he moved as though he didn't expect a tip.

Tim Jimpson was not a difficult old man. He was merely reflecting the general trend of feeling. The Vicar was much-loved, but his daughter was a different proposition. If she came home to stay, there was no sense in being anything but how they meant to be in the future to her, and even for the Vicar's sake, they couldn't bring themselves to be friendly.

'Where's the cab?' Hazel wanted to know, after she had negotiated the flagged steps on precariously high heels.

Elaine and Robert stared anxiously at each other.

'We walked,' Elaine said, looking down at Hazel's impeccable black suede court shoes. 'Across the fields. I naturally thought you'd wear something suitable . . . for the country . . .'

'Of course Hazel couldn't come in anything else,' Robert said, rushing in diplomatically. 'She had to go through Town, and you can't wear just anything—'

Elaine flushed, miserably aware for the first time in many weeks, just how shabby she must look, especially when compared with Hazel's immaculate black outfit with its light fur trimming.

Hazel ignored her, and turned to her father. 'Daddy! Haven't you got that car for yourself yet? You promised me you'd get one before Easter!'

The Vicar looked uneasy under Elaine's scrutiny. He rarely kept things from his secretary, but he had felt that this should be a private affair between his daughter and himself, and he had waited for her return before he attempted the difficult business of pointing out the question of income to her. All along he had known it wouldn't be easy. She was like her mother, sweet and affectionate when things went well, but wilfully incapable of understanding the true position when they didn't. Now he saw her as she had developed during the past six months she had been away from him, and he lost all hope. He stood silent, and the tension grew.

'You *ought* to have a car,' Hazel went on imperturbably. 'A man in your position can't go about on foot, or on a pushbike. It's just awful! Can't you see that, Daddy dear? Think of how *I* feel about you!'

Elaine cut in hurriedly, 'Hazel, let's talk about that later, not here. Haven't you any stouter shoes with you, that you could change to make the walk home?' she asked practically, looking down at the cases. The minute she had said it, she knew she had said the wrong thing. Hazel looked outraged at the mere idea of such an action as changing her shoes at the Halt.

Elaine bit her lip. 'Well, I'll 'phone Eb Wilkins for the car, if you like,' she suggested, then realized that Robert wouldn't like that idea. Such an act would complicate the housekeeping bills unnecessarily and irreparably.

There was another tiny pause, which Hazel noticed, and said with irritation, 'Don't bother about me—I'll drop in at Walpole House. I can take the lane—it's as much as my shoes will stand. Peter will run me home.' She broke off, and added, 'I suppose he *has* arrived?'

'Yes, he got home this morning,' Elaine said briefly, while Robert busied himself with picking up the hatbox and the largest case.

'I'll probably stay there to supper, then,' Hazel retorted. ' 'Bye, Daddy. Say hallo to Aunt Frances for me,' and with an airy wave of the hand, she left them.

Elaine watched her swinging along towards the head of the lane which ran down by the wall of the Walpole Estate, and eventually led to the main gates. Then she turned and picked up the third case, and fell into step with the Vicar.

He had said so very little, and looked so extremely hurt that she didn't know what to say, or how to begin to say anything. For the first time since she had come to live in his house, she felt that he had withdrawn himself a long way away, to somewhere where she could never hope to reach him.

Whatever Hazel had said in the past about the dreariness of the village and the Vicarage, she had never broken the age-old custom of going straight home and having her first evening with them. This time she had broken that custom so thoroughly that there could be no mistaking her intentions as to the future. First the little speech about the proposed stay in London, a plan that had apparently fallen through at the last minute; then the sudden decision to spend the evening with Peter Walpole and his sister.

She peeped up into Robert's face, and raked her brains for a subject for conversation, realizing that the longer the silence between them held, the harder it would get to break it.

'She grows prettier, Robert,' she managed at last.

'Yes,' he agreed.

'And such smart clothes. She pays for dressing well. She's got the figure the women's magazines rave about,' she added generously.

He didn't answer, but glanced at Elaine's old coat.

'And so poised and self-assured,' she went on manfully. 'D'you know, I felt quite juvenile and gauche. I'm glad she's growing up so gracefully, though, aren't you, Robert?'

They climbed a stile in silence, but because it was in the nature of a direct question, he forced himself to answer. 'Yes, indeed.'

'I expect she'll be thrilled about your book—going to a film company, I mean!'

A spark of life came into his face at last. He frowned. 'I don't want her to know,' he said, unexpectedly.

She was silent with astonishment. She had urged him into speaking, but this was the last thing she had expected him to say. She had anticipated, rather, that his reactions to his novel and the film company possibility, would veer in the direction of telling Hazel before anyone else.

He said, with a trace of hurry which indicated a need to explain himself before she could speak, 'It's not that I don't want her to know what's happening, you understand. It's just that it may fall through—it may not turn out quite as we wished——' He floundered a little, then tried again. 'Hazel has a bent for acting, as you know, and wants particularly to go on the films. I want no excuse for her to——No, that isn't what I meant to say.

What I mean is, it would be better to find out first if my work is suitable for filming. Then, if it is, and we accept a likely offer, we can then meet other eventualities. It may take a long time to settle, a very long time——I mean, perhaps by then, Hazel will be married to Peter——'

His voice trailed off in silence. Elaine's face cleared as she gathered what he had tried to tell her, but there was an ache in her heart. This was a confidence she hadn't wanted.

Robert looked intensely miserable. Between them everything lay open. There was no pretence, no more decent hiding of secret thoughts. They both knew what they must do for the Vicar's peace of mind. But Robert felt a traitor to himself and to his own child, and his young cousin felt an acute embarrassment that it was necessary for him to let her see into his mind like this.

They took the rest of the journey home in silence, and because of the effect of this new and unusual confidence he had been forced to place in her, the thing he had meant to discuss with her (about Andrew Farrar) passed out of his thoughts. In weeks to come, he was to feel anguish about it, but for the moment he had forgotten. To them both, a new twist had been given to their mutual lives. Hazel was home, and nothing would ever be the same again.

NINE

EVERYTHING changed, where Hazel was. She had the quality of spoiling things, so that those who lived round her were left regretting that things were no longer as they were.

Life changed not only at the Vicarage but also at Walpole House. Peter, the most placid of youths, had returned from college in excited mood. His sister was at a loss to know how to handle him. Hazel's visits were frequent and upsetting. As far as Judy Lassett could see, the girl simply came to wear off her own boredom, and finished up with tormenting Peter, until he, bad-tempered and frustrated, quarrelled with his sister and treated the servants badly. There was resentment and ill-humour everywhere.

In Robert's home, things were no longer quiet and well-ordered. Meals were kept waiting and spoiled. There were sharp voices raised at each other; Hazel's, her aunt's and Elaine's. Hazel's portable gramophone was heard at all hours. Elaine found herself more in the kitchen than at her typewriter, and often heard Robert laboriously tapping out his newest notes. She knew that he wrote his sermons by hand now, and he rarely smiled.

'I did think Robert would be able to let me have young Lizzie Ogg to help in the kitchen,' Frances said worriedly one day, as she uncovered saucepans and peered anxiously at the boiling contents. 'Hazel makes so much extra work, and you'd think Robert could afford help now he's free of her school fees.'

'It's all the added expense,' Elaine reminded her quietly. 'Hazel's bought a new summer outfit. Six frocks and three pairs of shoes. And a cartwheel straw that'll get spoilt in the first shower.' She said it without rancour.

Frances glanced sharply at her. 'I didn't know that,' she said, and sounded annoyed. 'I've had to get fresh curtains and covers for her room—she wanted a lilac floral design to match the new cream paint, if you ever heard of such nonsense! I told Robert not to give in to her, but he would insist on sanctioning it. He said that her room ought to be made pleasant and attractive, to make up for what she'd had all this time at school. He thinks because she's leaving her girlhood behind, that he owes it to her to give her a nice room. He'll be wanting to make over one of the empty rooms for a private sitting-room for her, next!'

It was a long time since Elaine had heard Frances get so annoyed, but in the six weeks that Hazel had been home from school, Frances seemed to have gradually lost that easy-going way which had made her so endearing. Frances, before Hazel's return, had been almost a substitute for the mother which Elaine missed so much. Frances, as she was now, was little more than a housekeeper driven beyond the limit of her frayed nerves, between the tightness of her employer's purse and the extravagance of her employer's daughter.

'I mustn't think like that,' Elaine admonished herself. 'Frances and Robert aren't really so estranged that they can't talk it over and come to terms. It'll work out all right.'

'What makes me so angry,' Frances went on, brandishing a wooden spoon, 'is the way she gets round her father. You'd think she had all the affection in the world for him, but I know different. Besides, she told me an untruth, and I can't forgive that.'

'Untruth?'

'Yes, she said the curtain material was the last thing she'd ask for, and now you say she's got a new summer outfit.' Two bright pink spots burned in her cheeks.

'Oh, no,' Elaine protested soothingly. 'She might have already asked Robert for them when she made you that promise. I don't think she'd lie to you, Frances.'

But Frances Boyd wasn't to be pacified. Her niece had considerably upset her little world, a world that had been unexciting but pleasant and secure while the girl was away at school. Hazel, too, had the same fine features of her mother, and the same extravagant tastes, and this was a perpetual thorn in the older woman's side.

'She's like her mother all over,' she muttered, glancing over at the sink to see if Elaine had finished the washing-up. The mere sight of the girl at the sink doing menial work, was sufficient to fan up the flame of resentment afresh over Hazel. Elaine was employed as a secretary. She shouldn't have to do kitchen tasks. Bad enough that she was dressed so shabbily, but now they were making a servant of her, Frances told herself furiously.

'She'll settle down, in time,' Elaine said doubtfully. 'It must all seem so different. I felt a little lost when I came home from school.'

Frances snorted. She could well imagine what it had been like in Elaine's home. She knew for a fact that the girl would have been allowed the barest week or two, before she had been sent to work, even had her parents lived.

'What did she do about the fancy dress?' Frances suddenly demanded, harking back to the subject of her niece.

'She kept it. She won't part with it,' Elaine said reluctantly. 'She got it torn a little at the school party, but she says it isn't fit to be sold, even if it could be repaired.'

Frances Boyd's unspoken thought was that it was Elaine's money lying idle, but she didn't enlarge on it, for with it came that other and more tantalizing thought: Where did Elaine get the money in the first place?

It had worried her ever since that day when Elaine had first said she'd get it. Frances herself would not go so far as to ask a direct question again, but she had kept making little openings for the girl to say where she had got the money, and it had grieved and puzzled her that Elaine hadn't been frank with her about it. It wasn't like her to have secrets.

It was Hazel herself who finally brought the matter out into the open.

Bouncing in one morning, late for breakfast as usual, she startled them all by demanding a portable wireless.

'Daddy darling, I simply *must* have one. I've seen a beauty for fifteen guineas—that's not a lot to ask, is it, sweet?'

The Vicar frowned.

She came over and stood behind his chair, and played with his hair. He laid his knife and fork down testily.

'Hazel, don't do that! You know I detest it!'

The other women looked sharply at him, but Hazel didn't appear to notice that anything was wrong. She crowed with glee like a child who has won its point.

'Then say you'll let me have it, or I won't stop, you old bear!'

'No. I've already told you—no more money!'

Frances and Elaine exchanged glances. This, too, was a change of front for Robert.

'Don't be a meanie,' Hazel murmured, still enjoying herself. Suddenly she dropped her bombshell, without even realizing what she was doing.

'You coughed up the fifteen guineas owing on the fancy dress, without a word. I thought there would have been a row about that, but there wasn't. So what's the difference?'

There was a strained silence. Elaine gripped her hands together in her lap, beneath the edge of the tablecloth. Frances nervously dabbed at her lips with her napkin.

'Would you mind repeating that?' Robert said evenly.

Hazel obliged, but with a little less confidence, and her enjoyment was rapidly waning. The thing was becoming too long-drawn-out for her fund of patience.

'Are you going to hold an inquest on a simple request like that?' she flung at him, as she took her place at the table.

'Have I seen this fancy dress?' he asked quietly.

She shrugged. 'Of course not. I didn't think you'd want to. Besides, it wasn't diplomatic to bring it up again so soon.' She thoughtfully manoeuvred with a grape-fruit, and looked up with her most dazzling smile. 'You could have knocked me down with a feather when the Head said you'd sent the cash by return, but who was I to ask questions? Don't tell me you're regretting your action, Daddy—that isn't what you preach, now, is it?' she added, maliciously.

'Hazel, don't talk to your father like that!' Frances burst out, resenting the slight on her brother's sermons more than the raking up of the unfortunate dress bill.

'No,' Robert said slowly. 'It isn't my way to regret an action of mine. If I consider it to be foolish after it is done, instead of regretting it I refrain from repeating it.' He crumpled his napkin and pushed his chair back, rising as he said, 'Which is what I propose to do now.'

They watched him leave the room, his food unfinished. Frances turned to Hazel, and said furiously, 'Aren't you ashamed, treating your father like that?'

'No, Auntie, dear,' Hazel said sweetly, 'and if I'm going to have a lecture from you with my breakfast, then I think I'd rather go without breakfast,' and she, too, rose and left the room.

Elaine looked as uncomfortable as she felt.

'It's come out, then,' Frances said, and waited.

'Yes,' Elaine said miserably. 'I wish she

hadn't said anything. Will Robert be angry with you for not telling him?'

'You heard what he said—what's done is done.' She still watched the girl speculatively, and waited.

Elaine began to get restive under her searching gaze, and raked her mind for an excuse to get away, before it was too late. Finally, she leapt up.

'Oh, crumbs, Robert will be in the study, starting work. I'd better go, too,' and she fled, before Frances could be tempted to ask the question still burning on her lips.

She talked it over with Robert, later in the day, when both girls were out. Robert was annoyed that she hadn't given him the bill. Curiously enough, he seemed to think that a bill for a fancy dress would have been a good excuse to stop Hazel's allowance, and in some measure to curb her extravagances. Ordinary clothes and bedroom hangings he felt to be too necessary to refuse to pay for. But he seemed to think he would have been strong enough to put his foot down on a frivolous request for money, such as the Persian Princess costume.

'Oh, don't talk such poppycock, Robert,' his sister exclaimed furiously. 'You know very well that fancy dress or ordinary clothes—it's all one to you! You give in to her, whatever money she asks for.'

He studied her, his anger evaporating. 'Well, you seemed to do the same thing,' he remarked reasonably. 'Where did you get the money, by the way? I didn't think you'd part with your precious savings for such a request.'

She flushed. 'That's just it. I didn't provide the money. I might have done, if only to save you at a time when you were in difficulties, but as it happened, I didn't have to find the money. *That's* what I wanted to talk to you about.'

'You didn't provide the money?' He stared. 'Then who—where——?'

She nodded. 'You might well flounder, Robert Boyd. Elaine provided the money, and what I should like to know is, where she got it from.'

'Oh-h!' His breath escaped sharply, and he looked decidedly relieved. 'So that's it!' He even managed a small chuckle, as he recalled the scene that day in his study, when Elaine was so angry and upset about small town bank managers. He related the incident to his sister, with more amusement than she appeared to feel.

'Well, Robert, a very funny story. But

where does that get us?' she asked, with some asperity, when he had finished speaking. 'You say Aruther Cheddle wouldn't let her have the money? What did she do then—write to the solicitors?'

'Why, no, I don't think so,' he murmured, looking worried again. 'No, I'm sure she didn't. You see, I impressed on her that she was still a minor, despite it's only wanting four months to her twenty-first birthday. She seemed to think it outrageously unfair that it was so near and yet so far. But I took it that she decided to leave the matter for me to think up something.'

'And did you?'

He looked a little shamefaced. 'To tell you the truth, I forgot all about it, Frances. She said that though it was important, she couldn't tell me what it was, and I confess I was a little piqued. It just went out of my head, in the press of other matters, and Elaine has never reminded me since. I never thought a word about it until this morning.'

'Well, she got the money from some-where. Where did she get it?'

'I'm sure I don't know. It's very disturbing and I can't very well ask her outright. You ask her, Frances.'

She looked severely at her brother. In

many ways he was utterly dependable, but just sometimes (as in this particular matter) he was inclined to shelve his responsibilities. It usually turned out like this when he knew he had to pry into someone else's affairs, and he always revolted.

'I have,' she said flatly.

'Did she refuse to tell you?'

'No-o, not exactly. But she did promise not to ask Mr. Farrar for it. At least, no—she didn't make any such promise, now I come to think of it. She just laughed at the idea of asking him, because he snubbed her at that time.'

'And he doesn't snub her now,' Robert said thoughtfully. 'Oh, no, she can't have done that. I refuse to believe that Elaine is so unprincipled as to borrow from a strange man.' He stared at his sister. 'But one has to remember that they aren't strangers any longer.' It was more a question, a desire to have his thought confirmed or disproved, than an actual statement.

When he was next alone with Andrew Farrar, he covertly studied him. He looked happier these days. The strain was going. He seemed to get a lot of pleasure from Elaine's company, though he did appear to be avoiding the Vicarage. Robert couldn't understand why, and wondered if such a thing as accommodation of money did exist between them, and whether any sense of delicacy forbade him coming to Robert's house while it did exist.

He worked near to the subject with all the skill he could muster, beginning with the sadness of young people having no money in youth, and not knowing what to do with it when it came too late. Andrew hid his amusement while he hazarded various guesses at what his old friend was getting at. When it was finally clear what Robert was leading up to, the question came as a shock to Andrew.

'Elaine borrow money from me?' he asked, in a dazed fashion. It was so far from the subject which he had thought the Vicar was getting at, that he was momentarily taken off his guard. He had been thinking that the Vicar was doing a little delicate begging for the youthful poor of his parish. That such a thought as he had voiced could ever have entered the Vicar's mind about such a person as Elaine, floored Andrew.

His hesitation was interpreted the wrong way by Robert. Even when a denial came, Robert fancied it was too emphatic, a shade too vehement to ring true. That he was upset was obvious, and Andrew wondered what could have been said or thought, to bring up such a subject at all.

Both men parted in a disturbed frame of mind, and when Elaine came face to face with them, each in turn studied her in a new way, and wondered if it were true. Oddly, both blamed the other, if it were. Robert felt that Andrew's obvious wealth had been an easy way out for Elaine, who wanted the money, and seemed determined to go against the creed of his house; he knew that she often chafed against his edict which prohibited borrowing, in any shape or form. Andrew felt that Robert worked her too hard on too small a salary, and that any girl who was forced to dress so shabbily would naturally come, at some time or other, to the point of borrowing, if not to other ways of obtaining money. Neither of them blamed Elaine, though both felt an acute disappointment in her, and a feverish desire to disprove their doubts at any cost.

Andrew couldn't get the subject out of his mind. He was still thinking about it when he went into Oakbridge. He had made up his mind to get her a present, just a small friendly gift, as a token of what she was doing for him. She meant, for Andrew, a new interest, and a new assurance that all women weren't like Sandra and Zillah. Her fresh country ways, her outlook and her sweet disposition all tended to put her in a special place, yet he was the last person to realize it. If he dissected his feelings at all, he put her down as a new interest in life sent by a merciful providence to keep him sane while he waited in terror for the dark days that were to come.

Oakbridge had a good selection of shops for a country town, but none which could help him in the difficult task of selecting a gift which was attractive yet not in the least intimate. It was to the bookshop he finally went.

Charles Ramsey had served him on several occasions since the night when Elaine had been in the shop. He fancied he knew his new customer's taste, and brought out the latest book on organ music.

'Not this time,' Andrew smiled, adding with diffidence, 'as a matter of fact, I want a book for a young lady and I don't know her taste. I think you do—she's a customer of yours—and I'd be obliged if you'd advise me.'

Charles cocked his head on one side and raised his brows in what he imagined to be an inviting manner.

'Customer?'

'Yes. Miss Harcourt. I've seen her coming into the shop, and I wondered . . .'

Something in the atmosphere became chilly and oppressive. For some reason best known to himself, the bookseller was not pleased. Andrew frowned.

'If you don't know her taste, then it doesn't matter. I'll compromise with a book token.'

'Of course I know her taste,' was the testy reply. '*I* should, if no one else does!' There was a meaning note in his tone, and he watched his customer anxiously to see if Andrew understood, but unfortunately he didn't.

'Oh, of course. You're the only bookseller in the town, and I suppose she always comes here,' Andrew said easily, and wondered what could be wrong with the fellow to get so nettled. These small-town shopkeepers set a devil of a lot on their pride, he supposed, with amusement.

'I meant that we were friends, good friends,' Charles insisted, but again Andrew didn't catch the significance. In his mind was the question of whether to weakly fall back on the book token, or whether he should tempt her to join him in his own absorption in organ music, with the book which Charles Ramsey had just offered him. Soon, very soon perhaps, he would no longer be able to read. It would be nice to have Elaine to discuss the subject with, and to be familiar with his own kind of books.

The telephone bell rang, and the other man left the shop with a muttered apology, to go to the little room at the end. Andrew could hear him fussing in the little office before he picked up the receiver. The door had been left ajar, and Ramsey's voice came clearly.

'Is that you, Elaine? What on earth——?' Stupefaction registered in his voice.

Andrew moved further away, wondering why she was ringing up, but still he paid no attention to the fact that she and Ramsey might be as friendly as the fellow had just been suggesting. He was still absorbed in the idea of the music book. He and Elaine were going out for their first date that afternoon. He had asked her what Belminster was like, and she had spoken of it in such glowing terms that he had asked her to go along with him. There was, she said, a concert hall, a museum, two super picture houses and one back-street one, a row of dress shops, three dance halls and nine cafés. It was, she asserted, quite a large country town, bigger even than Oak-bridge.

He thought of Elaine, out for the afternoon and evening, and considered it would be extremely pleasant. Probably the happiest stretch of hours he'd had for a long time. He was not unduly bothered about her shabby clothes. With Elaine, you thought of the kind of company she'd offer, and forgot the clothes she wore. They were, in fact, so much a part of her, that it was faintly ludicrous to imagine Elaine in smart clothes; she was so completely natural that it seemed right for her to be as she was. It wasn't necessary for Andrew to move out of earshot of the telephone. His mind was far away, in a large country town on a sunny afternoon at the end of May, and for once Sandra didn't haunt his thoughts.

Ramsey stood with the telephone in his hand, watching his visitor through the plain glass of the half-closed door. Elaine, it seemed, had had the same idea as Andrew. It had occurred to her that it was a nice friendly idea to give him a book, from the shop they both liked so much. Unlike

Andrew, she knew quite clearly what she wanted, but couldn't get away in time to choose it. She didn't specify over the telephone whom the book was for, but requested Charles concisely to parcel it for her and give it to the cleaner's boy, who was cycling out to the Vicarage within the hour.

Ramsey felt sick with fury. It was an odd situation to have these two people so close to him, yet he was unable to drive his claim home. If he didn't do something about it now, these two would get too friendly, and then he'd be pushed out. He had not found it easy to keep her friendship before this man appeared. He had little to offer her in comparison. On the other hand, Farrar had the lean good looks and dark features, together with the height, which appeal to most women. He had money, too, and time to loaf around. Ramsey still couldn't claim an engagement—at least, not in Elaine's hearing—but surely, he argued, there was something he could say which would give the desired impression?

Making up his mind, he said, 'D'you realise how much it will cost, Elaine?'

Andrew did raise his head at that, and unbidden came the recollection of the

Vicar's odd question regarding money.

Elaine, at the other end of the line, said impatiently, 'Good heavens, Charles Ramsey, d'you mean to tell me you're bothering about the mingy half-guinea for it? Can't it wait a few days?'

'Well——' he began, at a loss to know how he could make use of this opportune telephone call.

Elaine unwittingly supplied the answer. 'I'm not asking you to add it to the fifteen guineas I borrowed, if that's what you're thinking,' she said scathingly.

Charles smiled. 'Oh, never mind about the money you borrowed from me, my dear. You know I never mind your coming to me for money!'

She spluttered in fury. 'What are you talking about, Charles? That's the one and only time, and you know it! Charles, are you listening to me?'

'Of course, my dear, don't you worry,' he said easily, and put the telephone down.

He strolled into the shop, with a pleased smile on his sharp features. 'Oddly enough, that was the young lady we were both discussing,' he began conversationally, then noticed that the shop was empty. Andrew had gone, and the book on organ music lay on the small table where he had been standing.

TEN

JUDY LASSETT poured tea in the best Worcester cups and glared across at Elaine.

'Now there's a pretty mess!' she snapped disgustedly. 'Not one of us pleased about anything, and it has to be a soaking wet June! Oh, *hell*!'

Elaine watched the rain teeming down the windows and sighed. 'It is a shame, but you must admit it's the first time Hazel hasn't had everything just as she wanted it.' She grinned a little, to ease the suggestion of unfriendliness in her words.

'Hazel? Hazel? Who's talking about Hazel?'

'Weren't you?' Elaine sounded surprised. 'I thought you were referring to her party. It's to be at the end of June this year, though as a rule it's at the end of July. Hazel's idea, though it gives Frances less time to prepare. This year it's to be extra important to celebrate her leaving school.'

Lady Lassett snorted inelegantly.

115

'Damn Hazel!' she said, with feeling. '*I* was referring to Robert's Garden Party. Poor devil, every year it rains. Never has any luck, that fellow. Neither do I!'

She gloomily sipped her tea, and ate diminutive iced cakes.

'Oh, the Garden Party—I'd forgotten that,' Elaine admitted guiltily. 'Poor old Robert, he doesn't have much luck. Did he tell you they've rejected his manuscript?'

'No. Frances did. Who are these Pennington Picture people, anyway? Never heard of 'em, meself! Sounds a phoney name, if you ask me.'

'No, I don't think so,' Elaine said slowly. 'Robert said once that it was first mentioned to him by (or through) Andrew Farrar.'

'That fellow!' Judy Lassett exploded. 'That accounts for it!'

'Oh, I didn't mean to give the wrong impression,' the girl protested uncomfortably. She was well aware that the position between herself and Andrew was being eagerly discussed everywhere, and that popular favour was on her side. 'I was going to say that Robert started to tell me the day Hazel came home. We were waiting for the train. It came in just as he said that, and somehow we never got back to the subject. Robert seems very unapproachable these days,' she finished miserably.

'H'm, I don't wonder!' was the grim reply. 'But never mind Robert and his precious daughter. What about this Farrar fellow, and your own position, heh? You're not going to get out of it as easily as that, my girl!'

'Please, Lady Lassett,' Elaine began, but she could see it was of no use. Judy Lassett was a determined woman, and when she set out to be kind and helpful, she might trample down the unfortunate victim's finer feelings, but nothing on earth would stop her original intentions.

'Come along now, let's hear all about it. Been seen to cut you dead in the street, what? All over the place by now! Don't like to have friends of mine gossiped about without knowing the why and wherefore to put in a spot of defence meself!'

Elaine shrugged helplessly. 'Oh, everyone makes more of it than is necessary. To tell you the truth, I don't know what it's about myself. He's a queer person. I'm not going to bother any more about him.'

'But, my good girl, a fellow doesn't cut a girl dead in the street for no reason!'

'No, I know. I can't make it out. He had

117

been snubbing me, you know, ever since we first met. Then Robert said he'd hinted that he'd been jilted, and we supposed he didn't care for women much. I liked him, though, and I tried hard to make him be friends, and then one day he did stop snubbing me. Apologized, too, in a way. We got talking, and somehow we weren't bad friends any more. He's rather nice when you get to know him.'

Judy Lassett looked sharply at the girl, and wondered, as Frances had done, what Charles Ramsey would say if he heard Elaine talking like that about Farrar.

'You know, Lady Lassett, I don't think a man like that would act so strangely without good reason, and I think his reason is some inner trouble. I thought at first that there was something wrong with his eyes, but Frances thinks I was mistaken. Anyhow, we were going to Belminster one afternoon, and when I got to the Halt, he wasn't there. He didn't turn up, and I thought he'd lost the way, and went back. (I don't understand why he didn't use his car, either, but he seemed set on going by train, like everyone else.) I saw him standing talking to Hazel, and when I passed, he looked right through me.'

118

'Hazel, heh? Whenever anything's wrong, that damned girl's at the bottom of it! Shouldn't wonder if she isn't putting a spoke in your wheel. Better look out, my girl!'

'No, no, I don't think Hazel would do that. I do think that I'm not his type. Perhaps he needed someone to talk to for a time, when he was feeling lonely. Now he's seen Hazel he may feel he made a mistake, and was too embarrassed to say so. I don't know,' she finished helplessly. 'But I do know this—I'm sick of all this talk about my affairs and I wish everyone would mind their own business!'

'Meaning me?' Judy Lassett grinned.

Elaine flushed. 'I didn't mean to be rude, but honestly, I'm not ready to settle down, either with Charles or anyone else, and it seems that in a village everyone puts the pressure on, until you do start doing what they want.'

'That's the way of villages,' the other woman said happily. 'And why not? Young gal like you should think of settling down. I wish you would, anyway. I wish you'd get hold of this what's-his-name and take him off of Hazel, then that young scamp of a brother of mine would be happy and I'd get some peace. Though lord knows I don't want to wish you into a crowd like Farrar's,' she finished grimly.

'Crowd like Farrar's? What d'you mean?'

'Oh, the Merryweathers!' There was the familiar disgust in the older woman's tone, as she dismissed the most unpopular new-rich family in the district.

'But he doesn't know them—does he?'

'Doesn't he! When I met him in church I invited him to tea here. Only civil thing to do. Damme, I'm not going calling at The Crown! But when he didn't come near nor by, I began to wonder, and I've since heard that he's an old friend of theirs!'

'Who told you that?' Elaine wanted to know.

'I heard—La Rosa's back,' was the laughing reply. 'She's cursing the English summer in all directions—so her maid tells mine! I don't think she'll budge out of France next year, by the sound of it. Shouldn't be surprised if she doesn't sell The Chimes. Never heard of the female being so fed up before!'

'She's old. I don't blame her for not wanting anything but sunshine. She can afford it, too. Wonder why she clings to

Brookfield, anyway? I should have thought after that glittering career on the stage, she'd want to live where there was life and brightness.'

'She was born here, in those cottages we condemned last year!' Lady Lassett said.

'Was she?' Elaine gasped, and tried to fit in the curiously attractive old woman who had once been a famous Continental star, into those filthy old hovels at the end of the Walpole estate, now pulled down. She walked with a stick, a tiny figure whose features were buried beneath layers of make-up, and who wore her own style of gown, usually rich brocade or velvet. Her voice was clear and musical, an unusual, and very pleasant voice.

'I can't believe it,' Elaine murmured.

'Incredible, what? Her brother was head groom when my father was a boy, and her sister was my mother's sewing woman. Of course, the rest of the family's dead now; she's the last of 'em, but she's clung to Brookfield all these years.'

'And Andrew is friends with the Merryweathers next door,' Elaine said, and sounded as disappointed as she felt.

' 'M. Robert wouldn't care to have you mixed up with that lot, even indirectly,'

Judy Lassett told her.

Elaine looked curiously at the two houses on her way back to the Vicarage. Of the two, the old actress's house was the less vulgar and offensive. It was new, built within the last thirty years, and had more Tudor accoutrements than a genuine house of that period. Time and Nature, however, had done a lot to mellow the place. An old vine grew up the timbered walls, and a lot of the newness of it had been lost through its being shut up for most of each year. This, no doubt, was the old woman's dream house, the sort of house she must have promised herself as a girl, living barefoot and subservient in the workmen's cottages of the Victorian occupant of Walpole House. At the end of her life it was still to her a dream realized, a triumphant bit of individual achievement. She probably had no idea that it struck a discordant note among the matured property of the district.

The Merryweathers' house was frankly modern, and an eyesore. Even La Rosa had been heard to condemn it as an outrageous bit of architectural nonsense. It had a flat surface of white stone, with a bright green tiled roof. There were streamlined windows with iron frames to their casements, and these and the plain front door were painted scarlet. They called it The Wooky Hole, which further annoyed the owner of The Chimes next door.

Pip and Squeak Merryweather drove up as Elaine paused. She moved hurriedly away, annoyed with herself at having been caught staring at their house.

Pip was a large, fat young man tending to premature baldness. He wore a perpetual inane grin, and affected a monocle which was left dangling at the end of a cord rather than screwed into his eye. Squeak was small and unnaturally flaxen. The sort of little blonde who always wears black and looks overdressed in it. The villagers disliked her for many things; for her vivid scarlet lips and nails, her high metallic voice and overbold stare. And for invading the bar with her friends, where she drank too many straight whiskies and told smoking-room stories in a voice which couldn't be ignored. That Andrew was a friend of these people was a fact which would weigh heavily against him in Brookfield.

It was indeed all over the village. The information filtered to the Vicarage and was tossed between Frances, Elaine and Hazel over an otherwise silent meal. Robert rarely said much these days; indeed Elaine often found that his notes were left for her on her typewriter, while he went out. He had never been out so much in the past. Now he came back only for meals.

As he carved the meagre joint, Hazel said, 'Aunt Frances, is it true, what they're saying about the Farrar person?'

'*Mr.* Farrar,' Frances answered severely, 'is free to mix with whom he wishes.'

'But if he's friends with the Merry-weathers—phew! Can't see you inviting them here. Might be rather fun if you did, though.'

'Hazel, that's quite uncalled for,' Frances said, with a glance at Robert, who pretended he hadn't heard.

'Is he coming to supper to-night?' Elaine asked, with an attempt to appear disinterested.

'He broke a date with Elaine,' Hazel chuckled, and was rewarded by a furious look from her cousin.

'Oh, my dear, you didn't tell me,' Frances exclaimed, diverting the attention to Elaine, and appearing to be genuinely shocked.

'It's nothing, Frances,' Elaine protested, with an exasperation which Robert didn't fail to notice, though he still gave no sign of paying attention to what went on at his lunch table. 'And what were you doing talking to him that day, anyway?' she demanded of Hazel.

'I suppose I'm free to speak to any friend of my family if I want to,' Hazel said lightly, but with the sort of look which suggested (as she often did) that Elaine was too distantly related to be really considered a part of that family. 'Want to know what he was talking to me about? How to get to Belminster without going to the Halt! Could he have been avoiding you, d'you suppose?'

'Really, Hazel, that isn't a nice way to go on,' Frances said, and felt that Robert must think that she was always finding fault with his daughter.

'Aunt Frances, darling, don't fuss!' Hazel yawned, and got up from the table.

After she had left the room, Frances said thoughtfully, 'I wonder if it's true that Mr. Farrar is a friend of the Merryweathers? If so, then he must have been coming here to visit them, but he gave us to understand that he came through the village accidentally, without knowing just where he was, I mean.'

No one answered her, so she went on, 'But if so, then why does he stay at The Crown? Why doesn't he go to that awful house of theirs, if he's their friend, I mean?'

And still getting no answer, she tried staring at Elaine, who shifted restlessly.

'It's none of our business, Frances, now is it?' the girl protested, at last.

'Well, dear, I rather think it is. We have to be careful whom we invite here, don't we, Robert? If he is a friend of those awful people, then I don't think that *he* can be a very nice person!'

'Isn't that a rather narrow view, Frances?' This from Robert, speaking for the first time.

'Well, really, Robert . . . in your position . . . Vicar of the parish . . .' Frances floundered in dismay.

'Pooh, village gossip!' he growled. 'Does he go to The Wooky Hole? Does he ever stay in the bar when they come in? No. To the best of my knowledge and belief, he merely acknowledged them as they went by in their car one day, and even then they called out to him first. That doesn't make him a friend of theirs. It may be that they both know the same people, met in the same house.' He drew a deep breath, and looked

126

very disapprovingly at his sister. 'There's far too much gossip flying about since he came, and you, Frances, as my sister and housekeeper, should do your best to stem it, not to encourage it!'

But the gossip was too firmly entrenched for Frances to stop it. Andrew's arrival had caught the imagination of everyone, and he himself was something of a mystery to them. They had nothing to go on beyond his rather evasive replies to their leading remarks, yet from somewhere they had got the idea that he was something to do with the film world. Some even held that he was a screen actor. He was good-looking enough to be, thought Hazel, as she swung along the main road that afternoon in search of some diversion.

The rain had stopped, but everything was dripping wet. She had a townish-looking scarlet and white hooded raincoat slung carelessly across her shoulders, and extravagant scarlet leather shoes with platform soles. Frances watched her go, from the window, and there was frank disapproval on her face.

Hazel's imagination was caught by Farrar, and she was sceptical of the gossip about his friendship with her cousin. She put together all the scraps of carefully-hoarded information she had collected about him since her return from school. Not much to go on, but enough to build an intriguing picture. It was a small step from the film idea to connect him with the Merry-weathers, who were suggestive of the acting world themselves.

Squeak's jade slacks and black pullover with the jade snakes embroidered on it was enough to give that impression any day, Hazel thought with a chuckle. The Merryweathers must be rather fun to know, she decided, and it was a tantalizing idea that her father's new friend might well come from their world.

He was walking along ahead of her, taking a path through the woods. She didn't know it, but he came to the woods mostly because the light was subdued and softly green, and things had less of a tendency here to run into each other and become a blurry mess beneath his terrorized gaze. He stood leaning against a tree, and by the time she caught him up, he had got out an old leather pouch, and was thoughtfully filling a squat, rather foul briar.

'Why, it's Andrew Farrar,' she began, with a hint of mischief in her voice.

'Remember me? Hazel Boyd, the girl who sits facing you over supper at the Vicarage.'

'Hallo,' he said, without much pleasure in his voice.

She rested her foot on a nearby fallen tree-trunk. 'Not very pleased to see me? Or perhaps you'd rather I walked on?'

'The woods are free to all, I believe,' he said, without looking up from his pipe.

'Not afraid of me, are you?'

He didn't answer.

'You're a funny person, you know. Sometimes you're friendly, sometimes you're beastly. Only the other day you said I could call you Andrew.'

'You're mistaken, Miss Boyd. I said that I couldn't stop you using my Christian name if you wanted to. Just the same, I wish you wouldn't.'

'You're just the sort of man I like,' she told him. 'A pig!'

He wished she would go. He loved the woods round Brookfield. Somewhere a cuckoo was calling intermittently, and in this spot a squirrel usually appeared, if he kept very quiet. Strange rustlings in the undergrowth went on all the time, and sometimes a bird would dart out, almost across his face, as he walked.

'D'you think I'm pretty?' she cut in on his thoughts.

He stirred restlessly. 'I've just been talking to Peter Walpole,' he said, by way of a reply. 'That young man is drinking too much. He's a nice fellow, or he would be, if he wasn't worried and distressed.'

'Over me?' she exclaimed, and he imagined he detected a note of delight in her voice.

'Possibly, though I think his affection is ill-placed.'

'I know you do, darling! Oh, I like Peter all right, but we grew up together as kids. He wants to stay in this village all his life but I don't. Do you know what I want?'

'I have a fair idea,' he said dryly.

'Andrew listen. I want to go on the films, and you could get me there. Oh, you can pretend you're not an actor, but I know better. The Merryweathers are in the business, too, aren't they? But it's you who can help me,' she urged, suddenly serious. 'Oh, I know what you're thinking, just another silly kid film-struck, but it goes deeper than that. If I can't get into pictures, I'll try the stage, but it's films I want.'

He regarded her sourly beneath lowered eyebrows. This was the first time he'd seen her in serious mood, and he was almost taken off guard. Hazel, with frivolity thrust aside, could be enchanting.

'You're wasting your time,' he told her levelly. 'I'm not an actor, and if I were, I wouldn't help you. For one thing, I don't believe in influence. I'm not going to deny that I'm connected with the film industry, but that won't get you anywhere. I've seen too much of this business of pushing attractive young women into fat parts. My creed is start at the bottom, via the repertory company. That's where the best talent is taken from in this country.'

'Rot! There was a girl at school who had a cousin on the films, and he got her a decent part and she was noticed and in no time——'

'If you want the gloves off, young woman, right! May I remind you that your friend probably had something to trade . . .' He smiled a little grimly as she flushed.

'You *are* a pig!' she retorted, attempting an admiring tone.

'You're not fooling anyone, Miss Boyd. To be frank, I've a tremendous liking for your father, and I don't think he'd thank me for getting you into the film business. I wouldn't do it. You can pester me as much as you like, but it won't get you anywhere.'

'But I *can* act,' she said, and meant it.

He studied her. This was a new Hazel, and a not unattractive one. But he had seen so many pretty eighteen-year-olds who were convinced that they were ready to step into the big parts immediately.

She scowled at the derisive smile playing at the corners of his mouth.

'Don't laugh at me,' she said fiercely. 'I'll show you. What'll you have— Shakespeare? Shaw? I can do them all!'

She got down from the log and launched into Portia's speech, and saw with satisfaction that the smile vanished from his face. Here was no schoolgirl rendering, but almost finished acting. He knocked out his pipe in thoughtful mood, and gave her his full attention. She didn't wait for his comments, but slipped in and out of character. Now she was Desdemona, now Cleopatra. Hers was an intensely moving Ophelia, and when finally (and inevitably) she came to St. Joan, he was no longer offering her enmity. He was smiling, friendly, whole-heartedly admiring. She could, indeed, act, and he was not niggardly in his acceptance of the fact.

She stopped at last, and came slowly over to him, standing a fraction too close, studying his face. She was so still, it seemed she was scarcely breathing.

He had never lost the old thrill of discovering new talent, and he was as moved on this occasion as ever before. Looking down, he discovered that her skin was flawless, that her eyes were a clear, icy blue, with a bluish tinge in the whites, and that her lips were full, moist and inviting. He bent his head over her bright young face, until his mouth came close to hers, almost touching. Then he suddenly jerked himself up straight, angrily, and pushed her roughly away.

She was, after all, very young. She hadn't yet the skill of perfect timing. She had allowed an eagerness to creep into her face too soon; she had let him see a shade too early, the faint smile, at once mocking and triumphant.

'What's the matter?' she said softly. 'I *can* act, can't I? Yes, I can see it in your face. I suppose I'm poison to you, because you're soppy over that poor relation of mine!'

He didn't like her the more for that. 'You

can act,' he admitted sourly, 'but so can thousands of other youngsters! So what?'

He put his pipe away, and retraced his steps back to the village, and wishing with all his heart that he'd chosen a different walk this afternoon.

She kept in step beside him, blandly ignoring his dour expression and resolute silence.

'Can't you see when you're not welcome?' he put it to her brutally at last.

'Yes,' she told him sweetly; 'I told you I wouldn't let you rest. I'm not like my milk-and-water cousin. A few snubs won't send me snivelling back to the Vicar. I'm a sticker, and I'll wear you down yet.'

'I wonder,' he curtly remarked.

She didn't seem to mind what had happened. It was enough for the moment that she had almost trapped him into kissing her. She kept up a fund of bright chatter all the way back, but it did no more for her than to irritate him in the extreme, and to subtly remind him of Sandra and her crowd. The bright polished sophistication which Hazel was doing her best to acquire was a product of all he had left behind and wished most heartily to forget.

He tried again: 'Why don't you be nice to

that young Walpole? He's your age, and your type, and the best thing for you. Besides, it'd please your father no end, after all he's done for you.' It was sincerely meant, and in some way it hurt him to see this girl, who was hardly out of her teens, growing up so quickly and into such a brittle pretence of a woman.

She didn't receive it well. 'My dear Mr. Farrar!' she mocked. 'Are you so old that you can only deliver me lectures? Why have I been wasting my charm on an old codger?'

'Oh, don't be childish, Hazel! For heaven's sake think of your father for once, and stop playing at being grown-up.'

They had reached the end of the road which housed the Vicarage, and were about to turn down it when two people came out of a house beyond. He could just make out the distinctive shapes of the Merryweathers and the red blur which was to him the gate of The Wooky Hole. With a bit of luck, he thought, eyeing them warily, he could leg it to The Crown before they caught sight of him. He hardly heard Hazel's angry rejoinder.

'Look here, excuse me,' he said hastily. 'Some rather boring people coming whom I don't want to meet.'

Hazel looked sharply round to see whom he was evading and caught his arm.

'Oh, no, you don't, Andrew Farrar. You're going to do something for me, to atone for a very dull afternoon and some very bad behaviour on your part. It couldn't have been worse if I'd had to stay in with Daddy.'

'Let go, you little fool—what the hell d'you think you're doing!' he snapped, but she clung tighter, and waved at them.

They saw her, and recognized Andrew. Pleasure lit their faces.

'Dar-ling!' Squeak crowed at Andrew. 'Where've you been hiding yourself all this time? We've been trying to make contact, haven't we, Pip, but you're always with a church parade.'

'Oh, I say, rather!' her husband put in.

Hazel smiled nicely at him. 'So glad we saw you,' she told him. 'I've been wanting to meet you for ages, and at last Andrew's promised to introduce us.'

ELEVEN

LADY LASSETT'S gloom about the Vicar's Garden Party was well founded. The affair was an annual one in aid of the parish schools, and Robert had instituted it on his taking over the parish some twenty years ago. This year it was to be cancelled, for the first time.

'Damn good thing, too,' Judy Lassett said, when Frances told her. 'Though I'm sorry about poor old Robert. There's been too many outside elements this year to make a garden party pleasant.'

Frances knew what she meant, and didn't answer. It had been a painful time for them all, and Robert had been so wretched about it. It all seemed so unfair.

The baker's wife, who was on the committee and had looked forward to her little annual splash of importance, bridled when Frances broke the news to her that the Garden Party was off.

'I'm not at all sorry, Miss Boyd, reely,

137

I'm not,' she said, with a sniff. 'This year there's been too many outside——'

'Yes, yes, I know,' Frances put in hastily, and decided it was time to go before she heard similar home truths to those she had heard at Walpole House.

Israel Lincoln, and his two sisters (who ran the schools between them) had been nice about it, and showed a sympathy and understanding which Frances felt should have been shown by all, but Mrs. Everton was unexpectedly frigid.

Frances had not had a pleasant time at the Forge, either. Eb Wilkins, Junr. acted as carpenter for all village functions, and he had been counting on the money for the work, to pay for his wedding in the autumn.

'Now Prue Chibbetts will go off with the proprietor of the Royal Hotel, I suppose,' Frances thought, with a click of the tongue, as she went through the side door of the Vicarage to save the front step.

The house seemed very quiet. For once, Hazel hadn't got her gramophone blaring, although at first she had had to be reminded that her father was ill. Elaine's typewriter was silent, too, and that in itself was a sign that something was wrong.

Elaine watched the Vicar's sister as she

passed the study window in her old raincoat, clutching the Vicarage umbrella—a large one which lived permanently in the hall and was used by everyone. Overhead the sky was grey and heavy, and the air was chilly for June. There was contention in the atmosphere, as well as anxiety. And it all started one day at breakfast, a meal which was fast becoming one to be avoided at the Vicarage.

Elaine cast her thoughts back to that morning, and remembered the three of them in their dull, workaday dress, their careworn faces searching for the one thing missing—the brilliant splash of colour and the haunting suggestion of expensive perfume, that had been about the house since Easter. Hazel might be the main cause of discord, the draining power behind the Vicarage purse, and the most upsetting influence in the whole village, but she was also symbolic of life, gaiety, that easier way of living which they had become accustomed to do without. Once you had Hazel around, Elaine thought grimly, she was like a drug. You hated the thought of her, but you found you couldn't do without her.

Frances had sat staring at the empty chair, while she mechanically attended to her duties of the meal. Then she had started, in a bitterly complaining voice, 'Hazel's never at home these days, not even to breakfast.'

The Vicar didn't answer, and she repeated her statement, looking at Elaine for support. Elaine ducked her head, and pretended to be immersed in removing bones from her fish, but knew, with a sinking heart, that she wouldn't be able to steer clear of the discussion for long. Frances, these days, made her bitterness a family affair.

Roused at last, the Vicar said, 'Really, Frances, one would think the girl was incapable of doing right. When she *is* here, you don't like it!'

Animosity flared between them, the first time since the day Andrew had run his car into the churchyard wall. Frances started to cry, and to rail at her brother for being against her. The Vicar, once the cheeriest, kindest of men, took up the cudgels on behalf of his daughter, and tried in the most un-Robert-like way to make the taking of breakfast in someone else's house the most natural of everyday performances.

'Here they go, quarrelling again,' Elaine told herself with a little frightened turning over of her heart. With what was for her a big show of cowardice, she muttered an excuse about being wanted at the front door, and fled.

'I'm always making excuses to leave the table, and Frances is always complaining about Hazel!' she told herself wretchedly, as she sat down to her neglected typewriter and started working on some notes for the Vicar which should have been done a week ago. She was too worried for work, however, and tore sheet after sheet of spoiled copy out of the machine before finally giving it up.

This was the first year in which she had felt no joy in the preparations for the Garden Party. The weather was cold and wet, with sudden bursts of watery sunshine which acted as treacherous hope-lifters. Few people had much urge to cooperate this year—ostensibly because of the weather but (Elaine suspected shrewdly) in all probability because of Hazel.

No one had said as much, or even mentioned the girl's name, but it was there. That unspoken thought. Not long ago there wasn't a soul in the village who wouldn't have given their eyes to help Robert in his present trouble, but now it had all changed.

There was a change in Robert himself. She had noticed it imperceptibly creeping on, in the two months since the girl had come home. It was as though he felt that everyone was against her, and that rightly or wrongly he must range himself on her side.

Elaine was not the only person to see this, but few others had Elaine's loyalty, and the Vicar's popularity was on the wane. His sermons were poor, his work indifferent. He went about like a man whose thoughts were anywhere but in the welfare of his parish and his people, and those same people who had loved him so much, now felt that he had transferred all his attention to Hazel, and that they were the worse for it. They didn't like it, and were gradually showing it more plainly. Elaine was worried.

Hazel herself was curiously active regarding the Garden Party, and this—if for nothing else—was causing animosity, for her activity took a direction which no one appreciated. She had planned a tennis tournament, but as most of her new friends were of tournament standard, their entrance rather pushed out the local people who usually entered.

'We can't compete with them smart folk

from London,' was the general feeling. Mrs. Ogg flatly refused to enter, and went so far as to refuse to help at all in anything until Elaine persuaded her to reconsider, and Lady Lassett requested her not to be a fool. Even the Lincoln sisters felt they couldn't consider the tennis list this year.

The committee had split twice in the last week over it. Many felt that the mere presence of Hazel and the Merryweathers would make the day too unpleasant to contemplate. A few (such as Mrs. Harris, and Eb Wilkins, Senr.'s wife) were jealous of the money the Merryweathers' set were flaunting. They could do little to compete with the clothes those people would wear, and it was galling to have to go on foot along muddy country lanes, while Hazel's friends (who weren't staying with the Merryweathers) arrived with a flourish in a fleet of smart cars.

Others—among them Miss Trigg and Amelia Christmas—frankly disapproved of the friends of the Vicar's daughter and felt that Robert and Frances should 'do something about it.'

'What, may I ask?' Judy Lassett had demanded, to the confusion of the others. 'All very fine to talk of ''doing something''—I'd just like to see what sort of a fist you'd make of it, Muriel Trigg!'

Frances worriedly asked Robert if it might be as well to let Judy Lassett take over the arrangements and hold the affair at Walpole House. The estate staff could make the necessary items of carpentry and raise the marquees, whereas they themselves were relying on village help as usual, and owing to the storm which had boiled up, nothing had as yet been done, and the Garden Party was only three days away.

It was a suggestion sincerely meant, but Robert took it as a slight on his daughter's efforts, and promptly told Frances she had no right to interfere.

Elaine had broken in pacifically, 'I don't think Hazel's so keen on the tennis tournament, Robert, but if she were, I'm sure Lady Lassett would let her have it at Walpole House, just the same as if it were being held here.'

Robert had flushed, and said acidly that it had always been held in the Vicarage grounds, and always would be while he was Vicar. High words had flown between them all, and Hazel floated in and joined the argument with some scathing comments about her aunt having a 'down' on her.

And then in the confusion Robert had held his hand to his heart and tottered.

He was ashen white. His great bulk seemed suddenly to crumple, to lose something of its size. They were silent, as if someone had suddenly struck them dumb. He slipped to the floor, striking his forehead on the corner of a nearby chair, while they stood rooted to the spot in horror.

It was Elaine who came suddenly to life, doing what she could for him while she issued directions for fetching the doctor, and getting Robert upstairs to his room.

Afterwards she recalled how pathetically Frances had hung on to her words, and done everything she had told her. How Frances had not seemed to have a single thought of her own, but to act like an automaton.

Of Hazel, Elaine could remember nothing. Whether the girl had stayed in the room or not, she couldn't recall. It was Robert who filled her thoughts. Robert, who had stopped being the best friend she had, somewhere about last April, and who had developed into a person to be avoided because you never knew which word you uttered might turn into the spark igniting the flame of his passion, turning a light-hearted conversation into a verbal fury.

She couldn't bear the sight of those hunched shoulders on that frail little body, going past the study window, and the frail hands struggling to unfold the unwieldy old umbrella. It had always been at the back of her mind that in a crisis poor old Frances wouldn't be much good, and now her apprehension had materialized.

She put her work from her with a sigh, and got up to meet Frances as she slipped through into the lobby. It was a futile pretence, trying to work these days, for the Vicar's accounts were in such a hopeless mess that only he could ever hope to sort them into some kind of order.

'I've got the kettle on,' she told Frances. 'Would you like a cup of tea?'

Frances Boyd nodded. She and Elaine had had little to say to each other since the Vicar's seizure. There was so little one could say, without bringing Hazel into the conversation, and that was the least desirable thing. The one thing they could safely discuss was the temporary priest.

'How is Robert?' she asked instead.

'He was sleeping when I went up a little while ago,' Elaine answered, as she heated the teapot. 'How have they taken the cancellation?'

Frances sighed. 'Oh dear, it was very trying. I don't know why they set such a store on this garden party, I'm sure. It isn't as though it were the money—Judy Lassett is being so nice about it. She's practically promised to supply the identical amount last year's raised. She'd have a ''whip round'', she said.'

Elaine smiled faintly. Dear Judy, how like her to leap in on the essential point before any dismay could be felt in the Vicarage. Heaven knew what they were going to do for the money if she didn't help.

Frances went on, sipping the scalding tea gratefully. 'I'm sure I don't know what Robert will say about it, but I personally feel a little delicate about accepting such a kindness from her, with Hazel being so nasty to that poor Walpole boy.'

'Oh, don't let's mix Peter and Hazel up in this,' Elaine said, with a touch of impatience. 'For Robert's sake, let's just regard it as a tremendous unexpected gift, coming from the kindness of Judy's heart. There's no need to make it complicated.'

'There you go again,' Frances whimpered. 'Always against me. Everyone's against me.'

It wasn't possible to reason with her, so

Elaine poured a third cup of tea and took it upstairs. Robert was awake when she went in, and there was a change in his face.

In a way, it was a slight shock to her. He looked kindly at her, and with that faint touch of anxiety that had been in his face before Hazel had come home. For a second she wondered if he could have forgotten all that had gone by in the months between, as a result of his sudden illness.

'Sit down, child,' he said tiredly, and his next words assured her that he was suffering from no lapse of memory. 'I've been lying here so long, it seems, and there's nothing to do but think.'

He breathed a little quicker with the effort of talking, and she hurriedly said, 'Don't talk, Robert. It's bad for you. Just rest.'

He shook his head slightly, as though she was interrupting a train of thought, so she sat back quietly and let him go on as he wished.

'You've been rather elusive lately. There was something I wanted to say to you, Elaine. Something important. It's that I haven't forgotten. How close we were. You and I. But you're popular. Everyone likes you. Hazel has no one. No one who counts. I must be on her side.'

He peered anxiously at her, to be sure she caught the drift of his painfully brief sentences. She nodded encouragingly.

'I understand Robert. We're still where we were, you and I,' she lied.

Before Hazel came home, Robert wouldn't have been deceived. Now, so anxious was he to make his point clear, that he took her reassurring words at their face value, and hurried on.

'She's so like her mother. You didn't know her mother, did you?'

She shook her head, and as he waited, asked him, 'You loved her very much, Robert?'

'No,' he said, thinking. 'No. One didn't love Elizabeth. She was just a pretty toy. But she belonged to me. She was my own.' He turned his head until he could look straight into her eyes. 'That's what I wanted. To tell you. You've never had. Anyone of your own. Belonging to you. Even if you don't love them. It's a great thing. Belonging.'

Faint beads of perspiration started to his forehead, and he still had that ashen look about him. There was a bluish tinge to his lips that was rather frightening.

'Don't talk any more now, Robert,' she

urged, and prepared to leave him.

'Elaine,' he gasped. 'Don't go. Must tell you.'

'What is it, Robert? Another time, dear.'

'No. Now! Andrew Farrar—don't be harsh with him—he's going blind.'

TWELVE

PRUE CHIBBETTS climbed out of the old two-seater in the yard of the forge, and went to find Eb Wilkins, Junr.

His father looked up from a horse he was shoeing, and without a word pointed to the orchard at the back, and went on with his work.

She flounced through the arched doorway in the wall, and patted her hair into place as she made her way through the trees to where Eb was lounging, smoking a drooping fag.

'Well, I must say!' she greeted him. 'Fine thing if a girl like me is to marry a fella wot lounges all day! D'you know I've brought yon tin can all the way from Belminster, jest fer you? Because I thought you was working so hard you couldn't be spared to drive nowhere. Think I'd a' brought 'n if I'd known you was lounging, Eb Wilkins?'

'Oh lay orf me, woman. I've got things on me mind,' he protested.

151

'Oh, have you, now? Well, so have I! And one of 'em's that you'll be wedding some other fool come autumn, fer I'm going to the altar with one as owns a hotel, not a *part* of a dump like this!'

She waited for the effect and was rewarded. That brought Eb to life.

'You don't mean that, Prue Chibbetts, now, that I *do* know!' he urged, with more than a trace of anxiety in his voice. Prue was notoriously flirtatious, but there was no nonsense in her voice this time.

'Don't I, now? What's all this about Garden Party being put orf because you loafers won't get arrangements done in time? Weren't we needing that money for to be wed?'

'Oh, that!' He grinned a little in relief. 'That were put orf because old Vicar had a heart attack, that were!'

'Oh, yes, I heard that, too,' she told him, scathingly. 'Don't you think I won't look round for something better fer meself, though. I'm looking straight at that fella wot's staying in our best front. Got a fortune in the bank, they do say!'

'That Farrar!' Eb said, but it was uttered more in wonderment and awe than in any sense of rivalry. He knew, and Prue knew, that when she mentioned Farrar as a rival, it was flirting of the highest order. With the mention of his name, they both forgot their former verbal jostling, and fell in on the fascinating subject of discussing the possible calling of the elusive guest of The Crown.

'Could he be on that there Stock Exchange they talk about?' Eb hazarded.

Prue shook her head. 'No, he could not. I do believe he's something to do with the Pictures, that I do. He was talking about what went on in they studios last night, fit to knock you down. You'd think he'd been in film studios all his life, he knows that much on 'em.'

Eb considered the point, then slapped his thigh.

'I got 'un!' he shouted triumphantly. 'Fancy you, a woman, not hitting on it afore this. It takes a man, I tell you!'

'Oh, stop acting like a peacock, Eb Wilkins, and tell us what you're thinking in that pea-sized head of yourn.'

Eb blinked. 'I was only going to say he must be one o' they actor fellas. That'd account fer him knowing so much like, wouldn't it?'

Prue accepted the explanation with a

squeal of delight, and prepared to make off back to The Crown, to take up a tray of food to this fascinating person. That Eb had stumbled on the most logical solution to the riddle which had kept the village guessing for so long, bothered her not a little. He would never remember that he had thought of it, after she had told him several times that the idea was hers.

'Wait till I tell Bessie Harris we got a film actor right in our own house,' she crowed, and he watched her make her way through the trees a little way before he attempted to lounge after her.

Half-way back to the door in the wall, however, Prue whirled round suddenly and brought him up with a start.

'Does yore Dad know you're only lounging out here?' she wanted to know.

He grinned shamefacedly and nodded. 'He sent me out here,' he confided, kicking a nearby trunk of an apple tree. 'Ter think.'

'Ter think? Why, you couldn't do that *any*where,' she said scornfully. 'What're you supposed to be thinking about?'

'Whether I'd have yer in wedlock,' he said bombastically. Then, with a glance at his father's shadow in the forge beyond the wall, he added truthfully, 'and whether

154

you'd have me.'

She sniffed, and tossed her head.

'Father says to tell yer the forge and garridge'd be mine if you was to have me,' he offered, and as she slowed her pace to listen, he went on earnestly, 'Father says to tell yer 'e'd be retiring like, and'd give us a tidy sum ter carry on with, if yer was to be willing.'

There was excitement in her eyes, but she veiled them as he caught up with her and studied her face.

'Well,' she said slowly, scuffing the toe of her shoe in the soil for greater suspense value; 'well, I don't know, Eb Wilkins. What's a forge compared with a hotel—a hotel in a town like Oakbridge, at that?'

'*And* a garridge,' he added anxiously.

'Well, I'll let yer know,' she said, breaking away from him and running through the forge without a glance in his father's direction.

The horse was being led away by the time Eb came into the forge. His father, hands on hips, called to him, 'Well, will she 'ave yer?'

'Dunno. She said she'd think about it,' Eb said despondently.

'Ah! Let Seth Chibbetts' minx get the

better of you!' the old man spat disgustedly. 'I always said you was a fool!'

Prue Chibbetts wasted no time. First she called in on Bessie Harris, then the eldest Ogg girl; she met Milly Everton on the way to the Vicarage, and finally knocked on the study window and called her bit of information to Elaine.

'Our lodger's a film star!'

Elaine looked startled. 'What did you say, Prue?'

'It's all over the village!' the girl said, with truth, for she had made a lightning job of spreading it herself.

Elaine sat thoughtfully staring after Prue's plump back until she was out of sight. Since Robert had first told her that Andrew was losing his sight, she had been building a corrective picture of him in her mind. Now so many things were clear that might never have been. Surely a man of his background would take oncoming blindness very badly, and react to it in many strange ways. Might it not (she persuaded herself) account for the odd things he had said and done to her? She had got further bits of information from Robert in the days that followed. The Vicar had apparently discovered Andrew once in the woods, totally

156

blind for the moment, waiting for sight to return to him before he could venture to move at all. On that occasion he had admitted to the Vicar that these 'black-outs' were by no means new or unexpected, and that they would continue until blindness came on permanently.

'But can't they help him at all? Can't he wear glasses?' Elaine had said at once.

Robert had smiled. Though still weak and ill, he was now sitting up and talking, and taking a more active interest in the parish than he had done for some time.

'Well, my dear, to a man of his temperament, I should imagine that any such half measure as the wearing of spectacles, would merely seem to him a prolonging of the agony. He's been used to adulation, a public life, and to him I dare say a clean break is best.'

She recalled the day when he had been standing alone and a little lost on the river bank.

'Robert, you don't think—he wouldn't take his life, would he?' she whispered.

Robert hadn't answered.

It had seemed rather strange at the time that a business man—even a wealthy business man—should take failing sight so hard. What if he did have to give up the more public side of his life? Many men did.

Now, Prue Chibbetts had given the clue. If he were a film actor, and he went blind, of course there'd be nothing left for him.

Robert was in his dressing-gown, propped up against the pillows, when she went up to him that day. He had a wry smile on his face, and she saw to her astonishment that he had the copy of his MS. on the bed, fingering it ruefully, flicking over the pages as though he thought very little of it.

'Oh, Robert,' she began earnestly, 'don't look like that over it. It *is* good, and you know it. It's just a matter of finding the right people for it. Someone wants just that sort of story, if only we could find him.'

He smiled fondly at her. 'Yes, my dear,' he said.

'Oh, you don't believe me! I could shake you. Look, put it away until you're about again, then we'll talk about it some more. You're in a mood to destroy it now, I can see!'

She took it away from him, and carried it down to the study. She had meant what she said. It was a satisfying book, a book that she felt she wanted to read again and again. A book so different from anything else that

158

Robert had done.

If, she reflected, if only I could place it somewhere for him, somewhere worth while, it would do all the good in the world to speed up his recovery.

It needed just that, to get him well again. Dr. Everton said his heart was tired, and that he needed bucking up. They were giving him eggs, milk, all the nourishing things they could obtain. Lady Lassett had sent him some fine old wine from the Walpole cellars. Harris had sent from his Stores some invalid jelly and other delicacies. Everyone was so kind. Even old Mrs. Geddes had sent a few things over, things she had made herself for him.

It seemed that the Vicar's illness had brought to the surface once more all the love and affection they had once had for him, before Hazel had come home and made him so unpopular. Yet it seemed as though he needed just that other thing, the assurance that this—his best work—had not been wasted, and that his financial worries were over.

As she stood staring out of the study window, Elaine recalled Prue Chibbetts and the way the girl had darted up to the glass and pressed her fat button of a nose against it as she had called out so excitedly her news about Andrew. He was still an event in this village.

Elaine smiled. Andrew, a film star. Of course, they should have all seen that, long ago. He had all the assurance of one of those pampered screen idols, and all the reticence of one whose private life is an open book against his will. Andrew . . .

She pressed her forehead against the cold glass of the window pane and felt heartache over a man for the first time in her life. It could have been wonderful, if that friendship they had slipped into so naturally had developed.

She let herself dream, of a future in which they shared everything, even his oncoming blindness. She pictured herself doing his secretarial work. What did actors do when they gave up acting? Produce? Write books or scripts themselves? In her mind she was helping him to find work for other actors to do, taking down his letters and answering his fan mail for him, until finally she looked down at the Vicar's MS. through a mist of tears.

'I could even have taken Robert's MS. to him,' she thought savagely, as she went over again in her mind the strange way in which their friendship had stopped.

'I *could* take it *now*!' she told herself suddenly, and wondered why she hadn't thought of it before.

Would it look as if she was using it as an excuse to see him again, she asked herself anxiously, her pulses racing at the thought of what she proposed to do. Of course, the thing was mad. So obvious to anyone why she was doing it. She'd be the talk of the village—as if she wasn't being talked about enough already, over Charles.

She was at the point of discarding the idea when Frances looked in.

'Are you doing anything, Elaine dear?' she asked worriedly. 'I want a message taken to Mrs. Ogg. The wretched woman should have come over this afternoon, but I expect she's being tiresome about her duties because Mr. Harris' sister has been put on the Committee. I do wish they'd show a little more of the spirit they seem to admire so much in Robert's sermons.'

'All right, I was going out anyway,' Elaine said, making up her mind to visit Andrew after all. 'What do you want me to say?'

All the way from the baker's, she told herself she was being a fool for doing this.

161

'Can't you see, you idiot,' she muttered to herself in a savage undertone, 'can't you see that he doesn't want any more to do with you, or he'd have made some excuse, some sort of opening to see you before this? I expect he's got someone else already.'

Prue let her in, and showed her the way up to Andrew's sitting-room. 'He's havin' 'is tea, miss, and right miserable he do look,' the girl said, hazarding in her own mind the possibilities connected with Elaine's interest in him.

He didn't look very pleased to see Elaine, yet he had been listening to her voice as she came upstairs, and found his hand was shaking so that he had hurriedly put his cup down.

'I don't want to bother you,' Elaine said, as she sat down on a nearby chair and refused tea, 'but I did wonder whether you would help me. It's not for myself but for Robert. It's his book, the one I told you about.'

'Book?' he said vaguely, and her heart sank as she realized he had forgotten the very mention of the manuscript. She couldn't know that he was trying to see her face clearly through the mist that had been more or less permanently over his eyes all day.

'I believe it's a good story,' she said earnestly, 'and don't think I'm prejudiced, either. Frankly, I couldn't read any of the other stuff Robert writes, although it's popular and sells well enough. But this—this is a novel I can't leave alone. I rather thought it would make a good film, but we have tried one company already, and they've rejected it. So I thought I'd bring it to you and see what you thought. I mean—you've so much time, and—well, I didn't think you'd mind, for Robert——'

She broke off, flushing, and finding it much more difficult to put into words now that she was here, in his sitting-room at The Crown, in the light and under the direct and disconcerting stare of his, than anything she had ever had to do before. She was angry, too, at her own feelings now she was near him, and at being caught stammering and halting like a schoolgirl.

'What made you bring it to me?' he asked. 'I've been hellishly rude to you, and I thought I'd made it clear that I only wanted to be left alone.'

She got up. 'I'm sorry. I thought——'

'What *did* you think?' he persisted, rising uncertainly and holding on to the arms of his chair.

'Well, it's all over the village that you're a film actor, and I did wonder—I mean, I thought actors sometimes read stories for themselves, and I thought there might be a part in it for you——'

'You're mistaken,' he told her, harshly. 'I'm not an actor. I doubt whether I shall have much to do with the film industry again. In fact, I doubt whether I shall have much interest in anything, soon.'

Something about his eyes didn't look quite right, yet she couldn't lay a finger on what was wrong. He was focusing on things, yet there was a strange look about those dark eyes.

She sat down again. 'Andrew, I know about that. About your eyes, I mean. Robert told me about it,' she said gently, mastering her feelings with difficulty, and determining to take no notice of his brusque manner. 'I didn't mean you to *read* the book, naturally. I just wondered if you'd let me tell you a bit about it, and give me your opinion. You must be able to decide within a little whether the plot is suitable or the dialogue is weak, or anything.'

There was a little silence, in which she wondered uneasily whether she had done the wrong thing in mentioning what Robert had said. Suddenly his mouth twisted into a sardonic grin, and he started speaking in a clipped, bitter voice.

'So you know I'm going blind.'

He lowered himself into his chair again and sat staring towards her.

'Funny thing,' he continued, laughing savagely. 'I thought you were paying me a social visit. The thing about being connected with films is that no one wants you for yourself. You might fool yourself that they like your company, but no! Sooner or later it comes out just what they do want. No, no, don't say anything. Don't spoil the effect by making excuses. Have the courage of your convictions, for heaven's sake! Stick to your original line—you want something. Something for the Vicar. Well, that at least is better than for yourself, like your precious cousin. She made no bones about what she wanted. My late fiancée, now—she wanted something quite different. She wanted my money. She knew, as I've no doubt you know, that I've a tidy fortune. Outside my film job, that is. But she made the mistake of listening to others, and decided I wasn't wealthy enough.'

Elaine jumped up, and angrily gathered

her things together. 'Really, Andrew Farrar, of all the low-down, rotten——' she began, but he pushed her back into her seat.

'Oh, sit down, do! You've come to my lodgings to shamelessly ask me to do something for you. All right, stick by it! I'll do what you want, in my own time and my own way. Now, let's hear about the book. If it's any good, we'll have it. If it isn't, I'll tell you. Here, give it to me.'

Everything inside her revolted against his ungracious manner, yet she couldn't leave him. She watched with heartbreak his attempts to read the title page. He even directed the beam of a powerful torch on it, then threw the MS. back into her lap.

'You may laugh at my efforts if you wish. I'm sure you find them amusing. But I assure you it isn't amusing to see print dance and go into a blur of jumbled characters.'

She said, 'The title is *Deep is the Night*, and it's a little longer than the average manuscript, but Robert couldn't cut it.'

'H'm. Title's all right. Well, well, what's the setting? How many characters? Does the story move fast? Let's have a précis of the plot, and make it snappy.'

'It's about a man who loved a woman

madly, but he was inarticulate, and he lost her,' she began, and claimed his attention at once. 'He's quite wealthy, and though he showers gifts and things on her, she leaves him for a man without a penny to his name, because he has the knack of putting into words what he feels for her. The setting is London mainly, and a patch in the Belgian Ardennes.'

She let her stiffness slide from her as she settled back to tell him the story, and he forgot to remind her to keep it brief.

He had always loved her voice. It was low and soft and had a rather caressing quality which was as different from Sandra's assumed velvety voice as the imagination would allow. Elaine could tell a story well, too, and he could see that she was wrapped up in Robert's work. It was a matter of prime importance to her, what happened to Robert's book, and her salesmanship was of the highest.

He dismissed the story as being of good quality and quite adaptable for the purposes of his company. What concerned him now was how he could bridge the gap in their friendship, and bring her back to where she had been at first with him.

Sitting there in the descending darkness

of an overcast day in late June, he saw it was impossible. He hadn't got it in him to humble himself, as was necessary, and she would misconstrue, whatever effort he made. It no longer mattered a great deal about the money she had borrowed, though it mattered enough for him to strive to push the disagreeable thought to the back of his mind rather than tell himself that it was not even disagreeable and mattered nothing. His principles were high, and the women who took first place in his life must necessarily be high-principled, too. But he needed Elaine, and the knowledge that he needed her was sudden and overwhelming.

She said, 'Don't you think so?' and he didn't know what it was she was referring to.

'You haven't been listening!' she accused, flushing again. 'You've let me go on and on instead of saying right out that you didn't care for it at all. Just the sort of mean thing you would do!'

Nothing she could say did anything but leave a wound. 'Don't you feel you could give me the benefit of the doubt?' he asked sarcastically.

'No, you're just mean. I know you're going blind and that's a terrible thing, but

168

you don't have to be beastly to everyone and make them suffer with you, do you? In any case, why sit back and wait to go blind? Surely you can have something done about it? Can't you wear glasses, or something? If you did, you might be able to read for yourself, then you'd take your mind off your trouble.'

She meant it kindly, but her tone was exasperated. He had the knack of making her feel a fool, and life hadn't been too kind as it was. She, for her part, made him feel that he was making a big fuss over nothing.

'I'd rather die than wear glasses,' he told her simply. 'When I was a boy we made fun of near-sighted gentlemen with thick lens such as I'd have to wear. We called them ''blinkers''. In case your flighty cousin hasn't confided in you, let me tell you that all men are conceited, some more than most. I have an outrageous amount of conceit, and repeat to you in all sincerity: I'd rather die than wear glasses.'

'All right. Sit in your room and suffer, but I'm not coming to see you again. And if you'd been at all decent, you'd have said at first that you weren't interested, instead of making me sit here like a fool and entertain you all the afternoon.

'Oh, shut up, Elaine. The book's good. I've said so. My company will take it, if I say so.'

'Your company?' she asked quietly.

'Yes. Pennington Pictures. Didn't you know? Surely it's "all over the village"?' he mocked. 'I have the unique good fortune to own more than half of it, and to be on the board of directors, so you and the Vicar need not worry. So stop standing there shouting at me about being mean, and make your good-byes like a little lady.'

'Pennington Pictures,' she repeated dully. She pulled her gloves on slowly, staring at him.

'Well? Don't you care for the name?' he asked with heavy sarcasm. 'I think I could have it changed if you liked.'

'Don't bother,' she said bitterly. 'We've no further interest in that firm. They've already seen the MS. and rejected it.'

'Oh, that's all right,' he told her easily. 'That's just the Fiction Department. They'll alter their minds if I say so.'

She walked to the door, and there was something final about her going.

He opened his mouth to call her name, but the word stuck in his throat. What was the good of calling her back? There was nothing he could say, now. He had been insufferably rude to her, and if he could live the afternoon over again, he would no doubt say and do the same things. It was just the way he felt. He wanted her so badly, yearned for her so achingly, that when he was face to face with her it was necessary to be brusque, rude even, than to dare allow himself to behave like a fool.

He got up and went to the window, and watched her out of sight.

'I could put down on paper what I feel,' he thought feverishly. 'That's it, I'll write to her.'

He strode up and down the room, sorting out in his mind all he wanted to say. Words, as he would write them, flowed easily. They flowed easily and coherently because he wasn't faced by that clear gaze of her wide grey eyes, and because he couldn't see the sceptical look that kept creeping into her face every time he tried to be nice to her. It was all there, what he wanted to say. He opened his heart in simple language, telling her all he had gone through, what he had thought and felt since he came to Brookfield, how she affected him and how he was struck dumb and churlish when he was with her.

He even included the nagging doubt of the borrowed money, and the certainty he wanted to feel (even if he didn't quite manage to feel it) that she had borrowed it for some very good purpose.

Finally, he stood still, satisfied, and got out his pen and writing-pad. He had never composed such a letter before, never felt so clearly in his mind what he wanted to say and how he was to say it, before he put pen to paper.

He sat down to undertake the task, happier in mind than he had been for some time.

'Dear Elaine,' he began, and the still-wet letters writhed into their customary jumble.

'Oh, God, I forgot,' he moaned, crumpling over the table and burying his face in his arms. 'I forgot—I can't see to write. Oh, God, I can't see.'

THIRTEEN

TEARS blinded her eyes as Elaine ran downstairs and out of The Crown into the watery sunshine. The world of Brookfield looked dreary, despite the pale yellow light that was breaking through the heavy cloud banks.

A despondent duck wallowed in the mud at the side of the pond, and the leaves hung wetly from the trees and dripped with a resounding series of plops. Puddles were everywhere, and the clay soil looked like a grey sea of stickiness. The only bright thing in view was the apple-green saloon car pulled up outside the inn.

'Friends of the Merryweathers,' Elaine decided, dismissing them with contempt. Everyone belonging to the Merryweathers affected the brightest of colours and the newest of possessions. 'They must be as wealthy as Andrew,' she told herself, and with it came the thought that the two people slowly and self-consciously climbing out of the car must be visiting him.

From a discreet distance Elaine watched them. A slight dark girl and a short podgy man. The man especially interested her, he walked so energetically, and looked so pleased with himself—a dark, Eastern-looking little man with flashy clothes and a too-smooth grin over his coarse, olive features.

She walked back to the Vicarage without a glance at anyone, though the ladies of the Committee passed her in little groups smiling and half-bowing. Mrs. Ogg, still rankling over Frances summoning her to attend a meeting she was deciding to miss, made an audible remark to the effect that Elaine was fast following in Hazel's footsteps, but Elaine didn't even see her. She was picking her way along the tortuous path of her own thoughts, round and round the subject of Andrew, and Robert's book.

How was it possible that Andrew hadn't heard of Robert's cherished hopes regarding it, in all the times he had been to the Vicarage to tea and supper? How was it that Robert hadn't spoken to him of it, nor shown it to him? They had discussed books and authors on almost every occasion, and Elaine had heard Robert discussing his popular novels, on more than one visit to Andrew's.

'He must have known about it, and didn't want to bother,' she decided. But then the puzzling thought of how he hadn't mentioned to Robert the name of his own company cropped up. Was it possible that Robert hadn't confided to him where the MS. had been sent—Robert knowing before Elaine herself that Andrew was connected with film-making? That had to be abandoned with the other disconcerting reflections.

It was all beyond her, and though she spent considerable time going over the subject, the obvious reason eluded her. She had no idea of where she herself stood in Andrew's thoughts, nor had she any inkling of the possibility of his thinking too much about her to take much interest in the work or aspirations of anyone else. To Andrew, even Hazel didn't count, when Elaine was around, though Hazel had done her best to make him conscious of her personality.

It was Hazel who had indirectly prompted the visitors to call on Andrew that day. Hazel had been at the Merryweathers' playing snooker with their week-end guests when Zillah Carey had come in with Mark

Pelham.

'I want you to meet a good friend of mine, darling,' Zillah had cooed. 'Mark here designs glamorous bits of nothing to wear in the boudoir—I know you two pets will have a lot in common.'

In the week-end which followed, Mark and Hazel spent a lot of time in each other's company, and the little man found out just how the family set-up was at the Vicarage, and what Hazel's ambitions were. He also discovered her feelings towards her cousin Elaine, and her willingness to do anything she could to make her less favourable in the eyes of the 'one man who could get Hazel into pictures'. Mark didn't press for the name of this apparently important gentleman, but took his findings to Zillah for her advice.

'All thees ees vairy involved,' he complained to her, after Hazel had gone home. 'Eet seem to me, eef I get thees man to theenk the cousin Elaine she steenk, zen the leetle Hazel weel get into Peektures.'

'Wait a minute,' Zillah protested, laughing. 'Let's sort all this out. Oh, yes, I think I know whom she means. What about it, Mark? What's worrying you?'

He shrugged elaborately. 'Just where do I

feet een?' he wanted to know.

'Ah, now you have it!'

She thought a little, her small, pointed face shrewd, and hard as nails. He considered himself lucky, as he watched her, that he wasn't the unfortunate man who was trying to get her.

'Now, listen, Mark duckie. All you have to do is to follow little Zillah's advice. See? I'll go and interview this film wallah. You'd better come with me, in case I need you. (You can wait downstairs in the bar, if you promise me not to have too many.) You see, a mutual friend of ours used to be engaged to him, and I think he'd like to have her back. Yes, I think he would very much. I fix it, but we let Hazel think you were the good fairy. Get me? (No, no questions, and you'll be told no fibs!) Hazel will bestow on you her undying gratitude and devotion for scotching cousin Elaine who loses her beau, and you're sitting pretty for life, see?'

'No!' Pelham, said, blinking. 'I see vairy leetle. Thees Hazel want to steek the knife into her cousin, eh? Maybe she want to steek the knife in me some day, huh?'

'Don't be soppy, darling,' Zillah begged him. 'Girls aren't made that way. They only want to be rotten to each other, not to their

177

boy-friends. Don't you worry. She's the type who'll adore you for ever—you've got that sinister look that girls like Hazel just adore. I might go for you in a big way myself, only I've got a bloke, see?'

She playfully ran her hand under his chin and up into his hair, ruffling it, before taking out her make-up case and giving her face 'the works''.

'I hope you are right,' Pelham complained bitterly. 'Thees Hazel ees pretty—vairy pretty—but I theenk she has claws and I do not like women with claws.'

'Oh, don't be barmy, duckie. You can't have everything, you know,' Zillah assured him, briskly, and dragged him off to The Crown before he could change his mind.

'Did you see her?' Zillah hissed, as she hustled Pelham into the now open front door of the inn.

He blinked uncomprehendingly. Zillah shrugged impatiently, and wished he wouldn't look like that when he didn't understand anything.

'Angel, for a man of your pursuits and capabilities, you're singularly dense at times. That girl we passed just now—(here, in here. We'll get ourselves a drink before I go upstairs). That girl—that was the cousin

178

you're going to ''do''—see? Looked pretty wet, didn't she?'

'She looked a good woman,' Pelham said grimly and with distaste. 'I do not theenk she will be so easy to ''do''!'

By the time Zillah left Mark in the bar to go upstairs, Andrew had recovered a little. He was standing at the window, gloomily looking out at the duck-pond, and wishing he had never come to Brookfield. The village from this angle was at its best on a sunny day, but at the moment it was depressing in the extreme. His eyes, too, were always better in a poor light, which meant that he now never saw the village when it looked attractive.

'Hallo, duckie, it's me—little Zillah,' she began, throwing down her scarf and bag, and perching herself on the edge of the table. 'Been writing letters?' she said, putting out a hand to pick up the sheet on which Andrew had begun to write to Elaine. He forestalled her, snatching it up and tearing it viciously into small pieces.

'All right, I don't want to pry,' she said offhandedly, and lit a cigarette. 'As a matter of fact, I just dropped in to say hallo and to ask if you'd heard from Sandra.'

'No, I haven't, and I don't want to,' he

told her.

'H'm. Polite, aren't you? Oh, well, it looks as if you don't want to hear my news, so I'll keep it to myself.'

She got up to go.

'Look, Zillah,' he said, 'I know I'm damned rude at times. Lots of people tell me so, but I don't mean it. The fact is, it's hell, just now. Sandra knows all about it. She decided she didn't want to be tied to a man without eyes. Well, that's good enough. All I ask is to be left alone. I don't want to move on from this place—I like it. But if you and the Merryweathers don't keep out of my way, I shall have to. And I don't want to have to.'

'Darling, who's stopping you from staying here? I don't suppose I shall ever cross your path again. I just thought you'd be wild if you didn't hear about Sandra's trouble. You never know—someone else might tell you—then you'd think I was a fine friend, not to pass it on to you when I saw you!'

'What trouble?' He was belligerent and suspicious, yet obviously anxious to hear. She gazed wide-eyed at him. Was it possible that he still cared for that hard-shelled little jade he had left back in

Town?

'Well, her father,' she began, with a nice degree of hesitation. 'You knew he was broke, of course?'

'No, I didn't, but I'm not surprised,' was the grim reply.

'Oh, my dear—it's just awful for that family. They've had the brokers in—Sandra's had to give up her flat and go out to work—it's just heart-breaking. I don't think I can speak of it any more.'

'You're doing all right,' he told her, and waited.

'You are a stupid old thing, you know,' she told him, warming up to her subject. 'Fancy you swallowing that story she told you when she gave you your ring back. Any other man would have seen through that right away and demanded the truth. But not you. Just stuck your head in the air and marched off, offended. D'you think Sandra would leave you to face your fate alone?'

'Oh, come off it, Zillah!' he said, nettled. 'This is getting us nowhere. You know damn well Sandra got wind of my eye trouble from Burke's daft little wife. Bubbles! What a name—it suits her! Well, if Sandra had wanted to, she could have stuck to me then. But she didn't, so it's no use coming here spinning me that sort of yarn.'

She got up with dignity. 'I'm not. And Sandra would kill me if she knew I'd come here. She can get a man any day, with her looks. I don't know why she ever bothered with you. She knew about her father's financial state then, and wouldn't let you think she was sponging on you, so she chucked you up! She might have saved herself the trouble, for all you appreciated it. I told her she was a fool, but small thanks I got for it!'

'Wait a minute, Zillah.' He strode over to the door, and almost fell over a footstool he didn't see in time. 'You say Sandra knew about her father when she threw me over?'

She shook him off.

'Oh, what d'you care? You make me sick, Andrew Farrar! You think you're the only fish in the sea, just because you're lousy rich! I've told Sandra once, and I'll tell her again—I think she's well rid of you! A bigger swell-head I never ran up against!'

He watched her whip up her things from the chair and slam out of the room. Women seemed to be doing that to him everywhere. He wished Zillah hadn't come. She always had an upsetting effect on him. He wished she hadn't talked to him about Sandra, too. Useless to tell himself he didn't care. He knew he was no longer in love with Sandra, but she had that heady fascination that always intoxicated him. He thought of her now, and wondered how she was managing, without all the wealth that had always surrounded her. She had to have a good background, wonderful clothes, and loads of witty friends. He just couldn't see her in any other environment.

Then he thought of Elaine.

'I'll never get her. If I got her, I'd never keep her,' he thought bitterly, and forgot that that was how he had once thought of Sandra.

With Sandra, he had tried to appear impoverished, and that was the reason he had lost her—at least, he had thought so until to-day. With Elaine, he had hidden his wealth, and when he had disclosed it, she had run like a frightened hare. Or was it his wealth that came into it at all? Might it not be something in himself which made him lose his women?

He sat holding his head in his hands, thinking. Aching for Elaine, yet willing to snatch at the offer of Sandra's company and the background to which he had belonged, in his utter loneliness and fear of the future.

Prue Chibbetts came up to collect his tea-things, and to clear the table ready for bringing up his supper. There were smoker's oddments, a book or two, and the Vicar's MS. She lumped them pell-mell into a corner, on a small shelf, from which he later retrieved his pipe and tobacco, but pushed the other things to one side. Books and reading matter were daily meaning less and less to him.

Prue said, 'Mester Farrar, you've been around in Town and among folk. Could you advise a country girl what to do with a problem?'

'Oh, lord, have you got a problem, too?'

He grinned at her. He liked Prue. She always managed to say or do something that (for the moment at least) took him out of himself, and she never slammed out of the room in high dudgeon.

'A big'n,' she told him seriously. 'Ef you was me, would you marry a dafty with a forge and garridge, and a bit in the bank, or would you marry a real smart fella with a hotel in Oakbridge?'

He rubbed the back of his head, and hid a smile.

'Well, which one do you like best?'

'Don't like neither over much,' she said, dimpling at him. 'Guess I could make shift with Eb Wilkins best, come to think of it. He's young, and I'm used to 'n. Dan Overall, he's right smart and makes money fer to put in the bank, but bless me, 'e keeps it there. 'Tain't no good marryin' fer money in the bank, I s'pose, unless some of it gets spent on yer. Dan 'e ain't young no more, and 'e don't pinch and pet me, but 'e won't let folks put on 'n. That's something, I reckon. Yet I dunno——Eb 'e do make love to me shockin', and I can do anything with 'n I like. But which should I marry? Which would you say, Mester Farrar? You know so much about everyone and everything.'

He was touched by her appeal, but puzzled. Prue was so open and forthright, and had said how she looked at the problem. Might it not be the way most women looked at it? Supposing they each had more than one man, and simply weighed the pros and cons in this way? Was not all this talk of love a little over-rated?

'Well, put it this way, Prue. Suppose you had to lose one of them—suppose some fellow came along and said to you, ''Now, Prue Chibbetts, one of these fellows is going to be hanged, and it's up to you which one it will be!'' Which one would you say?'

'Would he be a young, good-looking fella who'd say it to me, now, Mester Farrar?'

'Why?' he gasped.

'Well, I was jest thinking like, ef he was young and goodlooking and got a bit by him, himself, I might say let both on 'm go, I'd take him instead!'

Andrew laughed helplessly. 'Oh, Prue, you do me good! You're incorrigible! You'd better stay an old maid till you know your own mind, I suppose. I can't help you.'

'No, 'tain't no use askin' someone who can't fix 'is own life, now, is it?' she returned smartly, flouncing out of the room.

'Heh, come back here!' he shouted.

'I didn't mean nothing,' she protested, flushing a little.

'Why did you say that?'

'Well, sir, seems like you want Miss Elaine, and don't just know ef you do. Seems there's someone else, yon painted hussy in a photo you 'ad out once when I made yer bed. Can't 'ave two women, and I don't see yer gettin' one at this rate—sir.'

'All right, you can forget the "sir". It

was a little belated, anyway,' he said testily. He sat back on the table edge. 'Well, I'll be damned! You don't miss much, do you?' he muttered, eyeing her warily.

'You don't have to tell me father, now, Mester Farrar?' she inquired, with a mixture of coyness and fear. 'He do take the strap to me when I'm forward like with visitors.'

'Oh, forget it,' he waved it away. 'Well, what would you say I should do, now you've raised the subject?'

'Stay as you are!' she said promptly. 'Don't take the one in the photo—she looks bad. And you can't 'ave Miss Elaine—not now. I know that look on 'er face. You won't do no good there. Upset 'er proper, you 'ave. And ef you 'adn't, Miss Hazel'd cook yore goose fer you!' she finished shrewdly. 'She won't let her cousin have no man of 'er own, not while she ain't settled herself. Nor she wouldn't ef she were settled, take my word for it!'

He sat on the table edge long after Prue had gone downstairs. The girl's words kept repeating themselves in his head. She was right, of course. It was hopeless, as far as Elaine was concerned. He knew in himself that he didn't stand a chance with her, now. Too much had gone by unchecked, for him to do anything about it at this late stage.

It left Sandra.

He dismissed Prue's suggestion that Sandra was bad. Sandra was too sophisticated for country tastes, so it wasn't a surprising verdict. But Andrew didn't think Sandra was anything more than selfish and mercenary. And what woman wasn't, these days? If you got someone who wasn't the victim of one of these vices, you were lucky. And he'd never had any luck.

He got out the photograph Prue had referred to, and studied Sandra in the loveliness of a softened studio portrait. Even at this distance, and after all that had happened, the photograph could still stir him. His blurred vision softened the outlines still more, and made her an ethereal thing, infinitely desirable at best, but in his present low state the one thing he needed.

He stuck it up on the chest, and stood looking at it until the light finally faded.

'I couldn't ask for more than to look at that face when my own light fades,' he told himself, with bitter pleasure. 'There's visual beauty, anyway.'

FOURTEEN

HAZEL was eighteen while she was still at school, and for this reason and because it was to be the last birthday celebrated at the end of the summer term, Frances had decreed that it was to be a special affair. This decision had been prompted, partly to propitiate Robert, and partly to forestall any complaints the girl might make about the plans for her first grown-up party.

The birthday party was usually fixed for the quietest day in the week starting the summer holidays, so that it didn't interfere with committees and church business, and to allow time for Frances and the rest of the village to recuperate after the exertions of the Vicar's Garden Party.

This year Hazel had altered the date. She wanted it in June. Finally it was put off until the middle of July, to enable the Vicar to get fit enough to come downstairs for it.

Hazel put in an occasional appearance to ruffle his hair and tell him he was a pet to make such an effort to get well for her party, but compared with other years her interest in the proceedings was small.

'She's disappointed about the alteration in the date,' the Vicar said worriedly. 'Did she say why she wanted it in June this year? I wish she'd let it be the same as usual. It's so upsetting to alter things unnecessarily.'

Frances sniffed. 'It's my belief that she's being as difficult as possible—as usual!' and glanced quickly at her brother. It was the first time since the Vicar had this attack that she had allowed herself the luxury of airing her views about his daughter, and too late she wondered if she had upset him again. He didn't appear to have noticed what was said, to her infinite relief, but was watching Elaine cutting flowers in the borders near the front fence.

'Don't work that girl too hard,' he said unexpectedly, still watching the girl with that worried air.

He looked smaller and rather thin, wrapped up in his blanket, in the old armchair from the kitchen as the nearest thing to an invalid chair.

'Well, who else is to help me?' his sister wanted to know. 'I've only one pair of hands, after all!'

'But we've had our youth, Frances, and she hasn't,' he answered quietly.

Judy Lassett came to see him that first day. She came on her bicycle, the one which squeaked, and which usually had to be walked back because bits of it fell off.

She said, as she shoved it through the gap in the fence to save the effort of wrestling with the stiff fastening on the gate, 'What-ho, Robert! About again, I see! A definite improvement on the acting Vicar! Am I glad he had friends in St. Mary's—bad enough to have him in church, but I couldn't stand him about the village! Well, and how are you feeling, Robert?' She went on without pausing. 'A fine disgrace to the neighbourhood, fainting like a woman!' He smiled delightedly. He liked her bantering. He often said, to his sister's constant confusion, that Judy Lassett was like a breath of fresh air going through the Vicarage.

'Come and sit by me, Judy, and tell me what's going on,' he invited.

'Ah, your nose is getting to its old length! When Robert Boyd wants to hear the local news he's getting well again,' she observed with satisfaction. 'Well, for a start,' she boomed, with a complete disregard for the nearness of Elaine, 'what about this Farrar fellow—heard the latest?'

Frances, from the kitchen window, saw Elaine lay down the flower basket and shears, and slip round to the back instead of crossing the lawn. She went to the back door to intercept her before she made for the back stairs.

'What have you come in for, Elaine? You know I'm waiting for those flowers.'

'I can't stay there, Frances. They're talking about Andrew. Why can't they leave him alone? Why does everyone—even nice people like Lady Lassett and Robert—have to gossip in this village?'

'If folks went on as they should, there'd be nothing to gossip about,' was the tart reply. 'Besides, I thought you didn't care one way or the other about him?'

Elaine didn't answer, and tried to squeeze past Frances, but the other woman made no attempt to move.

'Well, what were they saying about him?'

'Excuse me, Frances,' Elaine said, and slipped past and up the stairs.

Frances clicked her tongue. 'Why don't they tell me what's going on? I'll find out, see if I don't!'

Hazel came in presently, with a wry face. 'That old hag here!' she muttered, referring to Lady Lassett.

'What's this about Mr. Farrar that everyone's talking about?' Frances demanded of her niece, plunging straight into the subject in the firm belief that it was the only way with Hazel.

'Are they talking about him?' Hazel asked, in genuine surprise, and didn't wait for an answer.

Frances went back to her washing up, with an angry face.

'They won't tell me. Well, I'll ask Judy Lassett—I'll find out!' she told herself. No one ever confided in her, but she had never minded so much as since Hazel had come home, for from that date onwards gossip in the village had flowed thick and fast, and for the first time she felt that she was really missing something.

'God above, Frances, I don't know!' was Lady Lassett's blunt retort. 'I came for news of him, not to bring any!' But Frances wasn't deceived. She had seen the quick glance Lady Lassett had flashed at Robert before she spoke.

Robert, being the last in her company that night, had to face the brunt of her questioning.

'Oh, Frances, I'm tired. Don't bother me with such things. You should be ashamed, the way you pry into other people's business!'

'Then you should tell me, Robert! I'm your sister, and what have I done that I can't know what's going on? You've no business to confide in that Lassett woman and keep secrets from me. I suppose you're still gone on her—everyone says you always were, till you met Elizabeth!'

'*Frances!*'

Two pink spots burned in his cheeks, and his eyes were unnaturally bright. His appearance frightened her.

'I'm sorry, Robert. Pray don't excite yourself so. I'm sure I don't want to know about Mr. Farrar. I don't want to know about anything!'

'If you must know,' he said wearily, 'he's going blind. So blind that he can no longer read the newspaper, but has to have it read to him. *Now* are you satisfied?'

She looked eagerly at him, and waited, but there was no more forthcoming, and she felt that he had deliberately given her that bit of information to keep her from guessing the real news.

'And don't broadcast it,' he warned, as he lay down, exhausted.

Eb Wilkins and Jonas Trigg came over next day to put up the marquees and the wooden seats and trestle tables, and Eb's father came to superintend and see that his son wasted no time while Prue Chibbetts was around. One or two of the other men came in to help, and Harris came over for a private consultation as to supplies. Mrs. Harris was in charge of the female help, and she and Mrs. Ogg fought out their verbal grievances in the Vicarage kitchen while Frances fluttered helplessly on the fringe of the fray.

Elaine was kept so busy she hardly realized who was there and who wasn't. She sent out the invitations from the list she had with difficulty got Hazel to compile. There was the going over and choosing music for the village band to play on the lawn, and among other things a quiet superintending of Frances who was supposed to be in charge of everything.

Strange feet tramped all over the back lawn of the Vicarage for the next two or three days, and Elaine and Frances were run off their feet. The eldest Ogg girl and one of the Harris girls were put on the jelly-making and the washing-up, and so many people were in and out of the house that in the confusion Hazel's absence was scarcely noticed.

Robert was aware that his daughter wasn't there, however, and wondered. He had been advised by Dr. Everton to stay upstairs in his room until the day of the party, so that the confusion and noise didn't upset him, and he felt himself singularly fortunate in receiving such advice. It was from the window of his room, however, that he saw Hazel quietly leave the Vicarage each morning, before she could be roped in to help with anything, and she often didn't return until late at night.

Hazel herself kept the Vicarage activities well in sight. She watched it all with some amusement from the other end of the street. Squeak Merryweather stood behind her at the bay window, and made bright comments on the coming and going of the people whose job it was to make Hazel's party a success.

'Nice to be fêted and have nothing to do with the preparations, my sweet,' Squeak remarked, peering round into the girl's sulky young face.

'They make me sick,' Hazel muttered.

'Even over a party they go all soppy. It's no good staying there. Someone's bound to tell me I should consider myself a lucky girl, or that my poor father is working himself to a shred to provide the eats, or that few Vicars' daughters have such a gay time. Oh, God, it makes me sick!'

'Oh, well, angel, there's the seamy side to everything, y'know,' Squeak said, lighting a cigarette and fitting it into an impossibly long holder. 'Take us, for instance.'

'Not now, Squeak,' Hazel said, without preamble. 'Pip's told me all about it, anyway. You tell me about Mark Pelham, instead. What's his nationality?'

'Oh, he's a British subject, of course!'

'Yes, yes, I know,' Hazel said impatiently. 'But what's his real nationality, I mean? Is Pelham his real name?'

'Angel, we don't ask such questions in our set—it isn't nice.'

'Why isn't it? Has he got anything to hide?'

'Well, since we're in a mood for candour, you tell me why you want to know all this. If you're gone on him, that's different.'

'Can't you see—I'm breaking my heart

over him!' Hazel returned smartly. 'Oh, don't be soft, Squeak. Anyone can see he's got Continental blood in him, but what? It's nothing to be ashamed of—I just wanted to know, that's all. And if "Pelham" is his business name, so what? I don't suppose his own name is pronounceable—they never are!'

'Well,' Squeak said unwillingly, and ignoring Pip's urgent telegraphing not to say anything, 'he's a sort of mixture. Mongrel, I suppose you'd call him. He's got Armenian blood, and some Turkish or Persian, I'm not sure which. I know his mother was French—Moroccan French, I believe. He got "Pelham" legally, deed poll and all that, because no one could spell his own name and it was bad for business.'

'What is his business?'

'Hazel, darling, I told you—he designs clothes. I told you that when Zillah introduced you. Remember?'

'Yes, I remember, except that he doesn't know the first thing about designing anything, let alone female garments. I tried him, and he didn't seem to want to talk about it. Oh, I know he's got a gown shop—he owns it, that is. But he doesn't have anything to do with the business side.

He as good as said so.'

'I thought he was getting you some clothes, poppet?' Squeak said carelessly, but with a warning look in her eyes.

'I'm buying them,' Hazel retorted, lifting her chin. 'From him or from any other gown shop—it doesn't matter. I don't have to be nice to people to buy clothes from them, do I?'

Pip moved over to them and said soothingly, 'Now, now, Hazel, old girl—our rule is, be nice to our friends or don't come at all. I'm sure you think that's right? Mostly we don't ask our friends what their business is or anything about their private affairs. It isn't always wise to, you know, old thing,' and under the bantering tone was a warning corresponding with the look in Squeak's eyes.

'You make it sound as though there's something nasty to hide,' Hazel said contemptuously, and suddenly yearned a little for the security of the Vicarage.

Pip and Squeak were silent. She was conscious of their silence in a way which made cold creep over her. There was something that might have been merely unfriendliness, but she felt it was almost hostility. Something about their manner

199

made her feel very young and untried, sheltered almost, and she didn't like it. It was almost as though her father, aunt and cousin were near at hand, smiling kindly yet wisely, in an I-told-you-so manner. These people made her feel that she was a fledgeling venturing too far from the nest.

She flushed. 'I think you're both being unnecessarily secretive. Mark's a decent old sort at rock bottom, but he's gorgeously mysterious, too, and I did want to know a little about him. Now you've spoilt everything.'

She pouted like a pampered child, and their expressions cleared a little. They exchanged a rapid, reassuring glance, and the tension eased. Squeak flung an arm round the girl's shoulders and Pip suggested drinks all round. Zillah came in with Mark and some other friends and the conversation was forgotten for the time being.

But the damage had been done. Hazel's mind kept darting back to it. While she was dancing with Mark, she wondered how he could afford such expensive clothes, from a tiny gown shop in a back street in the West End of London. West End dressmakers made money, she was well aware, but since he knew very little about the work, she could only reason that he must have a competent staff, and coupled with the enormous overhead expenses which such an address must involve, it did seem odd that he still had so much to spend on himself. He had, she knew, a smart flat in Town, and a 'cottage' outside Oakbridge, which he had recently bought to be near the Merryweathers. Many of their friends were buying little week-end places in the district, and Hazel wondered if Andrew would do the same. That Andrew could still stay in the discomfort of The Crown was beyond her.

From the incomes of Mark and Andrew it was an easy jump to the Merryweathers themselves. Hazel had heard all the current rumours about them. She knew what talk went on about the whole of their crowd, but nothing that had been guessed or hazarded seemed to fit in with what she had seen from the inside of The Wooky Hole. The furnishing—if not her own taste—was, to say the least, costly. Squeak's wardrobe was large and extravagant, although in style she kept to somewhat unorthodox lines.

Pip himself was something of a dandy, and their staff of servants were male, efficient and essentially products of the Town. Where did the money come from?

That Pip did work for it, and that it was not inherited, was obvious from his compulsory (and somewhat hurried) visits to Town in his colourful roadster. But what he did to earn all this money was a mystery. Up till now, it had been a rather intriguing mystery, the sort of thing which happened on the screen, and which turned out to have a quite reasonable (and often romantic) explanation at the end. After to-day, the mystery of the Merryweathers' income was no longer romantic or pleasant. There was a faintly nasty flavour about it. It must be a rather shady occupation, Hazel felt.

Towards evening Zillah and Mark went out again, and came back later—cold and a little irritable—with a third person. After drinks round the electric panel fire in the big mirrored cocktail lounge, they brightened up again, swore lustily about the English summers, and introduced Hazel to the newcomer.

Sandra Standish. Hazel turned the name over in her mind again and again, while she chatted brightly with the other girl, and admired the superb figure and colouring, and the enviable poise. The men clustered around Sandra, though Squeak didn't seem to mind, and Mark—who had hitherto stuck by Hazel's side like a limpet—now seemed intent on getting the newcomer into a corner and talking earnestly with her.

'They're old friends,' Hazel thought with amazement, but whenever she withdrew a little to watch them, someone from the crowd happened to seek her out and draw her back into the circle of noise, smoke and laughter. 'They don't want me to watch them,' she decided uneasily.

Someone sat down at the cream-painted grand, and played a haunting tune, while Sandra sang. Hazel recognized superior showmanship, and asked a neighbour if Sandra was on the stage.

'Lord no,' was the astonished reply. 'She's half owner of the Blue Cockatoo in——'

'Darling,' Zillah cooed smoothly across the other voice, 'you're getting mixed. Our Sandra is the girl who was engaged to Andrew Farrar not long ago. You remember. She broke off the engagement because her poppa went bust, poor devil. Won't Andrew be surprised that she's here?' and taking the gaping young man by the arm, she manœuvred him through the crowd to the bar.

Hazel looked across to where Sandra

again sprawled on the divan, beside Mark
Pelham. Was Mark the other half-owner of
the Blue Cockatoo? Impossible to ask
anyone here, and the watchful Zillah would
probably warn them all, once she had gone
home this evening.

She thoughtfully twirled her glass in her
hand. An elderly man with a toothy grin
stopped at her side, ran a podgy hand over
her dark head and murmured something
about a raven's wing. He smelt strongly of
whisky. Squeak paused for a minute to ask
if she was having a good time, and didn't
wait for an answer. Through a gap in the
moving knots of people, Hazel caught a
fleeting glimpse of the couple on the divan,
and saw Mark Pelham slide something from
his hand to Sandra's. It was a slick
movement, the work of a minute, and she
would probably never have noticed it but for
her attention being caught by a superb
bracelet on the girl's wrist.

She thought of the incident in bed again
that night. 'It *was* slick,' she thought,
intrigued. 'They seem to be experts at
passing things. I bet I was the only one in
the room who noticed it. They made it look
as if he was meaning to hold her hand.
Clever!'

That Pelham should have turned his attention to another girl troubled her little. Something about his attentions to Sandra suggested that it was business which held them together for most of the evening. There was nothing amorous about their manner. Nothing in the little man's face to suggest that he had the interest in Sandra that he had shown Hazel.

Hazel knew he would come back to her. That she had not, in fact, lost him for a moment. Disturbingly she knew that she didn't care. There was something faintly revolting about him. Why she had anything to do with him at all, she couldn't have said. There was no need to bother with him. Many young men, interesting as well as young, came to the Merryweathers' house. There was always a new face, and many of them had shown interest in Hazel. It was her own loss that it took an embittered man like Andrew and a sinister man of Pelham's type, to arouse her at all.

She tossed and turned, and switched the light on to see the time. The floral decorations she had so recently chosen, now sickened her. They belonged to the period before she had met the Merryweathers. She switched off the light, and let the welcome darkness blot out the familiar background.

'Hell, why does everything have to be like it?' she muttered, and buried her face in her pillow. Sleep eluded her, and before her eyes for many hours danced the tantalizing enigma of Mark Pelham on the divan with Sandra Standish, passing slickly to her a small white package.

FIFTEEN

WHEN anyone got engaged in Brookfield-under-Woke, it was all over the village within half an hour. Elaine had often wondered idly how it came about.

Some people took tremendous pains to keep their engagement secret, especially that poor little Cole boy who hadn't a job, and was afraid his girl's father would take the horsewhip to him (and he did!) but it didn't help. No amount of secrecy could prevent the leak, and then the tongues would buzz. Future wedding plans would be discussed, and funds examined with regard to a wedding present. The wedding and the gifts were always the real point at issue—outside the subject of the engagement ring—and it had always amused Elaine that the suitability of the couple and their private feelings were not considered at all. The engagement was *news*. This being so, it was hardly surprising that the re-engagement of Sandra Standish and

Andrew Farrar should be known almost as soon as it happened, the day before the party. Andrew had been the chief topic of conversation since he first appeared in the village, and it had been hazarded in many quarters that one of the Vicarage girls would get him. Odds favoured Elaine, though two or three of the less friendly females backed Hazel as being the smarter of the two. That Andrew should finally choose to become engaged to a member of the Merryweathers' set (and a girl he had been engaged to previously at that) shook Brookfield more than anything had since the accident in the threshing machine.

Rumours flew about on the subject of the ring. Somehow it got about that the original ring was being used again, and this was voted to be poor taste, shocking, and 'not at all the thing', according to who was speaking at the time. Though why this should be considered so was very hard to say.

Other subjects were gone over. Miss Trigg said it was a pity the young man hadn't chosen a nice girl in the district—one whom she could have attended to for the wedding. One glance at Sandra's immaculate blonde head assured the little woman that her hairdressing services would assuredly not be called on, and for much the same reason Amelia Christmas was not at all enthusiastic.

The organist's two sisters stopped being nice for the first time in their lives, and voiced their true opinion of Andrew and the Merryweathers, an opinion that could hardly be considered flattering. Lady Lassett was reported to have sworn colourfully and at great length, though it was afterwards reported that the originator of this story had not actually heard her ladyship swearing, but had had it from the understable boy that someone had been swearing and her ladyship had passed that way a minute before.

Brookfield was tremendously upset.

Elaine took it more calmly than most, perhaps. Robert watched her covertly as she sat by his invalid chair in his room, quietly taking down notes for another book on which he had started. The rush of preparation for the party had worn itself out. There was little left to do, so she had urged Robert to do some work.

From the window by his side, he had a clear view of three separate groups of gossiping women. There was no doubt about whom they were talking. Occasionally they looked towards the Vicarage, once or twice they pointed up to The Wooky Hole beyond, and when Andrew's car went by with Sandra at the wheel, they frankly stared, turning to watch it out of sight.

Elaine sat immobile. She must have known what was going on outside. There was little opportunity of being unaware of anything in Brookfield. Yet she showed no more interest than the stub of pencil she kept licking.

'Elaine, child, are you sure you wouldn't like to go away somewhere, just for a change?' Robert ventured, at last. 'Don't think I don't notice how hard you're being worked here. Frances doesn't always think, though she's a good soul at heart. What do you say, now?'

As she didn't answer, he went on, 'I've been meaning to give you a little present for some time. I don't know what to give you, but it does occur to me that perhaps your railway fare and expenses for a little holiday, perhaps—while you look around for a job with brighter possibilities?'

His voice was as hesitant as he himself felt, yet it was something which had to be done. He couldn't sit back and see her

210

unhappy, as he was sure she must be.

She turned dully to him. 'Stop jittering, Robert. I'm comfortable here, as I've always been. And if you're thinking I'm fed up about Andrew Farrar, you'd better stop it. I couldn't care less.' She turned to her notes. 'Where did we get to?'

Frances made life unbearable for her, too, on that last day before the party. If she had been trying to be tactless, she couldn't have succeeded more.

'I never thought that Mr. Farrar would have the impudence to bring that creature into this house,' she began. 'I must say I did begin to think he was interested in *you*, Elaine, but if he wasn't, then all I can say is that his carrying-on with you like that was in very bad taste.'

'Please, Frances,' Elaine pleaded, as she pressed her one and only good dress for the party.

'That's it! Now *you* start hushing me! Everybody tries to hush me, and goodness knows I mean well. All I said was I think it's a disgraceful way to go on. I wonder you don't do something about it, Elaine. When I was a girl, we didn't let a man slip through our fingers in such a way!'

Elaine looked thoughtfully at her cousin,

211

an old maid of old maids, and left unsaid the words which rushed to her lips. She was too innately kind to speak her mind, so she finished pressing her frock, and took it up to her room without another word.

Frances followed her up, and went into Robert's room.

'What a time we're going to have! Really, Robert, the more I think about it, the more I dislike that Mr. Farrar. So inconsiderate to announce his engagement just before the party. Now the excitement will be most wearing.'

'I don't believe he *did* announce it,' Robert said mildly.

His sister looked suspiciously at him, but let the point go as she thought suddenly of something else.

'Why, I do believe that's what you all knew about, the day Judy Lassett came! So that's what you were talking about, and wouldn't tell me. Oh, Robert, how could you be so unkind to me?' she cried, and burst into tears.

Robert began expostulating and Frances sobbed out bitter words. All the little slights and secrets she had been bottling up for so long, came out now. Robert tried to soothe her by telling her she was worn out by the exertions of the party, and Frances retaliated by pointing out that it was for his daughter that she had worn herself out, and finally they got back to the aggravating business of whether Robert was indeed still hankering after Judy Lassett.

It seemed to Elaine (behind the shut door of her room which was ineffective in blocking out their raised and angry voices) that Frances was afraid of her own future. While Hazel was away at school she was fairly sure that Robert would make no sweeping changes. Now that Hazel was home, and rapidly shaping her own life, Frances was not so sure. Elaine pitied her, seeing too clearly how life would look to the little spinster if Robert again took a wife.

She went and knocked on Robert's door. Quietly she put her head round the corner, caught Robert's eye, and signalled that the windows were open. He looked alarmed at once, and did his best to quieten his sister, who was now bordering on hysterics. He looked ill himself, as he did every time Frances got in this mood.

'Robert, Robert, if I'd known how you'd treat me when I got old,' she was crying, when Elaine made up her mind. Walking quickly into the room, she took the older woman's arm, spun her round and smartly slapped her face.

'Elaine, you shouldn't have done that!' Robert said in a low voice.

'It's what you have to do for hysteria—I learnt it in First Aid class;' Elaine said, and pointed to two people standing at the Vicarage gate, taking it all in. 'Israel's sisters,' she said, and grinned a little ruefully at Robert as he stared down into their outraged faces.

'There they go, to spread the glad news. Seems to me that there's plenty of good material for cub reporters in this village—they certainly get on the scent of news quickly.'

Frances got up from the end of the bed where she had recoiled when Elaine slapped her. 'I'll never forgive you for this,' she said.

'Don't be silly, Frances. It was for your own good. Come downstairs with me and I'll pour you a drop of brandy. Do you good,' Elaine said in a rallying tone.

Frances turned, and said in an offended voice, 'I don't want you to do anything for me. Brandy from you would choke me.'

Elaine watched her go. 'What a house to have a party in,' she said.

She went back to her room and looked at the dress. It was a soft grey, and with it she was wearing a necklace of green glass. Green stones. She hesitated, then popped it back in a drawer, and got out instead a chain with a small locket attached to it. Anything rather than green stones. They were too close a reminder of the ring Andrew had tried to give her that day by the river.

At that moment Andrew was twirling it on Sandra's finger. 'You'd really rather have a fresh one, wouldn't you?' he asked, hesitating.

'No, angel,' Sandra said languidly. 'Let's keep this one. It kids me I haven't been foolish and nearly lost you. It almost kids me things are just as they were.'

'They are, aren't they?' he returned, without much enthusiasm.

'Are they?' she echoed. 'I don't know, I'm sure. I wish I did. But then if I did, I might not be as pleased with myself as I am at the moment, and that would be a pity.'

'Oh, stop talking in riddles, Sandra, and let's go down and get some lunch.'

'Andrew! In this dump? Not for me, thank you, and the sooner you pack your bags and get out of here, the better I'll like it. I don't like that saucy wench of a barmaid, for one thing, and if I weren't a nice girl I'd say she were a shade too familiar with you. Haven't encouraged her, have you, pet?'

He looked angry, for the third time since they patched up the old quarrel. She said hastily,

'All right, I take it all back. I forgot she was the proprietor's daughter, and a friend of yours. But promise me you'll get a decent house, or at least something on your own? We'll never have a minute to ourselves if you stay in this place, darling, and I do so want you all to myself for just a bit.'

'O.K., Sandra,' he said briefly. 'Now let's get lunch.'

'I've got a surprise for you,' she told him.

'What sort of surprise?' he asked, suspiciously.

'There you go again! Won't you ever believe that I act in your best interests? The fact is, I thought it would be rather good fun if we had lunch at the Merryweathers'—oh, before you explode, let me assure you it's a small party, and your Vicar's daughter will be there!'

Andrew looked at her. She was a golden

haze at one minute, the next a clear-cut girl with a beautifully chiselled face and a granite-like expression. He wished his eyes wouldn't play tricks on him, but to be candid, he knew that it wasn't entirely his faulty sight which made him doubt his own judgment.

He began to feel the old trapped feeling that he had had when he had been engaged to Sandra before. In the interim, he had forgotten that it had ever existed. In the anxiety of watching his own ability to see fading daily, he had not noticed overmuch the gloriously free feeling that had been his since Sandra had been out of his life. Now he remembered it, with a rush of sorrow, that he had let it go so lightly.

'All right, lunch at the Merryweathers',' he said shortly, and prepared to go with her. This, he decided bitterly, was how it had been once, and how it would be in the future. You did as Sandra schemed to make you act, and if you didn't, you had to fight. Sandra didn't give in easily, and she was only happy when she was getting her own way all the time.

He passed the Vicarage with averted head. He knew that if he turned his head slightly he would see Elaine's bright curls as she bent over her typewriter in the study, or as she sat at the window in the Vicar's bedroom taking notes. He didn't want to see her. The sight of her would only remind him more bitterly of what he had had within his reach and deliberately thrown away.

SIXTEEN

PETER WALPOLE came into the drawing-room and stared moodily at his sister's back. 'Judith, I'd like to go away,' he said suddenly.

Judy Lassett had been scratching worriedly at some account books. She never managed to work with a fountain pen without getting covered with ink, and had long ago gone back to the type of pen she had used at school; the same type of nib, with the same amount of noise. The persistent scratching sound, she often asserted, kept her company, and told her she was a busy wcman. Also, she was fond of admitting, the nib never carried enough ink to get on her fingers.

Now, with her brother's alarming request, she shot up from her work, dropped the pen, and knocked the ink bottle flying. A series of oblong blots imposed themselves in a more or less straight line across the carpet and up the wall, and she looked fixedly at the damage before turning round to her young brother.

'Damme, boy, d'you have to come barging in here while I'm wrestling with the accounts, and shoot that sort of staggerer at me? Now look what you've made me do!'

Peter's graceful yet none the less sincere apology couldn't have irritated her more at such a moment.

'For the love of all souls, why don't yer swear like me?' she cried, in exasperation. 'Swear, boy, don't apologize! Tell me it's me own silly fault if you like, but *don't apologize*! It's all you damn well do. Look at you! Why, save us, you're a walking apology! Come here, come here and sit down, do! I want to talk to you. Oh, you've interrupted me train of thought enough for to-day—I wasn't doing so good, and now my efforts'll be lousy, so let's pack it up and thrash out your problem. God knows it's big enough to tackle first!'

'Judith, all I want is to go away somewhere,' he attempted to explain, politely and patiently.

She slapped her thigh in extreme exasperation.

'There you go again—if you're not apologizing, you're trying to efface yourself, or trying to ·fade out of the picture altogether. You'll do no such thing, go away, indeed! You stay and face out yer puny little love troubles, or, woman as I am, I'll give you a damn good hiding meself!'

'But, Judith, it isn't because of—' he began. She impatiently cut across him.

'Oh, don't try and fool me, Peter, my boy! I've seen this coming, and running away will do no good. That little baggage of Robert Boyd's has got you on a bit of string—there's nothing she'd like more than to see you pack up your things and run. Well, you're not going to do it, I say! For one thing, you'll be master of Walpole one day, and you'll never look yer neighbours in the face after you've run away from a bit of skirt and had to be fetched back to take the estate over. And for another thing, there's not the money to go gallivanting. Better know it now as not. The fact is, I simply can't afford to let you go anywhere: much cheaper to have you stay here, if I have to go and bring that little filly to her senses meself!'

He had a faintly amazed expression on his face.

Everything Peter did was a faint

interpretation of the real thing, his sister thought, savagely, as she strode up and down, red in the face, quivering with justifiable anger. That a girl like Hazel Boyd could make her brother into a shivering ninny was unforgivable, and all the anger she could throw up herself would (she well realized) do nothing about it. Hazel was wayward, and far removed from Peter since that last term or two at school, while Peter had got her under his skin, and would never be any good without her.

'Judith,' Peter said, slowly and hesitantly, yet with a consideration for her feelings which hurt her in some obscure way. 'I've been meaning to tell you for a long time, but I knew you wouldn't like it a bit. You see, the fact is, I don't want to be master of Walpole. Ever. I want to go to Italy. To write, or study music.'

There was silence. A silence which lay as heavy between them as had perhaps ever fallen in Walpole House. He sat there watching the carpet, that same old carpet which was more holes and worn patches than pile, and reflected with a curious lack of feeling that for the first time in his life there was a fraction of time at Walpole without the baying of dogs, without a sound from the stables, and without the ever-soughing wind through the woods behind the house. It was as though everything were waiting, with him, for the explosion from his sister. For the vituperation which was more fitting for stable hands than the lady of the house, but without which it wasn't natural when his sister had been angered. And it didn't come.

When at last he managed to look up at her, she had lost that red flush of anger, and the fierceness in her eyes had died out. It was as if something had died in her.

'Yes,' she said at last in a low voice, 'that's what you want, Peter. I know. I think I've always known it would come to this.'

Her lips were white, and he didn't like the way she sat down so suddenly, as if her legs wouldn't hold her any longer.

'Is it such a tragedy?' he asked quietly and reasonably. 'We both know I'm no countryman. I've mixed with the other men in the village, in The Crown, and I've tried to get interested in their talk of crops, horses, dogs, weather. You don't know how sick of it all I am!' He was as vehement in his quiet way as if he had used the lustiest of stable oaths.

223

She looked steadily at him, an unfathomable expression in her eyes. Her stillness affected him strangely, as though she had somehow ceased to be his elder sister, and that he had to explain it all carefully to her, like explaining to a child.

'I've always known I couldn't take over Walpole when the time came, Judith. I'm ashamed to say I've shrunk from it. It's an earthy existence and, I think a meaningless one. Squeezing the last drop out of the soil to keep up the house, because Walpoles have always lived in it; squeezing the house to the last halfpenny on the mortgage to keep up the stock; bleeding the stock white to keep up the stables because Walpoles have always hunted; bleeding the tenants white to keep up the sort of existence that Walpoles have always done. It's like a tame rat going round in its cage. There's no end to the vicious circle. You try and beat the weather at its own game and you compete with your neighbours until you're all cut-throats and not neighbourly any more.'

He was very moved. His earnestness hurt Judy more than his efforts to make his explanation convey his thoughts. She dare not look at his eyes for fear of seeing tears there. Tears in a man's eyes sickened her, because it usually meant that his foundation was rocking. The men who meant most to her were those who ordered their existence in such a way that their emotions had no place. Hard men, earthy men (as Peter had said) earthy and tough—Walpole men.

'I want a gracious existence. I want to see beauty and peace and leisurely happiness. It is in the world, but not in my world. I wasn't born to take a place here, not really. Walpole is going down. I'm not the man to pull it up. You should have been that man, Judith. You ought to have been a man. You don't really care if you never hear the best music in the world, or see the miracles of architecture, do you? You never had the urge to visit other countries, in search of beauty, did you? You never felt you were imprisoned, here at Walpole, or that you were missing things in the world outside, things that are being destroyed one by one, and no one cares. No one cares while landowners like us spend our little lives on our own few acres, getting upset over trifles like the rise and fall of fat stock prices, or the vagaries of our filthy climate!'

'No, you're right, I never had the urge!' she said, speaking for the first time with a bitterness that shocked him. 'I never had the

225

urge to do a thing beyond saving Walpole, saving it from sinking down and down, losing acre by acre, losing head by head of stock, shutting the stables stall by stall, parting with servants one by one, cutting off our life blood! Cutting off our life blood, while slimy little whippersnappers like you sit around snivelling about beauty and the arts, and a gracious existence. Gracious existence, my foot! You were born a Walpole, and a Walpole you'll live and die, if I have to force you with my own hands and my last breath. I'll not bear the disgrace alone, you mark my words. There's precious little money left, and a thoughtful father provided that you shouldn't squander it on anything but Walpole. Did yer know that?'

She saw that he didn't, and his changed expression gave her no satisfaction.

'Well, you weren't supposed to know it,' she growled, 'But as I see it, now's a good a time to break a bond as any. I wasn't supposed to let you know till you came of age. I'm your guardian, and when you get your hands on the Walpole funds, I'm powerless to do any more. But there's others to take over. You can't do as you like with the money. It's for Walpole, every penny of it.'

She breathed loudly, and her old colour was coming back. 'I don't know if your precious Hazel knew this, or whether she's just got sick of you mooning around writing poetry! But I know this—I think if you were to stay and work out your own destiny (bleak as it looks and probably is) she'd like the looks of you better than she does now! Think that over!'

He got up and stood looking out of the window, at the rolling land that had belonged to his forefathers and would soon belong to him. His sister watched him anxiously, and her heart sank. There was, as he had said in all truth, nothing of the countryman in him. Neither pride nor joy lay in his face. Nothing to indicate that the possession of all this, the belonging to this stretch of land as far as the eye could see, gave him anything but misery. He was, indeed, imprisoned at Walpole.

He said, at last, 'Come here, Judith.'

She got up and stalked over to where he stood. Hazel was coming up the drive. Hazel on foot was a rare sight, but to-day she was obviously in the mood for walking. She wore a beautifully-cut coat of soft pale blue, and her black hair was secured from the wind under a scarf which had cost more than any head-scarf ought to. (Judy knew its price—she had already had it from Frances, with other details she would rather not have heard). And the shoes were as unsuitable for the country as the rest of Hazel's wardrobe—soft kid, dyed in a deeper blue.

'That's the girl you want me to marry? Is that the future châtelaine of Walpole?'

'I had a sort of rough idea that was what you yourself wanted,' his sister observed dryly, her anger evaporated.

'I've been trying to tell you, Judith, that that wasn't the reason I wanted to go away,' he said, running a sensitive hand over the back of his head and turning away from the window. 'I don't know why Hazel still comes here, unless it's to mislead her father. She is great friends with a man in that doubtful set she has got herself into, a man named Pelham. He's a foreigner, not a very good type. Much too old for her, too. I don't imagine the Vicar would care for the idea, if he knew,' Peter said, and Judy gasped at his lack of emotion.

'Damme, don't *you* care?' she gasped.

'No,' he answered levelly. 'Should I?'

'God help us, I don't know whether I'm on my head or my heels,' she exclaimed.

'Here I've been thinking that all these weeks you've been mooning around in the depths of dejection over that little chit, and now you tell me she's running round with someone else and you couldn't care less!'

'I did care at first,' he allowed, 'when I came home last April. She still looked extremely lovely, and a little fragile. Unattainable, too, and,' he said, with a suspicion of a wry smile, 'there I'm no different from the next fellow. I wanted her. But when I saw the sort of man she really liked—well, you know the old saying. You can tell a man by the friends he keeps. That goes for women, too. There's gossip about her, too. Unsavoury. The villagers are all against her. I don't hate Walpole so much that I want to instal that sort of woman for its mistress.'

He looked down at her, and read her thoughts. He was now a stranger to her. She had lost touch. A stranger, a lost and rather scared stranger, but a stranger nevertheless. She might never have had a brother.

'Why don't you marry again, and stay here, Judith? There's nothing against that in Father's will, and you'd make Walpole what it used to be.'

'Kind of you,' she snapped, with a return

of her old spirit. 'Now you've stopped talking like a man, and more like the schoolboy you are. Tom Lassett was all I wanted. I lived a damned fine life while he was alive, and when he died I lost my interest in men as potential husbands. He spoiled me for other men. But, by God, he was a *man*!'

Peter took the thrust without wincing. She wondered, once it had slipped out, whether he wasn't entirely in agreement with her. The boy was honest, anyway. In all probability he knew himself for what he was, and accepted it. Perhaps he preferred to lose the right to be called a man.

She watched him curiously over tea. He had stayed to receive Hazel, with all his old courtesy, and anyone but the Vicar's daughter would have seen with half an eye that he had lost all interest in her. But then, Judy reflected fairly, I don't seem to be much good at reading people. Perhaps Hazel does realize, and is playing up to him as always with the sort of face-saving that I wouldn't stoop to.

Being Judy Lassett, she couldn't let the subject of the Merryweathers rest. She probed throughout tea, and got heated and furious because it was Peter who parried all

230

her thrusts. She believed that if he hadn't been there, forestalling her attempts, she would have got all the information out of the girl that she wished. As it was, she got Hazel into a corner over where she spent most of her time, though the girl finally managed to wriggle out of it.

'Why, don't you know? I go to La Rosa's! Remember the old girl?' Hazel inquired with a nice mixture of innocence and amusement. 'The old dear knows more about backstage than I'm ever likely to. So I'm shamelessly pumping her, under the guise of a nice young thing visiting her elders. Just like me, isn't it, Lady Lassett?'

Judy Lassett stared blankly at her. There was enough conviction in her tone to make it seem impossible that it was a bit of acting. Yet Judy had never seen Hazel's performance at its best. She accepted the improbability of tongue-in-cheek visits to the old actress, and probed further, but without result. Neither could she get any more information about Andrew Farrar, and it was from others in the village that her ladyship heard eventually that Andrew and his fiancée didn't seem too happy together.

Peter did the unexpected thing and escorted Hazel down to the drive gates.

Judy couldn't imagine why he had done this, or what had happened to her brother to make him such an unknown quantity to her. Typically she blamed herself for the wrong choice of schools; alternatively she blamed the schools' choice of masters, in her opinion an unfortunate one. Someone (and the last person this someone could be in her view was Peter himself) had changed him lately. She didn't understand or like the change, and for perhaps the first time in her life she found herself wishing that the clock would turn back and leave them all as they were, instead of surging eagerly forward.

Her final visitor put the sting into her day. A very rare sight was La Rosa's old-fashioned limousine coming up the drive. The old woman never visited, neither did she encourage visitors. Lady Lassett watched curiously as the chauffeur helped his mistress out and, after taking her arm up the steps, resumed his place at the wheel to wait.

La Rosa. She had come to say good-day when she had selected the spot on which to have The Chimes built. She had invited Lady Lassett to come and see the house when she moved in. This, then, must characteristically mean goodbye.

The old woman rustled in, almost magnificent in sage green brocade, and wearing a necklace of rubies on her spare chest, a set of gems which Lady Lassett knew had been the gift of a prince. She walked falteringly, clutching her silver-knobbed stick with a beautifully-kept old hand, and in her simple way she had as much dignity as any duchess.

'La Rosa! How very nice,' Judy Lassett said, with genuine warmth as she went forward to greet her.

'It's Betsy Green, and well you know it, m'lady,' was the pleasant response, de-livered with a faint sweet smile, and a deprecating wave of the hand as the old woman took the armchair by Judy's side. 'It's been a long time . . .'

'Too long,' Judy told her. 'You should have come before. I would have invaded The Chimes, but you're there so rarely and we all know you loathe invasions of any kind.'

La Rosa nodded. 'Aye, they all know me. Ah, well, I've had a crowded life, and now I want peace. Don't want to see anybody. But,' she said, leaning forward confidentially, 'I do want sunshine. And I can't get any here. Confound the climate—never did like it! Going back to France—the South. Ah, there's sunshine for you! Warms my old bones.' She pursed her pale lips and nodded once or twice, repeating, 'Warms my old bones.'

'Do you expect peace there, or will you permit visitors?' Judy wanted to know.

'No. No. No visitors—no visitors anywhere. Can't stand visits either way. This'—she waved a hand again to indicate her own breach of her most important rule—'this is in the nature of a farewell. We both know we shan't see each other again. Just had to say good-bye.'

They chatted for a while. La Rosa's experiences could still be pithily told, and the old woman still had a chuckle for some of her reminiscences. But at last she began to look a little tired, and showed signs of departure.

Lady Lassett made her last attempt to get the information she wanted.

'You'll be seeing the Vicar, of course?'

'Yes. Boyd's a good fellow. The only churchman I could ever stand. But I shall have to do a bit of scouting before I venture there.' She leaned forward again, looking cunning. 'I shall send Beatrice—she likes a chat with Elaine. Beatrice'll find out for me if that hussy is there or not!'

'Eh? D'you mean the Vicar's daughter?'

'Oh, aye, I'm aware your ladyship is angling to get her for a sister-in-law, though I can't think why.'

Judy Lassett vigorously denied any such intention, and gasped, 'But I thought you liked Hazel! She told me herself she often calls on you, to get you to talk about your stage experiences. Isn't that so?'

'That hussy in my house?' La Rosa fumed. 'What lies is she telling now? I wouldn't have her within smelling distance! Can't stand the child! Haven't you heard?' and the old woman gave Judy Lassett her second bit of information about Mark Pelham that day.

After the old woman had gone, Lady Lassett went back to her desk. Mark Pelham, as Peter saw him, was bad enough. But Mark Pelham, as the old actress painted him, was so unsavoury that Judy experienced her first indecision about leaving well alone.

'So she didn't ever go to see La Rosa,' she said angrily to herself. 'Damned little liar!' But the disquieting thought of where Hazel might have been at those times, needed more than a little coping with.

The question was: did the girl merely keep going to The Wooky Hole to see Mark Pelham on all those occasions when she was supposed to be visiting the once-famous old woman next door? If not, just where did Hazel go, when Robert thought she was within earshot at the house up the road?

SEVENTEEN

'I LOATHE July,' Elaine told herself crossly, as she cycled into Oakbridge for some last-minute shopping. 'It's either raining when you expect sunshine, or it scorches you when you expect rain.'

It was the morning of the party. Robert, worriedly watching the proceedings, had called Elaine upstairs.

'How'd you like to get out of all this racket for an hour or two?' he asked her, in a low voice full of understanding.

'Oh, if I could!' the girl said wistfully, putting a hand to her aching head. 'You know, Robert, when Frances is in a flap, she makes everyone round her feel positively ill!'

He nodded. 'She always did. I'll tell you what you can do. Take a trip to Oakbridge for me, and if anyone tries to stop you, say I said it's urgent.'

'Oh, Robert, you're an angel! What do you want me to get for you?'

'I'm bothered if I know of anything I really want,' he said ruefully, and grinned at her. 'Well, make it some tobacco. Oh, and pick up a book on Central Africa that Ramsey is ordering for me. It should be in by now.'

'Oh, must I go to Charles' shop, Robert? I mean, there isn't a lot of time. Come to think of it, I don't think I ought to go into Oakbridge, as it isn't really urgent.'

She looked troubled, and glanced quickly away from his inviting expression.

'You haven't been into Oakbridge lately, have you?' the Vicar remarked. 'Israel Lincoln conveyed a message from Ramsey only last week. It seems he expected to see you before now, and is surprised that he hasn't.'

She flushed. 'Why didn't Israel tell *me* that?'

'Because he was asked (for some reason or other) to deliver the message to *me*,' was the collected answer. 'And don't think I'm trying to trick you into going to the bookshop against your will. I do happen to want that book, but if you don't care to collect it, I dare say someone else will.' Then, in a different, more friendly tone, Robert said: 'What is it, child? I don't have to have messages like that sent to me, to show me that there's something not quite right between you and Ramsey. I used to think it might be Farrar coming between you, but that can't be, as I hear he's got himself re-engaged to his former fiancée.'

He waited, but she obviously didn't want to answer.

'Well, well. I hoped you might feel that you could confide in me as you used to do. I shan't attempt to force a confidence—I know better. Run along, my dear, and do as you wish. Never mind my things, if you don't want to go.'

'Oh, Robert, it isn't that! Of course I'll go into Oakbridge. I'll even pick up your book for you, and bother Charles. You see—oh, I didn't really want to say anything about it, but I don't want you to think I'm withholding confidences. The fact is, I rather wanted to avoid Charles until next month. He's frightfully boring, you know, and to tell you the truth, he's being a bit of a nuisance. Over getting engaged, you know.'

Robert said nothing, but watched her steadily, with his special receptive expression which had often made the villagers open their hearts when they had no intention of doing so.

'I don't want to marry Charles, ever!' she went on, and there was impatience more than anything else in her tone. 'And I think it's mean of him to keep on about it, instead of taking ''no'' for an answer. I don't even like him any more,' she mused, adding swiftly, 'and it isn't because of Mr. Farrar, either!'

'No? Well, my dear, if there's anything I can do to help, you've only to ask me. But I shouldn't worry too much. You're young yet, and there's plenty of time. Ramsey, on the other hand, isn't so young, and you can't blame a man for doing his best to get the girl he's keen on, even if he has an unfortunate way of showing his affection!'

He had left it at that, and she had offered no more confidences. He watched her go off, on that overcast morning, clad in her old drab raincoat, and her workaday stockings and brogues. What had this village to offer her now? He had hoped that Farrar would choose Elaine to help him in his dark days. She would have been an ideal partner for him, the Vicar reflected. Now it was left to Charles Ramsey to fill the gap, and things seemed somehow to have slid back to the way they were on that day in

April when Farrar had run into the church wall. The same, the Vicar reflected uneasily, with the rather important exception that at that time Elaine had known no other man but Ramsey, and that in his way he was a 'catch', as far as income went.

A solid young man, with a thriving business and a gift for making steady money. The girl he married would never want for material things, but would that be enough for Elaine? Since that day she had met and come to know Andrew Farrar, he seemed to have made Ramsey very much less desirable in Elaine's eyes, though he had been (by all accounts) infernally rude to her.

'Charles!' Elaine muttered angrily to herself, as she cycled to the town, and when she got there and the sun broke through the heavy grey sky, she got angrier. 'Now it's going to be a scorching hot day. Now I've dressed for heavy rain, I can see that the overcast sky meant heat. Isn't that nice!' she jeered at herself, making for the tobacconist's first.

Having taken as long as possible over this purchase, she reluctantly turned her steps towards the bookshop, wheeling the bike to make the distance longer.

Oakbridge looked a pet of a town in the sunshine. The local council hadn't got the modernizing bug yet, and the streets were still cobbled, with the original gulley running down the centre. Fine old trees grew at the pavement edges, carefully kept and protected by iron cages. Here and there were rustic seats. Most of the shops had small frontages, and gay striped sunblinds. The square had a tiny patch of green in the centre, bounded by seats, and there was a clock tower and pigeons. The Town Hall was a gracious red brick building, and the main church had a green slate roof, and its bells chimed little tunes at mid-day.

'Oakbridge would have been such fun if Andrew—' Elaine began, and firmly refused to even think the rest of the sentence. She sighed. 'Why does Hazel get everything her way, and I *never* do?'

She stopped by one of the seats, and propped the bike against its back. The day was getting too hot to wear the raincoat any longer. She folded it slowly, and took as long as she dared to strap it behind the saddle, and all the time she thought of the injustice of things, and wondered why the day had to be so perfect for Hazel's party, and why everyone should do so much to make the party a success, while Hazel did nothing but loaf around and have a good time.

'She's even got two men crazy over her, and she's a fool not to have that nice Peter Walpole!' she decided, with a rare hint of bitterness, and knowing nothing of Peter's changed attitude.

'Oh, heavens,' she said to herself, suddenly, 'I'm being mean. I'll get warped and beastly if I don't look out. What have I got? Let's see, I've got the satisfaction of knowing I've never sponged on any-one—but I've borrowed. Mustn't forget that! (Still, I can pay that back next month, when I'm twenty-one.) Oh, yes, and next month I won't be a child any longer, and Hazel's still only eighteen and that's a rotten age to be. And—I've got Charles.'

She pulled a face, and suddenly started laughing. It was so ludicrous. After all she had thought and said about Charles, and after all she had said to his face, here she was in the middle of Oakbridge High Street, on the first hot day in July, counting him among her blessings!

'And what a blessing he is! Oh, well, beggars can't be choosers. Let's pick up Robert's book and get it over!'

Vaguely at the back of her mind was the thought that she might as well say 'yes' if he proposed to her again to-day. As far as she could see, she'd be in Brookfield for a long time yet, and the more she came into Oakbridge the more difficult it would become if she kept refusing Charles. It might make things awkward for Robert, too, since he used the only bookshop in Oakbridge so much.

There were customers in the shop, so she waited until they had gone, and quietly watched him as he attended to them. Little by little her good intentions fled, and she found herself counting up the things she didn't like about him.

'Oh, why does he stand there with his head on one side and his hands wringing each other? Why doesn't he stand up easily and straight?' and it was a very difficult thing not to add 'like Andrew'. She didn't like the pernickety way he wrapped books, and made parcels. Almost as if he were counting the cost of each sheet of brown paper, the value of each length of string. He was almost obsequious to the customers, yet when at last he was free, he turned to her with a change of manner, at once domineering and almost possessive. She felt he was regarding her as an asset, valuing her by the sum she had borrowed from him, and the interest it would have brought from anyone else.

'Well, Elaine, so the Vicar gave you my message?' he began.

'Not until to-day, and I wish he hadn't,' she told him. 'And I haven't come about that either, Charles. I've merely dropped in to see if the Vicar's book has arrived—the one he ordered. And,' she added firmly, 'I wouldn't have come in for that if my cousin hadn't specially asked me to.'

'I see.' His eyes raked her from head to foot, and she stood stiffly, enduring his scrutiny with a set face.

At last he said: 'I don't see you wearing the new clothes you bought with my money.'

'Am I supposed to wear them to Oakbridge so you can see them?'

'I've seen you several times. You didn't see me, oh, dear, no! You've never worn anything but your old things. It seems suspicious to me, Elaine. I'm almost persuaded that you haven't got those new clothes yet.'

As she didn't answer, but stood glaring at him, he went on slowly, 'I'm almost persuaded, indeed, that you never intended to get them. I should like very much to know what you wanted that money for.'

'Well, of all the nerve, Charles Ramsey! I bet you'd like to know! Well, you won't know. It's none of your business. And next month—just over three weeks' time—I shall be getting money of my own, and I'll repay you with all the pleasure in the world! And I'm never going to see you again after that. I think you're the meanest man I know!'

He raised his sandy brows and looked thoughtfully out into the street. 'I merely wanted to know, so that I could buy you what you wanted as an engagement present. I still want to hear you say you'll marry me, you see!'

'I don't think I've met anyone so thick-skinned,' she murmured angrily. 'Can't you get it into your head that when I say "no", I do truly mean it?'

'No, you don't, Elaine. All girls say "no" and keep on saying it until some fellow is strong enough to persuade the "no" to turn into a "yes". I'm one of those fellows,' he told her, with a meaning smile.

'It's no use talking to you,' she said, turning away, but she felt uneasy. Charles

Ramsey never smiled without reason, and she wondered what dirty trick he could possibly be planning.

'I had rather a nice thought, Elaine. Your cousin Hazel has surprisingly included me in her party, and it might be nice to announce our engagement then.'

'No! Don't you dare!'

'I'm only doing it for your sake, Elaine. To protect you against malicious gossip. You never know in a small place like this, if it would get out. Besides, there's the Vicar to think of. He's ill, and I think that if he heard you'd been borrowing money from me, it would upset him very much. Don't you?'

'Get me the book we ordered, Charles Ramsey. Get me the book if it's here, and let me get out of your shop before I say something I'll regret. And don't you dare say a word about this to anyone!'

He bowed mockingly. 'I'll bring the ring with me this afternoon. I've merely bespoken it, to avoid the unnecessary expense of buying it in case you proved headstrong, and decided to risk the Vicar's getting to hear of—er—our little transaction.'

EIGHTEEN

ELAINE'S memories of the party were confused. The heat of the day brought on a nagging headache. She was disappointed in her dress, too. It had seemed such a nice quiet grey, a simple dress which she felt became her, but when the guests began to arrive, she realized how sombre it was going to look against the gay colours worn by the Merryweather party, and the vivid patterned prints worn by the local women. Even the grass was a brilliant green, all fresh after the recent rains, and everything looked alive and bright and happy excepting herself.

Robert sat quietly in his invalid chair, a little apart from the rest, watching it all. Tea on the lawn meant the seating of the local folk at the trestle tables, with the Walpole party and Hazel's special friends at smaller tables. These were ringed round at the end, forming a horseshoe of the whole, in the centre of which was Hazel herself, looking superb in ice-blue crépe. Squeak Merry-weather wore white with tremendous success, and Andrew's fiancée contrived to look frail, feminine, and rather dream-like in pale yellow.

Andrew found himself a place to sit in the shadow of one of the great oaks and looked less strained than usual.

'He can see better in the shadow,' Elaine suddenly discovered, with a pang, and felt wretched for the rest of the day because of the times Sandra managed to drag him out into the glare of the sun.

'Everything looks wonderful,' everyone said, and sounded as though they meant it. Even Hazel's new friends said nice things, but as Elaine followed their glance round at the tables and the general arrangements, she wondered tiredly if they knew just how much hard work lay behind it all, or what crises and sacrifices had been in the forefront of their existence this last few weeks, to make Hazel's day so lovely for her.

The cake, for instance. Tragedy had overtaken the one which had been ordered, through an accident. It was really the fault of Frances, and to repair the damage, she and Elaine had made up a big rich cake and iced it as near as possible to the other one. But it was Elaine who had done most of the work, and dashed about secretly, getting the special ingredients, and in many cases paying for them. She did not know whether Hazel would notice the difference and realize what had happened, and at this stage she no longer cared.

Hazel's new dress, obtained from a big shop in Belminster (Robert had been unexpectedly firm in refusing to pay another London dress bill) had had to be fetched, as they couldn't get it sent in time. Hazel said she couldn't go herself, so Elaine had gone, and had staggered home with the big box, walking across the fields from the Halt to avoid the cost of hiring a cab.

There was hardly a thing which went towards the success of it all which hadn't gone wrong at first, or fallen on to Elaine's shoulders. Prue Chibbetts, hired to help with the waiting, was slow and inclined to flirt in odd corners and neglect her duties. She had to be watched, and occasionally jogged into action. The eldest Ogg girl and the Harris girl, however, though considerably younger, and very willing and quick, were inclined to be clumsy, and Elaine had to keep an eye on them to forestall unnecessary breakages and possible damage to the visitors' clothes.

'I'll be glad when this day's over,' she told herself.

She and Frances (who seemed to have forgotten the scene in Robert's bedroom the day before) snatched a hasty snack together behind the screens in the kitchen, at a point when tea was nearly over and the women helpers could carry on unaided. The heat grew in intensity, and someone said it looked like a storm.

'Never get a fine day but a storm brews to spoil it,' Frances moaned, and Elaine thought in amazement, 'Why, she looks more tired than I feel!'

Charles was never very far from her. Andrew always seemed to be a long, long way away, firmly clutched by the arm, Sandra obviously bent on reminding him of what the future would be like.

Whenever Elaine searched and found Andrew, although she didn't move, she was always conscious that Charles was following her glance, and in his eyes there was the smallest hint of a mocking light. It worried her, and she never seemed to get a minute to herself to think of a way out.

'Don't work too hard, child,' the Vicar

said once. 'It's all so nice, and it's all due to you.'

'Aren't you dancing, Elaine? You should be! Damme, let someone else do the waiting on everyone!' This from Lady Lassett, in a voice loud enough to be heard above the efforts of the local string band.

Peter talked to the older guests, and ignored Hazel once he had made his congratulations on arrival. He looked neither happy nor miserable; but he was older, much older, Elaine decided. In the last few months he had matured unbelievably.

Towards evening the sun went in and the air grew very close. Dancing was to be continued indoors, and all the windows were flung wide to let in the smallest breath of air.

The Vicarage, always too large for the family's use, now seemed to be crowded beyond belief. The 'empty' room had been flung open for dancing, the folding doors opening into the big musty parlour, and chairs brought from all over the house, ranged round the walls. Pots, buckets, vases and jugs, decorated with crinkled paper, stood at intervals, containing shrubs and flowers from the garden, and hot-house blooms which Lady Lassett had insisted on sending over. Extra electric light bulbs (a rare extravagance in the Vicarage) had been fitted into the central chandelier.

'My, it really looks lovely,' Mrs. Harris said, with satisfaction, and Mrs. Ogg agreed with her for once, though she couldn't resist adding, as she surveyed the scene and the improvised platform containing the string band surrounded by more plants and flowers, 'I'd like to see Vicar's face when the bill for all this comes in!'

Summer lightning began about seven, but after one or two gasps and comments, the party settled down again, and no further notice was taken of the weather. Hazel's crowd grew tired of waltzes and quicksteps, and chivvied the overworked musicians into producing rumba, tango, conga and the more rowdy eccentricities of the dance floor. Robert wrinkled his nose in distaste and retired to the study.

The older people resolved themselves into groups and sat talking in corners and round the walls. Some drifted out of the noise and movement into the little general parlour and tried to shut out the music and merriment by closing the door, but the french windows had to be left open as it was still very close, and the noise came in that way.

Elaine found the Vicar sitting back in his armchair by the big desk, an exhausted look on his face.

'Why don't you go upstairs, Robert, and rest? You've had a trying day, you know!'

He needed little persuasion. 'Make my excuses if anyone asks for me,' he said, and dragged himself out of the room. She watched him for a few minutes, until she was sure he was upstairs safely. Robert didn't like being helped, but he was a heavy man, and it seemed that it was taking so long for him to get strong again, strong enough to get about on his own.

She flopped down into the armchair herself, and reflected that there was at least one place in the house that was quiet.

Outside the sky grew darker, and the room was shadowy and hot. Lightning still flashed at intervals, but there was no thunder or rain, and so far only the threat of a storm. People's voices drifted in from afar, and faintly came the sound of the strings, playing a rumba. After a while she began to doze.

It was Andrew's voice, close at hand, which finally roused her.

'For heaven's sake, Sandra, leave me alone. Go off and have fun with the others. I shan't leave you, don't worry. But don't try to make me dance or clown about with that lot.'

'But, Andrew, it looks so rude, clearing off like this. Besides, what do you want to mope in the dark for? Why not grab as much light as you can, while you can?'

'Tact was never your strong point, my dear,' he said, wryly, and left her. Elaine heard him close the study door behind him and feel his way across the room. She wanted to call out that he was not alone; she knew she ought to, in case she startled him, or tripped him. But her voice dried up. She couldn't speak. Her heart was thudding. She knew he was trying to find the one armchair, the armchair she was sitting in.

His groping hand found the back of it, and his toe stubbed one of the feet. He moved round a little, and gropingly found the arms of the chair, and finally her hand.

His hand was suddenly still, resting on hers. Then, uncertainly, he ran his fingers exploringly up her arm and fingered her sleeve.

'Elaine?' he whispered.

'Yes, Andrew.'

She felt choked, frightened. She had never dreamed that his touch could stir her so. She could never remember him touching her before, not even to lightly hold her arm in crossing the road. The roads about Brookfield were not busy enough to warrant such assistance, and Andrew was the most correct of men.

His hand tightened on her arm, as he still bent over her, searching for her face in the gloom. Another flash of lightning lit everything up and showed him, tense and miserable, looking intently down at her. Hungrily, almost.

'Elaine?' he said again, and finding her other arm, pulled her slowly up towards him.

She made no resistance. She was deadbeat, and wretched. Everything was wrong with her world, and with his, also. She slid into his arms and let him search for her mouth with his own.

There was hunger and desperation in that first kiss, as though they were both drowning, and clutched eagerly at the same lifebelt. The fiddles and drums in the big room beyond were pounding out the heady rhythm of a conga. The shuffle of the dancers' feet, and the stormy heat, gave the atmosphere an exciting quality. This wasn't Brookfield Vicarage, where Hazel and her friends were having a good time, and two people called Andrew and Elaine were trying to heal their mutual despair. This was the jungle, this was a tropic island, this was anywhere far removed from the mundane everyday life, and they were alone and undisturbed.

Into the incoherence of her thoughts came little highlights, tiny things to be remembered afterwards. The rough touch of his tweed coat (he had refused to dress, much to Sandra's annoyance) and the tobacco smell about it. The prickly sensation when her hand crept round the back of his neck and encountered the place where his hair began. The firm, smooth warmth of his lips, the brushing of his eyebrows against her forehead when he moved to rest his cheek on hers.

His cheek was wet, and she found she was crying, and saying his name over and over again, in a choked little undertone. He said nothing, and she guessed he couldn't. He just held her close, and they stood by the side of Robert's desk, in a tight desperate embrace, an embrace which couldn't be broken hurriedly, because they both knew it might never happen again.

'I can't let you go,' he whispered finally. 'I need you. Oh, Elaine, I want you so much. I've wanted you all the time. I tried to write, but I couldn't see.' His voice broke without warning, and she found she was gripping his arms, comfortingly, reassuringly.

'It doesn't matter,' she kept repeating, and for a second it didn't seem to matter, though underneath they both knew it did. There was Sandra, and Charles. There was Hazel, Frances and the Vicar. There was Lady Lassett, and Peter; the Merry-weathers, the whole village, in fact. Engagements weren't taken lightly here.

And there was themselves.

'I can't break things up between you, Andrew.'

'We don't love each other, Elaine— Sandra and I. We've never known love. I think she doesn't even like me. I was a fool to slip into it again. I was lonely. I was miserable. Oh, Elaine, don't let me go.'

They thrashed it out, desperately, in a series of urgent whispers. It was deadlock. They knew that at the start. But they had to thrash it out.

Finally, Elaine gave up for the moment, and started another line of thought. If his eyes could be put right, surely Sandra wouldn't have so much her own way, might even find him less attractive and suitable to her purpose if his sight were repaired, and he were no longer virtually a sick man? She put it to him that if he tried, something might be done about it.

'Andrew, you don't really need to lose your sight, do you? You can have something done, can't you? With your money, there *must* be something!'

'I won't have operations,' he returned, a little too quickly. 'I won't let them tinker with me, to run up big fees. Quacks, the lot of 'em!'

'Andrew, don't talk like it. What caused it? Did you have an accident? Or is it hereditary?'

'Don't let's talk about it!'

'Yes! Yes, we must. If you got your sight put right, you wouldn't be so dependent on people. Oh, don't you see? I hate to see you like this—you're young, you shouldn't have to resign yourself to this. Andrew, won't you *try* and have something done? Please?'

'Elaine, don't let's waste the precious minutes arguing like this about me. I'm to

259

lose my sight, and I'm resigned. But I don't think I have to stay with Sandra just because of the conventions, nor because in a moment of hellish weakness I started bleating about being alone, and sent for her. Elaine, Elaine, if I got free of this engagement, would you——? Is that what you meant, about getting something done for my eyes? You wouldn't want to be tied to a blind fool either? Is it, Elaine?'

'Oh, Andrew, don't talk like it! Don't! Of course I wouldn't feel like that. It's just that I want you to have a chance of sharing things—oh, what am I saying? I can't break up someone's engagement. In my world we don't do things like that.'

'Stop fighting,' he murmured, his lips against her bright hair. 'I'll make a bargain with you. If you'll help me get free—if you'll have me afterwards—I promise you I'll move heaven and earth to get my eyes put right! I'll even let them operate. What do you say?'

She didn't answer immediately. She was too tired, too confused, to think clearly. She wanted him so much. She wanted him to get his sight back. She couldn't bear to see him fumbling about, as he had when he came into this room. It hurt her to see him creeping into patches of shade, sitting in the twilight, avoiding crowds and traffic, like a sick dog.

'You do love me, don't you? This isn't just . . . one of those things, is it? It is the real thing?' he persisted with heartbreaking anxiety.

'Oh, yes. Yes, Andrew, yes!'

'Then you will do this for me?'

'Andrew, I don't know. It isn't right—I can't think straight—what will Robert say? Oh, I'm so tired. Ask me tomorrow.'

'No, now. Now! To-morrow's no good. Tell me now, Elaine.'

Suddenly she could see his face, very close to hers, the eyes intent and demanding, the expression such that she had never dreamed of seeing in Andrew's hard young face. Just that brief flash of view, before his eyes snapped shut, and she realized that the reason she could see him at all was because the door had opened behind her, and the light from outside was on them.

She swung round. Sandra stood there in her filmy yellow, her face shadowed as her back was to the outside light. Behind her stood Charles.

'How cosy!' Sandra said, her voice brittle like chips of ice. 'Let's have some light, shall we? I, personally, don't care for dark places.'

She snapped the light on, and came in, closely followed by Charles, who carefully shut the door behind him.

Elaine felt suddenly angry, embarrassed, a little cheapened, as when other people come into the bedroom before the occupant has finished dressing.

'How dare you!' she flashed, but she was speaking to Charles. Sandra answered, with a bright tinkle of amused laughter.

'Well, for ever more! How dare I, indeed! Or didn't you know that it was my fiancée you were pawing in the dark?'

'I wasn't speaking to you, but to Charles. Since you seem to want to draw attention to yourself, let me remind you that this happens to be the place where I work and you're only a guest here, so would you mind getting out?'

Charles interposed smoothly. 'If you'd be good enough, Miss Standish, to take your fiancé out, I'd like to speak to Miss Harcourt alone.'

Sandra smiled. 'A good idea, Mr. Ramsey. I'm sure Andrew will think so, too, when I tell him what you are going to do. Did you know, darling, that this nice man from the Oakbridge bookshop is going to announce his engagement to-night—to—er—Elaine here?'

'It isn't true,' Elaine gasped, turning angrily to Andrew. 'Don't believe it! He's telling lies. He's trying to make me say I'll marry him because——'

She broke off, confused. Sandra and Charles exchanged glances. Whichever one of them had discovered that Andrew and Elaine were together in the study, they must have had a brief but revealing conversation together before deciding to burst in like this.

Andrew, speaking for the first time said, 'Don't worry, Elaine. I think I know. I had hoped it wasn't true, but it doesn't really matter. What does matter is that you don't want to marry him. You really don't, do you?'

'Of course I don't. But, Andrew, how did you know? Did he——' She turned accusing eyes on the smirking Charles. 'Did he tell you?' she asked in a low, furious voice.

'Not exactly,' Andrew allowed. He was angry, too. He disliked people who arranged scenes, and he couldn't decide whether it was Sandra or that slimy fellow from the bookshop who had arranged this one. He was furious at being caught at a disadvantage, and uncertain of how much they had seen or heard. 'As a matter of fact, I was in the shop when he spoke to you on the telephone about that money. I felt that it was damned bad taste—he must have known I could hear what he was saying.'

'So that's why you were saying all those peculiar things, Charles! You need not have mentioned that money at all!' Elaine cried.

'Might one inquire what all this is about?' Sandra said, with a mocking smile on her face.

'One might,' Andrew said crisply, 'except that it doesn't happen to be your business, Sandra. What does concern you is, I think you're behaving in a pretty rotten manner. I don't like it, and I wish to be free of our engagement.'

She flushed, and looked as angry as Andrew and Elaine.

'I bet you would,' she said, between her teeth. 'To marry the Vicar's little typist, no doubt. Not much, you don't! If you think you're going to put me in that position, you'll regret it. I'll personally see you regret it!'

Charles added softly, 'My offer still holds good, Elaine. I—er—hesitate to adopt

Miss Standish's line, but somehow I don't think you'll care overmuch for the discomfort which goes with—er—trying to change partners in mid-stream, shall we say?'

NINETEEN

'BLESS my soul, I don't know how things get about in Brookfield!' Robert ejaculated. 'Here we've been exercising all our energies to keeping this miserable business a secret, every day since the party. Two whole weeks of guarding our tongues and faces, of behaving more or less like international spies, and here I find, on my first trip round, that all my parishioners know about it! I can't think how these things get about!'

Judy Lassett poured him some more tea, and smiled tightly. At one time she would have guffawed heartily, but those days were over. Peter had left Walpole House the day after the party, and brother and sister had parted bad friends.

This much Robert knew, and wouldn't dream of asking for more information, and so far Judy hadn't offered it, even to him. He guessed that she was too badly hurt to speak of it, but didn't realize that it concerned the Walpole funds.

Judy couldn't bring herself to admit, even to Robert, that her reluctant disclosure of the bar on the Walpole money had been no brake to Peter's determination to get away, and that he had left her despite the fact that he hadn't a penny in his pocket.

While Robert talked, she went over that last scene in her mind. It had been painful. She and her brother, in their different ways, had been very angry.

'You're not having a penny out of me, damn you, and how far d'you think you'll get without it? You stay here, and do the job you were born for!' she had shouted at him, desperation driving wisdom out of her head.

'That's how your world thinks, Judith,' he had answered. 'In terms of money. In my world it plays very little part. There are more important things. In my own way I am as tenacious as you are. I want to get to Italy. I shall get there, with or without funds. Watch me!'

She had been staggered at his manner. Quiet, yet more angry than she had ever thought he could be. He had gone without bidding her good-bye, neither had he said good-bye to anyone else. The absence of his customary courtesy was a bleak pointer to his feelings. Brookfield was no longer home to him. It simply didn't count any more.

She said now, because the Vicar was looking anxiously at her distraught face, 'You know, Robert, you and I think we know so much, but I've got a feeling we're damn well wrong every time. I about Peter. You about Elaine.'

'Eh?' he gasped.

She nodded. 'Elaine is a quiet person, in the way Peter was. I've been thinking a lot about her since Peter went away. Damme, why haven't we seen she was quietly breaking her heart over that Farrar fella? And what's so bad about him? Why shouldn't she have him? Just because he knows that bum lot at The Wooky Hole, doesn't mean he's one of 'em, does it? No, Robert, we've been wrong, badly wrong over it. If we'd driven that girl into the arms of that nasty little bit of work in the bookshop, we couldn't have hoped to do worse!'

'But, Judy, I've never said——' Robert began, looking distressed and a little guilty.

'No, that's you all over. You've never said! But you've felt the same things, and probably shown more of what you were feeling than you think. And what's worse, a damned sight worse, you've let that sister of yours have her say, and what damage d'you think that's been doing, eh? Given Elaine a hell of a life, Frances has! Oh, it isn't hearsay—she's told me herself. And she blows hot and cold, that's the worst of it. When Elaine could have got Farrar for herself, Frances was always running him down. When it was too late and that Standish woman came back, Frances veered the other way—everything was wrong about Elaine's methods then. Why didn't she get him, Frances kept bleating—why didn't she grab the fella before the ex-fiancée came back? That's the way Frances goes on, and believe me, Robert, Elaine wouldn't have stopped in this village so long but for you. Know that, don't you?'

'Oh, dear, oh, dear, how difficult everything is,' Robert said confusedly. 'I must talk to Elaine.'

'Take my advice and say nothing about it, now. It's too late.'

'But, Judy, I've been urging her to go away for a long, long time. I know we've nothing to offer her! But no matter how strongly I urged her, she wouldn't go.'

'Of course she wouldn't not on your money, or at your suggestion. From what I can get out of her, she considers it her duty to stay. You'd know it, if she went, my boy! You'd see a change in that little nest of yours, without Elaine. Pity Hazel isn't more like her!'

With the mention of his daughter, however, Robert bridled, and Judy saw her mistake too late. Nothing more could come of such a conversation, so she let it go. Robert, in his turn, left Walpole House in a very disturbed state of mind.

In the last two weeks everyone had noticed an improvement in him, and it was generally felt that a return to his duties (with the help of the temporary priest) would do him more good than staying in the agitated atmosphere of the Vicarage. Only Robert knew what the effort of going out at all was costing him.

He looked his old self. The doctor had pronounced him as fit. But privately he knew that he would not be able to keep going very long. Brookfield as a parish was a turbulent one, a parish which needed too much holding down, and too much keeping at arm's length from his own doorstep.

He had made a complete round that day, an uneasy round of visits, during which he had discovered many things he didn't know about his own household, small things the parishioners dropped unconsciously in the easy conversation with the Vicar, the dear old Vicar who couldn't see what was going on under his very nose.

'Had a good day, Robert?' Elaine greeted him, with a crooked smile.

'Yes, my dear, and I've picked up some news. Some extraordinary news, in fact. I have learned that Frances no longer deals with the Oggs, but bakes her own bread. That Harris had words with her over a mythical matter of over-charging, which you put right with a degree of tact which staggers me. I've traced the coat I mislaid, and find that it was bought at the jumble sale for threepence and is now gracing the back of old Mrs. Geddes' idiot nephew. And,' he said, pausing, 'I've learned that Charles Ramsey is making himself particularly unpleasant—er—about you.' He fixed Elaine with a stern eye.

Something in Elaine snapped. It wasn't enough that she had somehow come to bear the complete burden in the Vicarage, but added to this she she had to be harried over the one small thing she had done which might have been expected to displease Robert, while his own daughter got away with so much.

It wasn't fair, she told herself wildly—it just wasn't fair.

'It's a pity, Robert,' she returned, with unusual asperity, 'that you have parishioners who think it worth while reporting on my activities, and not telling you more about Hazel. If you don't want her in trouble—big trouble—very soon, you might find it worth while making inquiries about the Merryweathers.'

'Elaine! Don't talk to me like that!' Robert shouted, goaded again by the mention of his daughter's name.

'Then leave me alone! At least I don't get in with a nasty clique like those people!'

She hurriedly left the room, ignoring his commands to come back. Robert in this mood could be a hectoring stranger; a man who assumed the mantle of a father, and a domineering father at that.

'I don't know what happens to him, to change him in a flash,' Elaine mused, miserably going out to walk in the sweet-scented dampness which followed the intermittent rain of the day.

Even in the dusk there was no peace, no security. She passed the Lincoln sisters, clad in rainboots and mackintoshes and clutching umbrellas, walking out with the dog for his evening run. Their tight smiles and sudden silence at her approach told her that the two little spinsters had just been discussing her.

Further on was the little row of cottages where Grannie Geddes lived. The old woman was leaning on her little gate, gossiping with Eb Wilkins' mother and Mrs. Jimpson. Again that sudden telling silence as Elaine passed.

'I suppose the gossip started by someone overhearing Charles at the party telling Sandra we were in the study together,' she told herself, wearily, and at last left the road to strike across the fields in the direction of the river.

The River Wid, a deep and fast-running waterway, was fairly narrow at this point, widening suddenly beyond St. Mary's until it reached Belminster, where it needed a ferry at the unbridged parts. It was a pretty river, but too treacherous for bathing and other summer activities. Owing to its vagaries, the old wooden bridges had long since been removed, and sturdy permanent affairs erected from the large white local stones.

Elaine paused in sight of the Brookfield

273

bridge. It was quiet here. Willows leaned over the water's edge, and the white bridge reflected itself in the swirling waters below with more beauty in this dim light than in the daytime.

She stood for a second on the steep bank, looking at the deep shadows in the water, and under the trees on the far bank. It was good to take in all this peace and quiet. After a while she decided it was time to be moving on. She went to turn and walk away when, without warning, her foot slipped in the squelching mud of the turfed bank, and she felt herself rapidly sliding down.

She cried out a little in surprise but managed to save herself from the quick-flowing waters by grabbing at a young tree-trunk. She laughed a little shakily as she pulled herself to safety and felt her way along to the bridge. This was preferable instead of attempting to climb that treacherous bank. Her stockings and one side of her coat and sleeve were coated with mud where she had skidded down, and her heart hammered unpleasantly.

It was a nasty experience, pregnant with terrifying possibilities, yet now it was over, she felt rather foolish.

Then she saw Andrew. She had been

conscious of pounding footsteps over the bridge as she was sliding down; they had stopped, and she had forgotten them in the relief at being able to save herself. Now she realized why she had heard no more. He must have seen her and run across the bridge, but daren't venture down the slippery bank where the shadows were.

'Elaine!' He grabbed her roughly to him, and hungrily searched her face. 'Are you all right? You might have been drowned! There should be a rail there! You aren't hurt—you *are* all right?'

'Yes, yes,' she said incoherently. 'Mind, I'm a mess, caked with mud. I'm wet, too, I think.'

She tried to push him away, but he held her closely.

'Oh, my dear, why did you have to come here, alone? I heard you cry out—I'd been watching you, trying to see if it really was you or whether my eyes were playing tricks. Oh, Elaine, don't do that again. It's hell, not being capable of helping you if you need me——' he muttered brokenly, and pressed his face into her hair.

'Andrew, for heaven's sake—we mustn't risk being seen here together like this. Oh, don't, Andrew, let me go—it isn't fair!

275

Don't you know what agony it is for me to be so close to you, knowing, *knowing*, I've no right to be? Andrew, please let me go!'

'No. I can't Elaine, I can't! Don't make me let you go. Don't you understand—can't you see *my* side? Sandra won't release me, but she's making life a hell on earth. You can see that! Elaine, let's go away together. If she won't release me, I'll jilt her. Heavens, it isn't as though she's already married to me. She'll find someone else easily enough. It isn't as if she's in love with me!' he argued fiercely, and resisting all the time Elaine's struggles to break away.

'You fool, Andrew, don't you see what she's really like? She'll sue you for breach of promise! Oh, yes, I know you can well afford it, but you don't want all that publicity, not with all you're going through with your eyes, do you? Andrew, leave it alone, darling! Leave it alone. Perhaps she'll let you go later on, if she thinks I don't want you. But don't do this—I've got to go on living in this village, and they're talking about me already.'

'You can't stand a bit of gossip?' he asked, disbelieving. He gripped her shoulders and lowered his face until it was close to hers. 'Elaine, do you love me?'

'Oh, you know I do! You *know* I do.'

'Then do as I ask,' he whispered. 'We'll go somewhere where no one knows us, and get married quietly——'

'And Sandra will trace you through your bankers or your solicitors, and then the trouble will start. Don't be a fool Andrew! And in case you don't understand why I'm making all this fuss, look at it from my point of view if you can! I love you—I'm silly about you, if you must know—but, Andrew, I want you to myself. I want a peaceful honeymoon and a tranquil married life, not a harried existence in the public eye with a lawsuit in progress and probably dragging on for years. She's got us where she wants us—she knows that! She knows that what she could do to us would not only bleed you white, even of all your money, but it would kill our love, yours and mine. If you're honest and stop to think, you'll admit it's true! No, Andrew, I can't do it!'

'Elaine, don't refuse me. You want to see me get a bit of happiness, don't you? Life could be so good with you! She'd never find us—I'd instruct my bank and my solicitors——'

'Andrew,' she broke in desperately,

'Andrew, I won't stay in Brookfield if you're going to keep on like this. Come to think of it, it would be better for both of us if I took Robert's advice. I should have done, when he spoke of it before. I should have left this village when you got engaged again to Sandra. That was the moment to go then all this wouldn't have happened. Robert's offered to pay my fare, and keep me going till I get a job somewhere. He knows, he can see farther than either of us. People always act silly when they're in love—it's no use saying it isn't so, Andrew. You know it's true! Look at us now, at this moment! Voices carry at night, especially near water, and in this place it's madness to give anyone the chance to gossip. Let me go, Andrew, please.'

'Yes, I'll let you go, if you promise me not to go away!'

'No, I won't. It's best for both of us. It's the only decent thing to do.'

'Elaine, if you go, I swear I'll take my life, and I'm not pretending. I mean it!'

'Andrew!'

'Think, Elaine. What have I got to live for, if you go? Oh, I know I should have thought of that before, but you weren't helpful, back in those days when we were

278

both free. But that's all past. We know what we want, and we can get it. If you take away from me that one chance of happiness, I'll—' He looked down, speculating, to where the river lay. It was almost dark now, but the speeding waters made a sinister, inviting sound as they rushed along. 'I'll go that way. It's easy, and sure. I mean it.'

She stopped her mad struggling and slumped against him. 'All right, Andrew, you win. I can't fight you on those grounds, because I can see you do mean it. I'm doing the wrong thing, but . . . I'll stay.'

TWENTY

THE last week in July was warm and dry and sunny, and the nights close with a suggestion of impending storm.

Elaine developed the habit of sitting at her bedroom window far into the small hours, long after the last lights had gone out in the village, wondering if sleep would ever come naturally again.

She was dead tired. Andrew and the scene by the river was constantly before her, and even the Vicar's latest urge to work on the new book did not take her mind off her own problems.

She found herself thinking about Andrew while she took down rapid notes, notes that still made excellent sense when she mechanically read them back.

'If only the weather would settle. First wet and cold, then stifling hot, then storms. Oh, how hot it is!' She fanned herself with a sheet of notepaper, and listened to the Merryweathers bidding a noisy farewell to their guests.

Up the street roared three large cars, carrying most of them away to their homes in the outlying district. Despite the most vigorous protests and the most belligerent complaints, from practically every inhabitant in the village, the noise still went on. Loud music, loud laughter and voices, loud good-byes, and loud car noises as their guests departed.

Hazel came quietly up the road some little time later. Mark Pelham was with her. Elaine watched them both come through the gap in the hedge (to avoid the creak of the gate, she thought, contemptuously) and quietly let themselves in through the french windows. After a while, the fat little man went out alone, and the stairs creaked as Hazel crept upstairs.

As a rule she went to bed in darkness, but to-night she switched on her bedside lamp, and it was on so long that Elaine began to be worried. The lamp cast a shaft of bright light down the garden. Elaine could see it from the side window of her room, Hazel's room lying on the other side of the corridor, and overlooking the garden at the side of the house. Neither Robert nor Frances would be able to see that light, their windows facing

281

other directions, and for this reason Elaine doubted whether either of them had any idea of what time Hazel came in at night, or whether she came alone.

This started her worrying afresh; should she risk another scene by telling them, or should she let them remain in ignorance, and chance Hazel's getting into the trouble which Elaine had been half-anticipating for so long?

At last she dragged on a light coat over her nightdress and went out into the passage. There was a bar of light along the floor at the end. She went straight to Hazel's door, tapped lightly on the panels and walked in without waiting to be invited.

Hazel was writing in a small, thickish book which Elaine guessed to be a diary. Her back was to the door, and she was so engrossed in what she was doing at the little escritoire that she hadn't heard her cousin knock or open the door.

Elaine said quietly, 'I saw your light go up, and I wondered if anything was wrong.'

Hazel spun round, her face white and angry. As she moved, her hand knocked the book off the desk, and sent it flying. It landed with a thud at Elaine's feet. Elaine stooped to pick it up, and Hazel leapt up in an effort to retrieve it first.

On the open page, under the day's date, Elaine caught the words, 'Mark more urgent than ever, but I——' before her cousin snatched it from her.

'Rotten little sneak, coming prying in here . . .' she began, but Elaine swiftly intervened.

'Shut up! You'll wake the whole house.' She went over and closed the door, and turned to Hazel again. 'Make no mistake, I'm not interested in your business. I can't help noticing a light switched on when it isn't the usual thing, and I wondered if you were ill or anything. As you're not, I've no further interest. If you don't care what people say about you, I'm sure I don't.'

'What do they say?' Hazel asked, her lips whitening.

'They say what you'd expect them to say. That you're fast, and that you keep company with an elderly foreigner and a lot of queer people.'

'Oh. Is that all?' The girl's colour came back swiftly, and she began to look angry again as her fear evaporated. 'I suppose you encourage them to talk. I suppose you watch for me to come in, to see how late I'm going to be?'

'Oh, save your cheap sneers, Hazel, do! I told you, I'm not interested. Watch your step, that's all. None of us in this house can help you if you get in a mess. It's a bit out of our line.'

'What d'you mean?' Hazel was scared again, and Elaine wondered. There must be something deeper going on than she herself knew about. Hazel didn't get frightened easily, young as she was.

Elaine shrugged. 'How do the Merry-weathers get all their money? What makes them have peculiar people go to their house? Doesn't smell ''above board'' to me!'

'You should talk! Hazel retorted. 'They're friends of your fancy boy!'

It was Elaine's turn to be angry.

'You brat, I could kill you for that,' she said, through clenched teeth. 'You bring everything down to your own cheap level, don't you?'

Hazel laughed happily. 'Well, you ask for it, don't you? That touching scene by the river the other night—the odious Winnie Ogg saw it all and broadcast it, with frills on. The old hags are now all watching your figure with interest—you know how they always fear the worst!'

'Yes, I know,' Elaine muttered, hardly noticing she spoke. She knew too well how even a hand-clasp, between two people who hadn't the conventional right to it, could be misconstrued and enlarged and speculated on, until the story finally circulated made the village too unpleasant a place for either to stay in. Whispers. Nods and winks. Suspicion. Insinuations. The whole hateful pack of godly people in Robert's parish were outside baying, like wolves, for herself or Hazel—it didn't matter which. And Hazel would do her share to aid the wolves and save her own skin.

Andrew. Andrew and herself, and their love. The thing that was too big for either of them to spoil. The thing they were striving so hard to keep above common gossip and suspicion. The best and finest thing that had happened to either of them.

'No one wants us,' he had told her one day in the woods as they went over the scene at the party and its implications. 'That bookshop fellow doesn't love you. Sandra doesn't really care for me. Why shouldn't we be in love, marry and get a bit of happiness? *Why?*'

With his desperate voice in her ears, and her own misery threatening to choke her, she slapped Hazel a stinging blow on either cheek before she was aware that she had moved. There was a mist before her eyes, and she was talking. Talking in a low, vicious undertone. Hazel's frightened face was before her eyes, one hand to her reddened cheek.

She heard herself say, 'What does this Mark Pelham mean to you? Are you living with him? Where do you get all those new clothes? Not out of Robert's allowance, that I do know! What are you getting up to, you little fool? Get out of it while you can, or you'll have us all in it! Think of your father and that shaky heart of his, if you won't think of yourself!' and she found herself hitting Hazel again.

'I can't get out of it,' Hazel said, in a frightened voice, and shielded her face. 'It's no use hitting me for what everyone else is saying about you—you should have thought of that before. And it's no use flinging my father in my teeth—I can't get out of the mess I'm in, now. It's too late. I've got to go on. I've got to!'

She wasn't angry, now. She sat back suddenly on the stool at the escritoire and looked blankly at Elaine, bending over her and still blazing with fury. Elaine was hot and gasping for breath, but Hazel was cool; so cool, she might have been a detached onlooker.

Elaine suddenly realized that the girl hadn't really any more feelings about anything. Now that she knew her cousin had guessed at some of the things that were going on at The Wooky Hole, she cast her fear and anger off her like a discarded cloak. There was nothing more to feel about anything. She was spun out.

Elaine sat down and faced her. 'What mess are you in?' she asked, in a husky whisper, and leaned her elbow tiredly on a nearby small table, and rested her cheek in her upturned hand. 'What mess . . . what *sort* of mess?'

Hazel said flatly, 'I'm in debt. The sort of debt that doesn't get paid in money.'

There was no drama about it. It was just a fact, and she said it without any emotion. She had been over it too many times in her own mind, to make any real sense or meaning out of the words.

Elaine had a swift picture of Hazel lying in her pretty bedroom at night, sweating with fear over just that sentence she had just uttered, while during the day she put on an elaborate yet convincing act of a girl getting more than her fair share out of life, and enjoying every minute of it.

'Father and Aunt Frances are such awful fools,' she went on, in that flat, unnatural voice. 'They never raised any protest when I started going up the road,' and she jerked her head towards The Wooky Hole, though it wasn't really necessary. 'They ought to have known what it would come to, though I don't suppose I would have listened,' she said, with unnatural fairness. Again she spoke as an onlooker, not as a participant. 'Now no one can help me.'

She started to laugh, a funny, silly little laugh, like someone who has had too much to drink and is about to get mawkish, sentimental.

Elaine said thickly, 'Don't be a fool. What sort of debt was it? Drink? Clothes? And what does it amount to?'

'More than you'll ever dream of,' was the response.

'Tell me,' Elaine said, shaking her, and raising her voice a little from that savage whisper she had been using, for fear Robert would hear.

Hazel suddenly sprang to life as though a button had been pressed.

'Oh, go to blazes! Who d'you think you

are, coming prying in here, catching me in an off-moment, and making me say God knows what! Get out, I say—get out!'

She sprang up in a fury, and the two girls struggled for a minute, Hazel trying to hit her cousin, Elaine desperately holding down her hands and urging her to keep quiet. D'you want the whole household to wake up, you little fool?' she cried.

They stopped struggling, suddenly, as a folded piece of paper fluttered on to the carpet. Whether it came from Hazel's pocket, or blew out of one of the pigeon-holes with the draught they made, Elaine never knew. She swiftly retrieved it, and held Hazel off while she opened it. It was a dress bill. Whether the entire amount, or just one of many, she didn't know. But the total stupefied her.

'But clothes *can't* cost that much!' she gasped. 'It must be for something else as well?'

She looked blankly at Hazel, who snatched at the paper and sulkily stowed it away in the pigeon-hole out of which it had presumably fallen.

'If I spend the whole of my legacy, it won't cover that,' Elaine mused, in horror.

'Who wants you to?' Hazel said, in a

bitter voice. 'You keep out of this. I wish to heaven you hadn't found out,' she cried, in sudden hatred. 'I wish it had been Aunt Frances or Daddy, but not you! Not you! Anyone in this village rather than you!'

Elaine recoiled as though her cousin had actually struck her.

'I don't think you really meant that,' she said. 'I think you're just tired and fed-up. At least, that's what I'm going to believe. And I'll do what I can to help you, though goodness knows how!'

TWENTY ONE

ELAINE put down the receiver and left the call box. She was glad it was a nice, sunny day and that Oakbridge looked so inviting. That telephone call had left a nasty taste in her mouth. Bad enough to be calling up Mark Pelham to make an appointment to see him, but to have to go out to his cottage, in the evening at that, was beyond all she had anticipated.

'Can't I come in the daytime?' she had asked. She had been barely polite. He seemed such a nasty little man at best, but realizing what he was doing to Hazel, who was, after all, very young and inexperienced, made him so vile in her eyes that she couldn't even bring herself to say 'Mr. Pelham'. Her voice, to her own ears, had sounded curt to the point of rudeness, but he hadn't seemed surprised. In fact, it seemed that the telephone call hadn't surprised him, either.

'I'm glad to see you theenk such a beeg

debt should be settled,' he had said. 'Eevening ees the only time I can see you—when the day's work ees over,' he had said, with the suspicion of a grim chuckle.

Elaine shivered.

'I'll go and look at the shops, to take my mind off it,' she told herself, 'but I'll steer clear of the bookshop. I'm simply not in the mood for Charles to-day.'

Somehow that telephone call had done one thing for her. It had made her feel that she was on the way towards doing something for Hazel, which would ultimately help Robert. To let this thing go on any longer was unthinkable. She had visions of Robert hearing of it and collapsing again. Of Frances throwing another fit of hysteria, and of joyfully spreading it about the village, because she hated Hazel so much. Of neighbours and friends, raising eyebrows and gossiping, calling to commiserate and to pick up odd bits of information that Frances had not provided.

The possibility of newspaper publicity was a grim horror, for Elaine had a feeling that the subject of the dress bill was in the nature of small fry, where Hazel's particular mess was concerned. She couldn't have put into words what she thought was behind it all, but try as she would, she couldn't put away from her the thought that there was something sinister and very wrong in that house up the road. Hazel, she was convinced, wouldn't look so hopeless over the matter of a debt—even of that size—nor would the suggested method of payment scare her. Hazel, for an eighteen-year-old just out of boarding-school, was tough.

She had proved how tough she was, in developing a taste for that crowd at first. No one made her join their ranks. She had moved heaven and earth to do so, despite everyone's doing their best to prevent her. That she was now saying that Robert ought to have stopped her, was characteristic of Hazel. Apart from that, she was a badly frightened girl.

Hazel herself was at that moment in a rage.

Sandra, in pale green pyjamas, was lounging over the cocktail bar in The Wooky Hole, with Squeak beside her. Both were looking at Hazel in an oddly calculating manner.

'Mark,' Sandra began thoughtfully, as she studied the contents of her glass, 'has telephoned to say you've been on the 'phone to him. Now, Squeak and I know you've been with us all the morning.'

'Yes, angel, you couldn't have spoken to him,' Squeak put in.

'What was the call about?' Hazel wanted to know.

'The call was about . . . the settling of your little debt, Hazel,' Sandra murmured.

Hazel flushed. So Elaine was trying to fix things for her, after all. If she wasn't careful, Elaine would break the thing wide open, through that hateful, straightforward way of hers. The whole business had to be tackled with skill, under cover. Not by lumbering in, as Elaine would no doubt do. Besides, Hazel felt she would look such a fool, if these people found out that her cousin was trying to help her. The one thing she had been cautioned not to do (threatened, perhaps, was the right word) was to let out a single word of all this at home.

Hazel said, 'What are you looking at me like that for? What if I did manage to slip out and telephone Mark?'

'But you didn't,' Sandra purred. 'And someone has telephoned him. We want to know whom it was, because they gave him the impression that it was you, and it isn't easy to kid our Mark.'

Squeak said uneasily, 'Give her a shot of snow, eh? Buck her up a bit.'

'Shut up,' Sandra snarled, without looking round.

'Oh, it's all right, I know you all take dope,' Hazel said airily, and not pulling off her nonchalant manner very well.

'I'm aware that you know, my pet. That's why I want to know who telephoned Mark. Come on, tell!'

Hazel hesitated. 'Well, I don't know, and it's news to me that he was telephoned. I wasn't going to do it yet. But if someone did, I suppose it's that interfering cousin of mine. Oh, don't worry, she just thinks I'm in debt—she's going to borrow on her legacy to pay it back in money, I think.' Her lips curled in contempt. 'Her legacy is a flea-bite to what I owe Mark!'

'You should be worrying, honey,' Sandra warned her grimly. 'Mark has a trick of preferring early payment.'

'Look, Sandra, I wish you'd do something to help me. I can take care of myself, but I do wish you'd see Elaine Harcourt and stop her interfering. You met her at the party—you know what she's like. Will you? I loathe her guts but I can't keep her nose out of my affairs!'

'Can't you? Then I must do something about it,' Sandra said, smiling.

'You will?' Hazel was naïve in her eagerness.

'Yes, I'll do something,' Sandra purred.

'Take it easy, duckie,' Squeak warned. 'The Harcourt woman is no simpleton. I've given her the once-over.'

'I know,' Sandra agreed. 'But you see, I'm not going to deal with her myself. I'm going to be a little more subtle than that. I think Andrew should be useful here.'

The day grew hotter. That evening Elaine wore her thinnest dress, a plain white cotton, tailored, to answer the purpose of summer frock and tennis dress.

'It makes me look positively plain,' she sighed at her reflection in the glass, 'but I can't help it. It's the only thin frock I've got, so it will have to do.' Her shoes were plain, too, and the last vision of Hazel flicking out of the front door in jade leather sandals and a jade and cream printed silk frock, didn't help.

She took the bus to the last stop before Oakbridge. The journey was hot and dusty. A small boy near her smeared his toffee-apple down the side of her skirt before she could move out of the way. Women jostled her with their market bags. She was damp and tired long before she got there.

Mark Pelham's expression as he opened his front door for her, conveyed an accurate idea of how she looked. He didn't say anything. He just shot his thick black brows up, popped his tarry black eyes, and deliberately raked her from head to foot in an all-embracing glance.

'What ees thees?'

'Good evening, Mr. Pelham,' she began crisply, and with more politeness than she had managed earlier in the day. 'I telephoned you this morning and you made an appointment to see me, about my cousin Hazel.'

'You? *You?* Eet was Hazel—I thought she was the one who spoke to me——' he stuttered, and his rage mounted.

'May I come in?' she asked icily.

'Your voices are alike,' he said accusingly, as he stood aside to allow her to enter, and she realized how difficult the interview was going to be.

'Just what do you hope to accompleesh?' he began abruptly.

'Hazel has a dress bill for a very large

sum. I saw it by accident. She was very angry about it, but that can't be helped. I want to settle it.'

'Why?' His tone was uncompromising.

'In this country girls are not of age until they are twenty-one,' she began, when he broke in,

'Then why do you come here? Hazel has told me you haf a twenty-first birthday . . . next month. You are not of age yourself!'

She flushed at his smart move, but she was surprised that Hazel should mention her at all, and curious to know what brought her name into the conversation with this man. She said as much.

He shrugged. 'I haf no weesh to hide anything. It does not matter one way or the other. Your cousin has beeg claws. Pairhaps you know that. She was anxious to haf me know that you were the poor relation—no parties, not even for the twenty-first birthday wheech seems so eemportant een thees country. Hazel, on the other hand, she has beeg parties for *any* birthday. That ees why she told me. But,' he added, with another shrug, 'she might have saved her breath. I do not care eef that ees so. All I care about ees that thees debt ees paid . . . by Hazel.'

'Look,' Elaine began earnestly. 'Hazel's father is a good man. He's got a weak heart. He's just got over one serious illness. Now, you understand why I'm so anxious to settle this up, if I can. I just can't let him know about it. I can't risk his getting ill again.'

He strutted up and down the room, thinking. His little podgy hands were clasped behind him, and she noticed there were thick black hairs curling down the back of them. His neck was hairy, and his chin blue. His skin had a greasy quality that brought to mind the common native of the Adriatic regions, and this fancy grew in her brain as she took in the colourful details of his dress. There was something obviously and unpleasantly un-English about him.

She disliked him. She disliked his cottage. She disliked the whole atmosphere, and for one panicky moment she half-decided to throw up the whole idea and go home, even at the risk of making Robert ill again when he inevitably got to hear about what Hazel was doing.

'How much money haf you?' he suddenly wanted to know, stopping in his tracks and leaning over her. He smelt of perfume, brilliantine and unwashed body. She wrinkled her nose in distaste and he noticed the action.

'I haven't enough, of course, but given a little time, I think I can get enough.'

'Huh!' he grunted, as though he were thinking, 'just as I thought!'

He took a few more turns up and down the room, then came back to stare at her. She flushed again, as she realized what he was considering now. There was an intimate, insulting quality about that stare which could mean one thing only. Before she could say anything, however, he wrinkled his nose, delicately shuddered, and resumed his pacing.

Somehow his action piqued her. She would have been outraged, beside herself with fury, if he had made the suggestion. As it was, she was angry to think that Hazel's body appealed to him more.

She jumped up. 'Well, will you take the money I have as a first instalment, or not?'

'No.'

'I see. It's not money you want, but Hazel. Is that it?'

He didn't answer, but grinned at her in a particularly nasty way.

'You must want her badly, if you're prepared to break up a home and hurt nice people like us. I don't care so much for myself, but it's the Vicar.'

He stopped grinning, and merely smiled, and to her amazement it was almost a kindly smile.

'You do not appear to know your cousin very well,' he said mildly. 'And that being the case, you cannot hope to know what all thees ees about. I ask you, let eet alone. She will manage.'

She went over the whole interview again, as she stalked out of the place and down the lane to the bus-stop. The bus, a little early, was just whirling past, but she was too preoccupied to be annoyed over losing it. Without being conscious of the thought, she decided to walk back the whole way from Oakbridge, principally to gain time, and to think.

A car whizzed past her, a car which should have been familiar to her, but she didn't notice. Sandra was at the wheel, and Andrew was beside her. They had been parked in the opening of a field facing Pelham's cottage.

'I still think it was foolish of you not to tackle her, Andrew, and find out what she was doing in there,' Sandra murmured. 'After all, she's the Vicar's cousin, and it isn't nice for anyone in his family to be visiting a man's house alone in the evening.'

'Let it go, Sandra,' he begged, for the fourth time.

'I'm surprised at you, darling. I thought you were such a friend of the Vicarage family.'

'I thought you had a little more decency in you than you've just shown, Sandra,' he observed tartly. 'You deliberately brought the car this way and parked it in that gateway, a gateway leading into a field, carefully secluded under a clump of trees. Very well thought out. I congratulate you. Even then I might not have seen Elaine coming out of the cottage if you hadn't drawn my attention to her, and asked me if it was really Elaine. Why go to all this trouble? Aren't I supposed to be engaged to *you*?'

'Angel, I don't believe this tale of yours that you and she have decided to do the right thing about our engagement. I know human nature. That's why I wanted you to see what sort of girl she is. I don't mind admitting it. I'm not ashamed of it. It does seem rather a waste of time making this car trip, though. I wouldn't have done it—I'd have taken the easier course and told you where she was going to-night, but for the fact that a knight-errant like you wouldn't have believed me. So you see, my sweet, you just had to see for yourself!'

'And where has all this effort and scheming got you, Sandra?'

'You tell *me* that, my angel, when you find out what went on in Pelham's cottage. Up till now, you've only seen Elaine come out.'

TWENTY TWO

SETH CHIBBETTS wiped down the bar counter with satisfaction. Andrew Farrar's coming had brought him luck.

All these weeks since just before Easter, Seth had been receiving good money for the use of his two best fronts, and generous tipping for every known service, and for other services which he had never dreamed merited tips in the big cities. Now, he was to have other visitors, visitors who filled the remainder of his vacant rooms upstairs. The generous Mr. Farrar's future in-laws.

Andrew had demurred when Sandra told him they were coming to Brookfield. When she told him they would be staying at The Crown with him, he had frankly revolted. Unfortunately he was now no longer in a position to revolt. Even Sandra could see how uncertain were his movements these days, and how he hesitated slightly before recognizing anyone.

Sandra said, 'Well, Andrew darling, they

can't stay at The Wooky Hole,' and he agreed. 'Pip and Squeak are good scouts, but you know Mother and Dad. They simply wouldn't understand. No, angel, stop being selfish, and let them come to The Crown. Give you all a chance to know each other, anyway.'

Andrew fretted over the press of circumstances. He dare not try and see Elaine, though he would have given a lot for just the chance to talk things over with her. Brookfield had looked like a haven of peace to him, just three months ago. But for the fact that he had not bothered to ascertain if anyone in the village was known to him (and this, at the time, had seemed a coincidence too absurd to be likely) Brookfield had looked the perfection of a place in which to stay when he could no longer get about at his old speed. Now it was a hotbed of misery for him.

'Sandra, why do we have to rush this marriage? There are so many things to be done,' he fumed.

'Nonsense, darling. There's nothing at all to be done. Better marry me before the worst happens, then I can take care of you when you can't do it yourself. Besides, what have we got to wait for? Is there anything you want to delay our wedding for?' she thrust at him.

'I did want to go to that specialist fellow again. I'd rather like to have another opinion. I don't see the point of living, without sight.'

Her eyes narrowed. Who had put that idea into his head? Up till now, he had vigorously protested against going back to see Burke, and had made it clear that if his sight were to fail, he'd rather it did so in its own time, and without anyone trying to delay the event. Now, he was all agog to prevent blindness coming on. Definitely the idea had been implanted by someone, and must, Sandra decided, be plucked out before it took root.

'This is a new theme, Andrew. I thought you didn't want them messing you about any more?' she put to him, smoothly.

'Did you imagine I wanted to be blind as a bat?' he returned harshly.

She shrugged impatiently. 'Andrew, you're not the first person to lose his sight. There must be millions of blind people about, and you've got wealth to help you. What about the poor devils who are so hard up that they have to live in institutions? How would you like that? I think you're selfish, wanting to delay our marriage while you're in a nursing home being tinkered with. Why can't you wait until we come back from our honeymoon if you must indulge in such things?'

'Because if I waited until then, I'd never get the thing done. You know that! Besides, if there's nothing to be done for me, I don't think I want to live, let alone be married.'

'That's nonsense, talking that way. Besides, we both know it's no use going back to Burke.'

'Oh? Why isn't it?' he had asked, in a dangerously quiet voice.

'Well, to be frank, I've already done so. I had to know the truth—I couldn't rest till I did. And,' she said in a voice of triumph, 'in spite of the truth, I still want to marry you, Andrew.'

'What's the truth?' he asked her savagely, feeling for her and missing her as she adroitly eluded him and put the table between them.

'Now, darling, you'll have to be brave and take this. As a matter of fact, Burke's opinion is there's nothing to be done. Nothing at all. It's the result of the accident, you see. I forget the exact technical language he used, but that's the general drift. Oh, Andrew, let's forget all about it and have a good time. We can, you know, you and I!'

'Oh stop wheedling, Sandra. I don't believe it—Burke would have got in touch with me. He wouldn't have told anyone else who happened to inquire.'

'Of course not, darling. Very discreet is old Burke. I didn't ask him. I got Bubbles to look at his casebook and tell me what it said, over the telephone. Simple, but I wanted to know, you see.'

He turned on her, angrier than she had ever seen him. 'You damned women, why can't you stop poking your noses into everything? If I want to know about my eyes, I'll go in the orthodox manner and see the man himself, not have a parcel of women going behind my back and prattling about it over the telephone.'

'What a sour devil you're becoming, Andrew. I hope you won't let Mother and Dad see you like this.' She smiled. 'Of course, it won't make any difference. They want you so badly as a son-in-law that they'd forgive you anything, but you might as well let them see your nice side, mightn't you?'

Trapped. He reviewed the situation after

she had left him. Rapidly going blind and trapped into a marriage he hadn't really wanted. He fumed over it all that day and over breakfast next morning, the fatal day on which his in-laws were to arrive.

At last he made up his mind, and rang for Prue Chibbetts.

'Prue, can you drive a car? You can, can't you?'

'I certainly can!' she told him stoutly.

'Will you take me out for a drive? I'll make it worth your while, if you can get your father's permission to knock off your work here.'

'Drive *yore* car, sir?' Prue breathed excitedly. 'Oh, sir, she's a *foine* bit of tin!' Her round face grew pink and shiny, as she dived out of the room. 'I'll ask me Dad.'

'Nip round to the Vicarage and ask Miss Harcourt to come along,' he directed Prue, as she did a nice job of manœuvring the big car out of the difficult turn at the double gates of the inn. 'And make sure no one hears you. I've private business to discuss with her.'

She came back alone. Elaine, she had been told, had gone to Oakbridge, to pick up some things for the Vicar.

'Then take me to Oakbridge, Prue.'

'What bus did she catch?' he asked, as Prue drove into the square with a flourish. 'Did you think to ask?'

'I did, sir. The eleven-thirty, and here it comes, late as usual. Oh, look, there's Miss Elaine. Shall I go and tell her?'

'No. Is she coming this way?'

'Yes, sir.'

'Well, I'll get out and wait for her. You can take the car back. I'll come back by bus. And remember, don't drop a word of this to anyone.'

Elaine stopped at the sight of him, standing all alone in the square, jostled by marketing people, and apparently unconscious of the swirling life around him.

'Andrew! Andrew, darling, what are you doing here?'

As she came close, he saw her, and grasped her hand.

'Elaine, I *had* to see you. Let me tag along with you while you do your shopping. Then we'll go back on foot—that's if you don't mind the walk.'

'Andrew, you know we ought not to! How did you get here?'

'Prue Chibbetts drove the car in. There's such a lot I want to talk over with you,' he said urgently.

310

She took his arm and guided him through the crowds, letting him talk all the time. She kept him by her while she went to the Post Office, the bank, Robert's favourite tobacconist, and the little drapery store to pick up knitting wool for Frances. At last they left the town behind and he took a deep breath.

'D'you believe there's nothing to be done for me? Am I going to be blind for ever?'

'No, Andrew, I don't believe it,' she answered firmly.

He drew a deep breath again. 'Must I go through with this marriage, just because there's pressure on the part of Sandra's wretched family?'

She was silent for a while. He waited, with bated breath, for her answer, and wasn't really surprised when it came.

'Yes, Andrew. Anyway, you've answered your own question.'

They came to a stile, and she put her basket down.

'Andrew, there's something else, isn't there? What's on your mind?'

'Mark Pelham,' he said simply, and told her what had happened that day she went to the cottage.

'Andrew, knowing that, knowing how

311

ruthless Sandra can be, you still plan these meetings with me, to ask me silly questions such as whether you still must marry her? You know you must, don't you? You can't fight her, she uses such dirty weapons.'

'Can't we fight her together? Is there something between you and Pelham?' His question was almost piteous, he wanted to know so much, yet he couldn't bear to wait in dread for the answer.

She hesitated, then shrugged. 'I'll have to tell you, Andrew, because knowing you, it would be asking for trouble to leave you in doubt. But it does rather seem like betraying a confidence.' She sighed deeply. 'It's Hazel. I went to see if Pelham would leave her alone. I didn't want to go to his rotten cottage—I hated the whole interview—and it was all for nothing. No good came of it at all!'

'Elaine, are you crying? Oh, God, I can't see—don't, Elaine, don't.' He held her roughly against him, trying in his clumsy way to comfort her, while his mind darted back over all the doubts and fears of the past.

'That money you had from Ramsey——' he began, with hesitation.

'Andrew, you're still fretting over that?

That was for Hazel, too. It was to pay a dress bill at school, so Robert shouldn't be worried. It's all for Hazel. All,' she sobbed. 'You can cut off your limbs, one by one, to clear up the messes she gets into, and you'd still never be done.'

'Oh, my dear, my dear—I thought—I've been thinking——' he murmured, incoherently, but she hardly noticed, so preoccupied was she about Hazel and Pelham.

'That nasty little man wouldn't let me help her. I even offered him my legacy, when it comes. But the bill was much more than that, and I didn't know where to get any more money. It's always more . . . and more . . .'

He patted her shoulder, and frowned. 'What puzzles me is why you didn't come to me for help. Didn't you realize what a compromising position you were putting yourself into? Why, something might have happened to you—oh, damn it, Elaine, if you go through life doing silly things like that for other people——'

'How could I come to you, Andrew? You're not mine to come to when I need help,' she pointed out, as she pushed him away and began to mop her eyes.

313

'My offer still holds good, for us to belong to each other,' he said. 'All you need do is to pack a bag and come with me to London. A little matter of obtaining a licence and selecting a registry office is nothing to a man of my means,' and there was a trace of bitterness in his tone which she noticed was always there when he spoke of money. Apparently his income had brought him no joy.

'What would you do about Major and Mrs. Standish—everyone knows they're going to stay at The Crown and why they're going to be there. A church wedding, Andrew, with Robert officiating. Everyone's talking about it. In confidence, it's what everyone expected. Reporters from London. The Crown doing a wonderful trade. Local people called in to help. Publicity. Oh, Brookfield is no better than anywhere else, when it comes to trade booming and newspaper publicity,' she said tartly. 'If you try to push all that aside, you are going to have trouble on your hands. It's too big for you, Andrew. Too big for me, too. How I wish I'd gone away at first.'

'Would you go away, then come to London and meet me—if there was any hope for my sight, I mean? You see, that's what I've in mind to do. Go back to Burke and see if Sandra was speaking the truth. I should have gone before, I suppose, but you know what a horror I've got of operations and all that fuss.'

'If I go away, Andrew, I won't be seeing you again.'

'No, I can't let you go . . .' he began.

She stood up straight, and pulled her dress down. It was a defensive movement of putting her appearance right, and her life right. There was so much to straighten out. 'I'm going out of your life, Andrew, just as soon as I can think up some solution for Hazel. If only I had enough . . .'

'Elaine,' he broke in, 'I don't like Hazel. I think any young girl who goes into a friendship with a man like Pelham is asking for all she gets. But I'll settle her debt—not for her, but for you. Now will you rest on that score?'

'No, Andrew, I can't let you do it. It's nothing to do with you . . .'

'It has everything to do with me,' he returned crisply. 'If I don't do something about it, I'll never rest, for thinking of what idiotic action you'll take to help that girl. Don't you see, Elaine, you mean everything in the world to me. Get that into your head,

315

my girl, and you'll see how I feel about your precious Hazel's debt. Will you promise to leave it to me?'

She looked doubtfully at him.

'Oh, Elaine, be your age, my sweet. I shan't go myself. I'll get in touch with my lawyers and let them do the dirty work. Now, how's that?'

She looked easier, and managed a smile.

'Well, now we've settled that, what about my more urgent worry? Will you marry me?'

She started to laugh, and he shook her a little.

'Don't, Elaine! You're getting excited. All right, my darling, I take it back. I'll ask you again some other time, when you're more composed.'

He took her in his arms and kissed her tenderly before he let her guide him over the stile.

Robert said, that afternoon, 'Elaine, you've been out so much to-day, we haven't had a chance to tell you the news.' He looked uncertain before continuing. 'I hope you won't be upset, my dear. It's about Andrew Farrar . . . his wedding arrangements, to be precise.'

She shot her chin up, like a startled

animal.

'I wouldn't have mentioned it, but for the fact that his fiancée's people are here in the village. They seem to have decided on a distressingly big show, and want to come over and discuss the arrangements.' He looked anxiously at her over the top of his reading glasses. 'For courtesy's sake, we invited them to dinner to-night.'

'The Standishes here?' She panicked. 'Is—is Andrew going to be here, too?'

'Yes, and his fiancée,' Robert said.

'Oh. Oh, dear,' she cried, showing an amount of distress foreign to her nature.

'If it's going to be too much of an ordeal for you, child, then don't appear. I'll make your excuses,' he offered kindly.

'What nonsense you do talk, Robert, to be sure,' Frances said, coming into the room at that moment. 'Just fancy giving a dinner-party without Elaine. How d'you suppose I'm to manage, with all the extra work. I've only one pair of hands, you know.'

'All right, Frances,' Elaine said wearily. 'I'll be there. Don't worry.'

She went up to her bedroom, and leaned her head against the cool of the window pane. 'Two weeks to my twenty-first birthday,' she whispered. 'It's August. Harvesting. The Festival. My favourite month. How I'll remember this year.'

She struggled with herself for a few seconds, and managed to stem the tears that seemed too near the surface since the night of Hazel's party. 'Oh, Andrew, Andrew,' she whispered to herself, 'why did you ever have to come to Brookfield?'

TWENTY THREE

THE Vicar had always liked a good dinner-party. He had always regarded such things as among the major pleasures of life. A few friends, good, simple food, and a bottle of some of the wine made in the village, or sent from the Walpole cellars, and some intellectual conversation. Frances at the end of the table acting hostess (which she did with a quiet charm of her own, if there were someone like Elaine around to take the burden of the organizing) and the comfortable assurance that there were one or two local women in the kitchen, doing the jobs which soured his sister's temper. A good dinner-party.

To-night he looked round his table, and felt a pang of disappointment. His daughter was absent, though she had promised him earlier in the day to be there. Hazel had looked distraught this last day or two, and there had been a feverish glitter in her eyes. He had meant to ask Frances to do something about it, see if the girl were sickening for a chill or something, but when it came to the point, he had refrained from mentioning his daughter's name, so that there should be no agitation in the atmosphere to-night.

Elaine looked far from well. He had asked her if she were fit, but her reply had assured him that it was not her health which was troubling her.

Andrew Farrar, seated opposite, looked anything but a happy bridegroom-to-be. He ate uncertainly, in the hesitating fashion in which he did most things lately, and the Vicar could feel inside him the morbid fear the young man was harbouring, that he would drop his food or spill his wine.

The only people present who appeared satisfied with everything were the Standishes. Sandra, glamorous in white; her mother, a small, bird-like woman, beautifully gowned in grey lace; her father, a seedy-looking ex-Army man, whose conversation so far pronounced him as a shocking bore.

Frances appeared faintly bewildered. She strove to catch Robert's eye from time to time, to give a signal to him which he couldn't interpret, so he spent most of the evening avoiding her beseeching glance. The Standishes did most of the talking. The Major told of marriages made in India between Army people while he was out there. Mrs. Standish told of smart English village weddings they appeared to have attended in the past, and of her hopes for her daughter's wedding in this village.

Sandra spent her evening reminiscing for Elaine's benefit, of incidents and events experienced with Andrew long before Elaine met him. Andrew did his best to keep out of all this, and Elaine sat enduring it with a composure which the Vicar felt would surely desert her long before their guests went home.

'We must have a choral service, dear Mr. Boyd,' Mrs. Standish said, every other word italicized. 'And incense. Do you have incense in St. Chad's? No? Oh, dear, how tiresome. *All* our friends have *incense.*'

'By Jove, I well remember (speaking of incense) that time when young Nolan of the forty-third (you recall Nolan, my dear, don't you—married Stevensen's niece—old Stevensen of the ninth) he was sent out the night before his wedding——Gad, never heard anything so funny in me life——'

'Daddy, darling,' Sandra drawled, 'Mr.

321

Boyd doesn't want to hear your Army stories, do you, Mr. Boyd?'

Robert appeared as embarrassed as she had made him feel. Frances said, 'Oh, dear, how the time does fly. Perhaps we had better go into the small parlour and start discussing the actual arrangements. So much to discuss—Elaine and I have work to do in the kitchen, but all you dear people go with my brother——'

They trooped into the small parlour, and never more reluctant a group of people discussed a wedding. Andrew professed an ill-concealed indifference, and Sandra soon began to show an irritation with him that she usually managed to hide. Even to Robert it soon became clear who was to pay for all this extravagant show to be staged in his church.

Seth Chibbetts had done his best to put the news around in good time, and where he hadn't succeeded, Prue had done the rest. The Lincoln women eagerly discussed the organ music with their brother, who for once was showing a little interest in local gossip. Amelia Christmas dropped in to borrow some church magazines, and to wonder if anything had been said about the school children attending the wedding to reinforce the choir, and whether any of the mothers would be wanting new dresses made for them.

The Oggs, who were still very much put out over their 'words' with Frances, hoped it would rain, or that the organ would give out, as it had on the occasion of a wedding once before.

Eb Wilkins was so excited over the talk of someone else's wedding that he absent-mindedly put the question to Prue again, and she was excited enough to say 'yes' without having to be given time to think.

The only person who wasn't very interested was Lady Lassett, who was in the stables helping to foal a mare, and was still very much distressed over Peter's not having sent her a word to let her know where or how he was.

Back at the Vicarage, Elaine said: 'Leave me alone, Frances. I don't want to discuss it, not to-night, anyway. I'll tell you about it to-morrow, but for to-night I'm fed up with Andrew and his beastly wedding!'

They were alone in the kitchen. The hired help had gone back to the village to report on the situation as they had heard it in snatches of conversation through closed doors, and Frances had seized the opportunity of questioning Elaine on the truth or otherwise of the gossip she had heard about the girl meeting Andrew 'on the sly'.

'You have a horrid way of putting things, Frances, and if you're not careful, you'll soon find that no one will want to tell you anything at all. You don't invite confidences—and don't start crying, or you'll look too much of a sight to go back to the parlour and hear what's going on!'

Frances realized the justice of that, and sniffing in an indignant manner, she flounced out of the kitchen, leaving Elaine to set the breakfast-table by herself. It wasn't often Elaine spoke to her like that, and Frances had enough sense to know when she had gone too far.

Elaine didn't hurry. There was no need to go back in there too soon. She would hear all that went on, when Frances saw her the next morning.

The next morning . . . 'Must I?' she whispered, as she took off her apron, and went to the back door for a breath of air. 'Must I stay in this house to see another morning, and endure another breakfast-time with Frances going at me?'

She leaned against the lintel and pursued

the thought further.

'Where would I go, if I went away? Let's see—trains leave the Halt to Belminster fairly late. From Belminster, where could I get? Burnleigh, Harringford, Chislewick Halt, Briarchurch. Briarchurch, I think. For a day or two. Then I'll go on to the Midlands. Have a look at my home town. Look up old friends. Yes, that's what I'll do. If I run short of money, I can look in on the solicitors while I'm up there, and collect what's due to me.'

She went slowly out into the garden, to walk round for the last time before she went upstairs to fling a few things in a week-end bag.

'I'll write and ask Robert to get my trunk sent on, or perhaps I'll make do without it. 'M, might be as well if I started this wonderful new life with a few fresh clothes. Come to think of it, my wardrobe is hardly adequate for the town. Hardly adequate for the country, either, I suppose. I'll have to get some new things to wear before I can start looking for a job, anyway.'

She strolled unseeingly round the garden. Now that the time for parting had come, it was hurting badly to think of living elsewhere. To work for anyone else but

Robert would mean a big wrench. But to live anywhere else but the Vicarage was unbearable. She thought of her old home, a flat grey house in a square, overlooked on three sides by other flat grey houses, with a patch of dying grass and a few starved trees in the centre. Tall railings fenced in the miserable foliage, as though it were the best there was to offer, and was for looking at only, and not for walking through or touching.

She turned sharply to go in, and ran into Andrew. She hadn't heard him come up behind her on the soft turf, and he hadn't seen her standing there. The impact was sharp, but as she went against him, he caught her to him and held her close.

'Not here, Andrew! What are you thinking about?' she gasped.

'Yes, here! It's about all I shall ever have,' he told her roughly. 'I'm caught, Elaine. I can't get out now. I've left it too late. They've fixed my wedding up, and the rest of my life, too, it seems. They might have discussed it with me first!'

'They were afraid you'd wriggle out of it,' she reasoned. 'After Sandra finding us together that time.'

'And apparently she knows about all the

other times,' he said bitterly. 'News flies fast in your precious village.'

'Yes. That's why I'm leaving. Don't try to talk me out of it, Andrew. I'm going to-night. I just can't stay here now. There'll be talk of your wedding on everyone's lips. They'll stare at me, and I shan't be able to bear it, thinking of you and her . . .'

Surprisingly he didn't try to stop her.

'You'll be all right?' she faltered anxiously.

'If you mean, will I try the river, no! I can promise you that! I'll just have to go on, with Sandra shoving me where she wants me to go, and her precious parents tagging along, the three of them spending my money for me. All I shall have to do is grin and bear it! Perhaps there'll be a way of stopping this miserable business yet, but I doubt it. I feel like a male slave in the open market, with my bags of gold slung round my neck to make weight.'

'Don't. Don't joke like that, Andrew. I can't bear it.'

After a while, he walked her back towards the house. 'Where are you going?'

She told him her plans. 'There'll be a train to Belminster from the Halt. I must be slipping away soon. Will you tell them I've gone upstairs with a headache? I don't want anyone to know until I've got clear away.'

He said he would. There was a dead sound in his voice, that worried her, as though nothing mattered now, not even the business of staying alive.

'I don't want them to know where I am, Andrew. I'll use the Post Office for correspondence.'

'Will you—I suppose you won't write to me?' he said, with difficulty.

'No,' she returned, in a choked voice.

'Where will you stay to-night?'

'Belminster Hotel. It won't be difficult—they know me. The receptionist used to live in Brookfield. Besides, Frances and I stayed there once or twice before, when we got late shopping.'

'I can't offer to drive you to the station . . .'

'Don't worry, Andrew. I'll be all right.'

'You won't walk? It's across the fields, isn't it? You can't go alone!'

'No, I'll take the road,' she assured him. 'I'll go on my bike, with my case strapped behind. I can leave the bike at the Halt. Someone'll see to it for me.'

He refused to say good-bye when the moment came.

'Hate good-byes. So damned final,' he told her.

The last she saw of him was standing at the foot of the stairs, with a look of anguish on his face that haunted her all through her packing, her rapid exit from the Vicarage back door, her ride to the Halt and her train journey beyond. She couldn't get it out of her mind. When at last she was in bed at the hotel, it was before her through her troubled sleep.

She had always liked Belminster as a town. She recalled that this was the place they were coming to for their first real date, she and Andrew, that day when he hadn't come to meet her as he had promised.

An afternoon in Belminster. The town of the concert hall, the museum, the two super picture houses and one back-street one, the row of dress shops, the three dance halls and the nine cafés. She had lunch in one of the nine cafés, while waiting for her connection to Briarchurch.

When she finally went to get her ticket, she decided to miss that nice little town, and go straight on to the Midlands. 'I might as well—I'm not feeling happy enough to take a few days' holiday yet. I'll wait a bit, I think.'

She reached the terminus that evening, and waited another half an hour in the great, teeming booking hall, until it was time to pick up the connection for the little town in which her parents had lived.

The evening papers were out, and because it was so rare to see a London paper, she bought one in preference to the local one.

She took it to a seat occupied by one other person, a large woman with a round, comfortable face, and the resigned air of one who is waiting to meet an incoming traveller and not making a journey personally. Elaine glanced briefly at her before opening her paper.

After scanning the headlines, she decided with some disappointment that the great evening papers were either less well done than they used to be, or that she had lost touch through getting acclimatized to the local ones.

She was about to fold it up again and take out her magazine, when a tiny picture caught her eye, down towards the bottom of the front page.

It was set in a strip of three paragraphs, about a suicide in a village called Brookfield-under-Woke.

The newspaper slipped from her nerve-less fingers. The booking hall grew suddenly dark, and the noises receded. The fat woman on the seat beside her grasped her arm, and said, in a far-away voice: 'Are you ill, dear?' One or two people passing paused and someone picked up her handbag for her.

After the fat woman had taken Elaine to the ladies' waiting-room, someone said, 'D'you suppose she was wandering? She said, "Hazel always wanted to be front page news!" '

TWENTY FOUR

THE train steamed into Belminster on time, and Elaine got out. It was just a week since she had passed through this town on her outward journey. Just a week since she had left the Vicarage, yet it seemed in another life.

The fat woman, who had been waiting on the station seat to meet her niece, had taken Elaine home with her, and let her rest and get over the shock.

'Friend of yours, dear?' her new friend had wanted to know, when she had by painstaking questioning drawn from Elaine the information that the newspaper story of the suicide had been responsible for her being taken ill at the station.

'My cousin . . . third cousin, that is,' she had replied, dully but with accuracy. 'I lived with her family.'

'Oh, relation, eh? Well, you'll be wanting to go home, then, won't you? Always like to be at home when there's a death in the family, myself.'

Elaine winced. 'No, I don't want to go home.'

In truth, she didn't. She had left in a way intended to be quiet and unassuming. If she went back now, there would be a touch of drama about it, and Elaine had no taste for drama. It was the sort of thing poor Hazel would have done.

Besides, she didn't think she could bear to see their grief, Robert's and his sister's. And if she knew anything of the people of Brookfield, they, too, would be loud in their grief. Hazel, who had been everything that was bad in life, would in death take the form of an angel. There never would have been a girl so good, sweet or misunderstood, in their way of thinking. It was a sort of code to speak well of the dead, however much you spat at them while they walked the earth.

No, better to stay away, she decided.

Her new friend liked having her in her house, and went so far as to invite her to stay indefinitely.

'Get yourself a job at my niece's place; you'll be a companion to her,' she was advised, and for the moment the idea was as good as any.

She had only been going to her home town for the sake of fixing a definite destination. There was nowhere else she particularly wanted to visit.

So she stayed with the fat woman, and the pleasant girl of her own age who had been met at the station. They lived in a good residential district of the city, and the niece had a good job as a typist in a motor tyre manufacturer's office. Safe, the girl assured Elaine. 'Safe', Elaine decided, was a good word.

The fat woman was very obliging, and scanned the London papers each day for further news, but the affair was small, and of little national importance, beyond the fact that through the dead girl an organization peddling dope was traced. This intrigued the fat woman and her niece, and they begged Elaine to tell them what Hazel was like.

Elaine considered the point before she answered, and her answer was fair and just.

'She was lovely to look at, headstrong, and she loved pleasure. There isn't really anthing else. There was nothing bad about her. She had only just left boarding-school.'

'Ah, inexperienced,' the fat woman said sagely, nodding her head. 'They always grab the inexperienced ones. You see it every time.'

Through her and her constant newspaper reading, Elaine learned that the inquest had taken place in Oakbridge, and that the verdict was brought in as death by misadventure. Elaine knew that it was really as the first report surmised: suicide.

Hazel had been found in the river. Certainly she herself had nearly been drowned in the Wid, but it was a usual thing for her to go to the river bank. She loved the river and its surroundings, and went there for pleasure. Hazel, who hated the countryside and made no secret of it, would not have gone near the river for all the gold in Egypt, unless it was with the idea of taking her own life. And she had so much to cause her to want to end it.

It never occurred to Elaine that Robert and Frances would want her to come back. If she thought about it at all, she reasoned that Judy Lassett was on hand to help them, if they needed help, and she always thought of Andrew as being as much a friend of Robert's as of herself.

She forgot that she had given Andrew the Briarchurch Post Restante address, and that of her home town, but if she had remembered, she would not have gone to those towns to look for mail. At this point she wanted no contact, and she felt safe . . . safe from the old life and all its complications. They would not be able to find her.

It was with considerable surprise, therefore, that she received a message (on arriving back at the house after a walk) that there was a visitor for her. The fat woman was in a pleasant flutter of surprise and curiosity, but Elaine—after experiencing freedom for a whole week—was not so keen to see who it was.

He was a hard-bitten elderly man, in a quiet suit and a raincoat, and a dark hat. He came to the point straight away and told her he was a private inquiry agent engaged by Mr. Andrew Farrar to locate her, and to ask her to go back to the Vicarage at Brookfield at once.

'A detective! My, how thrilling,' ejaculated the fat woman, throwing up her hands. 'I've always wanted to meet one. How did you find her?'

'Oh, by routine inquiries, and a large slice of luck. One of the porters remembered hearing someone speak about the newspaper report of the suicide and the girl who was taken ill in the booking hall. Dates and descriptions were all that were needed to be checked up. Someone else heard you, ma'am, tell the young lady here where you lived, when you asked her to go home with you. I'd have found her eventually but time was the main factor. The Vicar is dangerously ill,' he added to Elaine.

'It's just like a story at the pictures,' the fat woman said with satisfaction. 'Good thing they didn't put out an S O S over the wireless.'

'Why?' he wanted to know.

'We haven't got one!' she said triumph-antly.

After he had gone, the resourceful fat woman dispatched Elaine out to the shops. 'Get yourself a black outfit, dearie, if it takes your last penny. It simply isn't respectful to the dear dead to go back looking like that.'

Elaine studied herself in the glass. Her new friend was right. It simply wouldn't do. She realized with a shock how little heed she had taken of her appearance during the three years she had been in Brookfield. Somehow there had just never been enough money, and it hadn't seemed to matter, anyway.

'Have you got any ready cash, dearie? Don't mind me asking, but it's for an important thing, you know. Can't be too careful about mourning.'

'I haven't got much money,' Elaine admitted frankly, 'but I can give them my cousin's name and address and leave a deposit, I dare say.'

'Go to the Prince Regent Stores, where I've got an account. You can use it if you like, and send me the cash after. I'm a good judge of faces, and I know you won't dish me!'

Andrew was waiting to meet her on the platform at Belminster, with the watchful Prue Chibbetts standing a little way behind him. She had, he told Elaine, brought him in his car, and was a first-rate driver.

It was a moment for formalities. Elaine hadn't expected him to be there to meet her, and was struck dumb with emotion, and dare not trust herself to speak with Prue Chibbetts looking on.

Andrew felt strange and awkward with this new Elaine. He had never seen her in new clothes before. She was wearing black; a black soft suit with a scrap of white at the neck, and a little black straw bonnet against which her reddish-brown curls glowed richly. The fat woman's niece had urged her to wear make-up with it, as the black made her complexion look a little sallow, and the girl had supervised the application of it. Something in the outfit, or perhaps the fact that instead of being dug deep in her pockets, Elaine's hands were encased in new black kid gloves, made her seem a different person. When she started to hunt for her ticket, instead of scrabbling into the deep, shapeless pocket of her old coat, she self-consciously opened a shiny black satchel bag which swung from her shoulder and extracted a minute and rather frivolous little purse.

He took all this in, and didn't know whether he liked the change or not.

She wanted to cry out, 'Andrew, darling, you came to meet me in spite of Sandra and all Brookfield?' but instead she managed a formal 'Andrew, how nice of you to come and meet me,' and that again sounded to him strange and unreal.

In turn he asked if she had had a comfortable journey, and she replied that she had. They were like two chance acquaintances, walking side by side without touching, Prue trailing a little behind with Elaine's week-end case and the extra bag she had bought and filled.

In her new polite voice, Elaine told him what had happened to her since she left Brookfield, and he listened with his head slightly on one side. His heart was hammering madly, and he wondered how she could act so coolly. And then someone bumped into him, and Elaine disregarded Prue and firmly took his arm, leading him out to his car.

The little action seemed to break the barrier that had for a few moments been between them.

'Andrew, how's Robert? Is he . . . *how* is he?'

He hesitated. 'Well, he's . . . very ill, Elaine.'

'Is he . . . dying?' she whispered.

'I don't quite know. I don't think they feel he has much chance.'

In the back of Andrew's car, separated from Prue at the wheel by a closed glass screen, they forgot their former constraint, and sat close together, while he told her all that had happened.

'They found Hazel's body just below the Brookfield bridge—where you slipped that evening. She was caught in the roots of a willow, otherwise she would have been carried downstream. No one knows why she did it, but I should be prepared for a battery of questions if I were you, my dear. Frances had a pretty firm opinion that you know more about it than anyone.'

She didn't answer that, but pressed back to the one subject of interest to her.

'Robert? How did he take it?'

'Some fool from the village rushed to the Vicarage door yelling the news when the body was found, and the Vicar heard it and collapsed. It was the shock that did it—so soon after his last illness.'

'The funeral?' Elaine faltered. 'Who . . . saw to it?'

'Lady Lassett came over. She's been at the Vicarage all the time. They say she and the Vicar . . . years ago . . .'

'Yes, it's true. They were going to be engaged, but Robert met Hazel's mother and married her instead. I'm glad Lady Lassett was with Robert. I'm afraid Frances isn't much good in a crisis.'

'The visiting priest hadn't left St. Mary's when it happened, which was a good thing. He stayed on and took over. Poor chap, he seems quite a bit bewildered by everything.'

'You look worried, too, Andrew,' Elaine said, searching his face.

'Well, I can't help feeling it was my fault. It happened while we were there discussing my wedding. My wedding!' he said, with great bitterness. 'I never told you but some time ago Hazel asked me to get her into films. She was a born actress. Really good. I should have done something about it, but at the time I was annoyed with her. You know, she had a trick of annoying one, sooner or later. I refused to get her a part, so she retaliated by tricking me into introducing her to the Merryweathers.'

'But, Andrew, that doesn't make you responsible for—the way things turned out,' she protested.

'Yes, it does. I wouldn't let her go on the screen because I thought she was too young and inexperienced. She would have been safer there than with that rotten bunch.'

'The newspapers hinted at dope traffic. Was that true?'

He looked quickly at her. 'Aren't you going to ask me how it is I'm able to come and meet you openly like this? Don't you want to know where Sandra is?'

She shook her head, her eyes glistening. 'No. I'm just being grateful for the little things. But I will ask you if you want me to.'

'The Wooky Hole is empty. Cleaned out and left open as though burglars have been there. It was like that next morning when Hazel's body was found.'

'Wha-at?'

'At about the same time Seth Chibbetts found his front door undone, and Sandra's parents weren't in their rooms. They'd gone, the whole lot of 'em, in the night.'

'But why?' Elaine asked, in a bewildered voice.

'Pelham's cottage was in the same state, but the police raided his gown shop and his flat in Town.'

'Andrew, I don't understand . . .'

'I've had my lawyers trying to trace Sandra, to clear things up between us, but her apartment is empty. Zillah Carey has vanished, too. What does that suggest to you, darling? Elaine, think—what does it suggest to you?'

'But—isn't Sandra still engaged to you?'

'I don't think she'll dare do anything about it now, wherever she is. As for that ill-fated ring, well, I never want to see that again. I've come to loathe green stones.'

'What does it mean, though?' was all she could say, and even when he carefully explained that she could now consider him free again, he could see she hardly believed it.

It was a long time before she could take it in, but for the moment there was Robert. Robert, who—propped up against the pillows in his shaded bedroom—looked not so much a sick man but a man who no longer had any wish to go on living, and was fast letting go of his hold on life.

He didn't speak at first but looked steadily at her, nodding a little and grasping convulsively at her hand with his own nerveless one.

'How are you, Robert? It's Elaine—Andrew said you wanted me to come home.'

He nodded again, but said nothing about her sudden departure, evinced no curiosity at what had happened to her nor how Andrew had found her. It was as if he were waiting for her to start talking about something, as a sort of signal for himself to speak.

'Andrew told me . . . about everything,' she said at last, not daring to meet his eyes.

She need not have worried. There was, strangely enough, no grief in his face, but as he started speaking, she grasped that what he wanted to do most was to establish the fact that while she lived, Hazel had been all that he had wanted her to be.

'She was very beautiful, wasn't she?' he asked, in a thin, tired voice utterly unlike his own.

Elaine agreed, which seemed to prompt him to add, 'And happy, too, I believe. She *was* happy, wasn't she?'

'She was happy,' Elaine confirmed gently.

'You two were good friends really, weren't you? Under the friendly arguments and scuffles, I mean?' and he smiled a little, as he recalled (or thought he recalled) such incidents.

'Well, cousins, you know . . .' she murmured, smiling back at him, and he seemed satisfied.

'I used to think that she wasn't popular at Brookfield. That was sinful of me. I know that now. Everyone has been so kind, sending loving messages . . . and flowers . . . and kindly remembrances . . . They couldn't have been like that if they hadn't loved her, could they?'

'No, Robert. They all loved her,' Elaine said bravely.

When she went downstairs, Frances rose to meet her.

345

'I want to know,' she said, with hard eyes and tightened lips. 'My brother is dying, dying believing that hussy was a saint and that he misjudged her. I'm going to put that right, if it's the last thing I do, and you're the only one who can help me. I'm not going to let him depart this life blaming himself. He had nothing to blame himself for.'

Elaine looked faintly bewildered. She recalled too well the times Frances had rebuked Robert, and the way she had talked about him behind his back, for spending money wrongfully on Hazel, when things were needed so badly in the house.

She said, gathering her forces, 'Anything I know, Frances, is locked away in my mind. Hazel is dead. Robert's happy thinking well of her. You don't get a word out of me!'

Frances barred her way out of the door.

'There was a night, not so long ago, that I lay in my bed listening to you quarrelling. I couldn't catch everything that was said, but I heard a dress bill mentioned. Ah . . .' She finished on a long-drawn sigh of satisfaction. 'Just as I thought. So she was in that sort of position with the little foreigner. And there's a diary too, isn't there? Yes, your face gives everything away.'

'All right, Frances. There was a diary. You seem to have done a fair share of listening-in, and it seems pretty improbable that you heard all this from your bed, behind closed doors. But if you think I'm going to stoop to diary-snooping, you're wrong. If you want to have such an act on your conscience, go ahead. But don't tell Robert. I'm warning you! Don't upset Robert, or I won't be responsible for what I do!'

The older woman wavered a little, under the girl's fierce tone, but Elaine could see that whatever she said would have very little effect. Frances had made up her mind to turn out Hazel's little desk. Why she hadn't done so already was hard to say unless, before taking her life, Hazel had locked it.

'I won't be able to stop her doing this,' she said to herself worriedly, 'but she may not do anything for the moment. I think I must get Judy Lassett over. She'll know what to do.'

She went to find Andrew, but they were delayed by Prue not being free to drive the car. Finally they persuaded Eb Wilkins to take them up to Walpole House.

'I'm damned glad to see yer back, Elaine.

Now perhaps you two'll have some sense and get married before the Sandra woman turns up again!'

'I don't think there's much danger of that,' Andrew smiled. 'I should think Sandra and her friends have made a run for it. Their activities aren't looked on kindly in this country.'

Elaine said urgently, 'I'm terribly worried. About Robert,' and got Judy Lassett's attention at once. 'I know you've been at the Vicarage all this week, and you're needed here now, but I do wish you'd come back with us and do just one thing. I want you to stay with Robert for a bit, to prevent Frances getting to him. She's going to upset him again.'

She told Judy of the conversation with Frances over the diary, and finally Lady Lassett decided to go back with them in the car.

They hadn't been very long out of the Vicarage, but one glance at Robert told them that Frances had already done the damage. The house was empty, and Robert was sitting bolt upright in bed, staring ahead of him, his face grey, and a bitter, down-turned twist to his mouth.

'He knows,' Elaine whispered, in dread,

and backed out of the bedroom, Andrew following her. Lady Lassett went and sat by the bed.

'Andrew,' Elaine said, going through the deserted house, and stopping to look in Hazel's room at the rifled escritoire, 'I don't know what's going to happen now. What does a dying man do, when he gets a shock like that?'

'Where's Miss Boyd?' Andrew wanted to know.

'Oh, Frances will have gone to spread the news around. Hazel's diary had everything in it, to judge from the bit I saw.'

'But she left her brother like that, a man in his state?'

'He probably ordered her out,' Elaine said, with a wry smile. 'He must have been very angry and upset.'

Andrew said nothing, and Elaine added, 'I'd like to do something to prevent her ever speaking again—she doesn't know when to shut up!' with a vicious tone utterly foreign to her. 'Poor old Robert!'

'Don't worry,' Andrew counselled coolly. 'I think it's done him good. He was ready to die in peace before. Now it's given him something to think about. He looked like a man who had been cheated, I thought.'

'You really mean that, Andrew?'

'You think a lot of the Vicar, don't you Elaine? Well, so do I. He's a good old scout. And I've been a selfish ass, too preoccupied with my own affairs to do the one thing for him I ought to have done. That book of his—heaven knows what I did with it. It's somewhere in my room at The Crown. I'll take it up with my company. It's good material, and I think the knowledge of that will make him want to get well. Yes, my darling, that's going to make you happy, too, eh?'

'Oh, Andrew, Andrew!' She rested her head against him for a minute, then looked up at him. 'No. No, that's not enough. There's just one thing more that I must have, to make me happy, apart from Robert's recovery!'

'What's that? You've got me—what else do you want?'

'Andrew, you're priceless in this mood! No, I haven't got you yet, and neither will I have you till you make a promised visit to Town. Remember?'

She got her promise, and characteristically she decided to make tea on the strength of it. 'Judy and Robert have been together long enough—perhaps they'd like some tea.'

Judy heard the kettle whistling through the open window. 'Good girl,' she approved. 'Nothing like a cup of tea at this stage. By the way, have you thought just what you're going to do without that girl, Robert?'

'No, I daren't think, Judy.'

His voice was quiet, but steadier. Judy, as he had said once before, was a wonderful tonic, a breath of fresh air. Under her brisk verbal administration, he looked a different man.

No one ever found out what went on in that room after Elaine and Andrew left them together, but Robert had lost that look of anguish and bitterness. He never mentioned his daughter's name again.

'Well, have a shot at thinking,' Judy reminded him, 'and buck up, old lad. I've got to be getting back. We're shorthanded with the cows.'

'What am I supposed to think?' he asked, smiling a little.

'Don't yer know? Well, I'll help you. Want to live the rest of yer life with that sister of yours?'

'No. No,' he said, almost shuddering.

'You're done as a Vicar. Know that,

351

don't yer? Everton says rest, and nothing but rest.'

'Yes. I know that. I've no wish to deprive that poor new fellow of a job.'

Judy chuckled but pursued her theme ruthlessly.

'That leaves your books. You'll always write, I suppose?'

'I don't know. I've had Elaine for such a long time, and without her help . . .' His voice trailed off miserably.

Judy strode up and down. Cups were rattling below, and the kitchen door had opened. Andrew was talking, and his voice sounded nearer.

'God save us, do I have to put the words in the man's mouth? Robert Boyd, you're a lonely old man and I'm a lonely woman. I've got a damned big house and I need a man around. Well?'

'What are you suggesting, Judy?' he gasped.

Red in the face, she stopped and placed her hands on her hips. Elaine's steps were on the stairs, coming up.

'You're too late! Here comes Elaine with the tea. You've missed a damned good offer!' But she grinned a little at him over the tea-tray as Elaine put it on the small table by the bed.

'Well, this is a change, Robert!' the girl said, looking at his face with a pleased smile. 'Almost looks well enough to hear our news, eh, Andrew?'

Judy Lassett quickly intervened. 'If you two mean you want Robert to marry you, it's the wrong tree you're barking up! Robert's not doing any more work—he's retiring!'

Andrew broke in quietly, 'It's the Vicar's novel *Deep is the Night*. My company are going to take it for filming.'

'And now you've got over that bit of excitement,' Elaine said, when they had exhausted the subject and expressed every tiring emotion from astonishment to a rapid calculation of what the film rights would fetch, 'I'll tell you our next bit of news. Andrew's going back to see the eye specialist for a final opinion. It may mean an operation.'

The Vicar settled back on his pillows, with a peaceful smile on his face, and left the women to do the talking. Andrew walked carefully over to the window and stood looking out (through the now perpetual haze) at Brookfield on a hot afternoon in early August. He recognized

Frances coming in the gate with some groceries under her arm. The Ogg child, who delivered the bread, chased up the street with a skipping rope. Somewhere a dog barked and cattle lowed in the distance.

In the room behind him, the two women quietly chatted, and Robert lay listening, the strain and bitterness wiped from his face. They discussed the coming Harvest Festival and the way the new priest was coping; the two latest births in the village, and the number of children leaving school to start work; inevitably they came to weddings—Prue Chibbetts' and Elaine's.

'I would have liked Robert to officiate,' Elaine said wistfully, and now the conversation had taken a personal turn, Andrew came back from the window.

'Perhaps the Vicar will come to our wedding as a guest,' he said. 'He'll be fit enough for that.'

Judy Lassett snorted.

'He may not have the chance, that's if he has any sense. I've just made him a damned attractive offer and he's let it slip through his fingers.'

Elaine's eyes widened, and she beamed at them both. 'No!' She grinned roguishly at Robert. 'You've got to choose, you know,' she told him. 'Author or farmer?'

'Well,' Judy remarked, 'now you've let out about the book, and the money he's going to make, you bet I won't let him escape the next time I ask him, not me!'

In the general laugh that followed, Elaine said to Andrew, 'I've got an idea,' and whispered to him.

He nodded, smiling.

She turned to Robert. 'Be an angel and put Judy out of her misery, or my idea won't work.'

'What idea, Elaine?' he asked, amused.

The bells of St. Chad's started to ring for mid-week evensong, and the scuffle of worshippers' footsteps started down the road.

'Let's have a double wedding!'